THE LONER

Recent Titles by Clive Egleton from Severn House

A DYING FALL

THE LAST REFUGE

THE LONER

NEVER SURRENDER

THE RENEGADES

A SPY'S RANSOM

THE SKORZENY PROJECT

THE SLEEPER

THE LONER

Clive Egleton

This title first published in Great Britain 2006 by
SEVERN HOUSE PUBLISHERS LTD of
9–15 High Street, Sutton, Surrey SM1 1DF.
First published in Great Britain in 1978 under
the title *The Mills Bomb* by Hodder and Stoughton.
This title first published in the USA 2006 by
SEVERN HOUSE PUBLISHERS INC of
595 Madison Avenue, New York, N.Y. 10022.

British Library Cataloguing in Publication Data

Egleton, Clive
    The loner
    1.   Espionage - Great Britain - Fiction
    2.   Revenge - Fiction
    3.   Suspense fiction
    I.   Title
    823.9'14 [F]

    ISBN-13: 978-0-7278-6410-9
    ISBN-10: 0-7278-6410-6

All Severn House titles are printed on acid-free paper.

Printed and bound in Great Britain by
MPG Books Ltd., Bodmin, Cornwall.

For my good friends, Terence and Susan

And also, Jeanne Mills

"After the third man, the fourth man,
after the fourth man the fifth man,
who is the fifth man, always beside you?"

– Cyril Connolly, *May 1951*

1

SERGEANT GEORGE CHESTERMAN stole another look at the photograph in his wallet and then returned it to the inside pocket of his jacket. Someone on the Assistant Commissioner's staff had obviously gone through the reel and selected the best exposure but even so the colour blow-up looked grainy and out of focus. The downward angle suggested that it had been taken with a telephoto lens from one of the administrative offices above the exercise yard, while the shadows seemed to indicate that it had been shot towards mid morning. To cap it all, the photographer had caught Mills half in profile as he turned to face the sun, with the result that the left side of his face was indistinct. In the circumstances, Chesterman thought it was just as well that Special Branch had his mug-shot on record; the pictures might be ten years out of date but they were a far better likeness than this latest effort from the Crime Lab.

In a few months time, Edward James Mills would be the wrong side of forty and his age was beginning to show in small ways. His fair hair was a lot darker and streaked with grey and the fleshiness had gone from his face so that his features now looked as if they had been chiselled out of stone. According to the pre-release medical, the ex-SIS man tipped the scales at one hundred and seventy pounds and was a fraction under five eleven which meant that somewhere along the line he'd lost more than an inch in height. He'd also lost one lobe from the right lung, the result of a lobectomy for pulmonary tuberculosis. Albany, Durham and Leicester had certainly left their mark on him, and not only in a physical sense. Hard, embittered, violent and dangerous were just a few of the adjectives used by one psychiatrist to describe his personality. There had been a time when none of these epithets applied but that was more than ten years ago and as Chesterman's superior, Chief Superintendent Wray, had often observed, prison could change a man out of all recognition.

Chesterman pushed his cup of coffee to one side and glanced at the clock inside the entrance to the buffet. The public address system had been unusually silent and in the absence of any announcement to the contrary, he thought it was safe to assume that the nine-thirty inter city from Leicester was on time. In less than fifteen minutes the train would pull into Platform 8 at St Pancras and then the fun would begin, if you could call surveillance fun. With Johnson loitering by the Arrivals and Departures Board ready to pick him up as he came through the barrier, and Hales covering the main entrance from W. H. Smith's bookstall on Platform 1, Mills was certainly getting star treatment for a thief.

So far as the SIS was concerned however, he was a thief with a difference. Back in '64, one million dollars worth of Bearer Bonds had gone down the sink in Geneva and thanks to him, the Department of Subversive Warfare had also lost a couple of agents in Prague. Knowing Mills had engineered the whole set-up was one thing, proving it had been quite a different matter. The SIS had started the ball rolling but they had been unable to break his story and Special Branch had had him under surveillance for the best part of a year before the phone tap paid off.

Perhaps after more than a year he'd thought it safe to cash in some of the securities and buy himself a nifty little villa in Juan les Pins. But, for a supposedly clever operator, Chesterman could never understand why Mills had chosen Janet Rayner to act as a go-between. He should have known better than to expect an ex-girlfriend to keep her mouth shut; less than five minutes after the title deeds to the villa he had bought in France arrived through the post, she had been on the phone to ask what gave him the right to use her flat as a forwarding address. The lead had been passed to the Fraud Squad and they had done the rest, patiently building a case that would at least nail Mills for theft even if they couldn't get him for treason.

After the trial at the Old Bailey it was common knowledge that the Director of Public Prosecutions had thought the sentence of seven years too lenient by half but, in the event, Mills hadn't made it easy for himself. Loss of remission and a vicious assault on a cell mate had led to another five years for Grievous Bodily Harm which ensured he stayed inside for ten. Of the one million dollars only one hundred and fifty thousand had been recovered, a fact that still rankled with a lot of people in high places. There was, however, a distinct possibility that Mills would lead them to the rest and putting him under surveillance from the moment he stepped off the train at St Pancras was to be the means to that end.

Chesterman glanced at the clock again, saw the minute hand jump forward and decided it was time he moved out into the concourse.

*   *   *

The train crawled by a gang of platelayers working on the down line, passed under a bridge and then slowly gathered momentum again. As it clattered through West Hampstead station, Mills reached for his pale blue holdall in the luggage rack and stepped out into the corridor. Although they had ignored one another on the platform at Leicester, he knew that Ray Walters would now be moving down the train to meet him, carrying an identical holdall. Sliding the communicating door open, Mills walked through the buffet car and entered the next coach where he found Walters standing in the passageway outside the toilet.

Walters exchanged holdalls with a broad grin and said, "We can't go on meeting like this."

"I know," said Mills, "people might talk."

"Since when have I had a loose mouth?" The smile was still there but it looked tight.

"You're on the wrong track, Ray. I was referring to my friends in the Special Branch."

Walter's jaw dropped and his throat worked up and down as if his mouth had suddenly gone dry and he found it difficult to swallow. "You didn't tell me you were mixed up with that lot," he muttered.

"There's nothing for you to worry about, they just like to keep in touch with me, like an old acquaintance." Mills weighed the holdall in his hand and wondered if Walters had put one over on him. "I suppose you managed to get the merchandise all right?"

"It's all there, everything you asked for. You'll find the keys and the parking ticket in the envelope on top of the parcel.

9

I've left the car where you said and I've marked the parking bay and registration number on the ticket. You couldn't ask for more, could you?"

Mills studied him thoughtfully. He was cocky and fly, very fly, the sort who'd lift pennies from the eyes of a dead man. "The Mini's not hot, is it, Ray?" he asked softly.

Walters looked disgusted. "Would I do a thing like that?" His voice rose indignantly. "Look, I've only been outside for a month and I'm still looking around. I'm not interested in doing a pissy-arsed little job like nicking a car. That isn't my style. I got a middle man to hire it from Avis."

A middle man? Well, that figured; Walters's every instinct would be to cover himself in case anything went wrong.

"It cost a bit and I'm short of the readies."

"You'll get paid," said Mills.

"When?"

"Early this evening, at your place."

"All two hundred?"

"All two hundred in fives and tens." Mills slid the communicating door open. "I reckon this is where we part company."

"Sure. Then I'll be seeing you tonight?"

"Of course you will," said Mills, "and thanks for everything, Ray."

The compartment was just as he'd left it and nobody looked up or paid the slightest attention to him. The two middle-aged housewives on a cheap day return for a shopping spree in London were still deep in conversation, the smartly dressed woman who looked as if she might be a buyer was still enthralled by *Vogue* and the sales rep in the corner was still avidly reading his glossy brochures as if they were the sermon on the mount.

The train rumbled over the Grand Union Canal and began to slow down as it approached the signal box on the outskirts of St Pancras. A few moments later the vacuum brakes came on with a harsh, grinding squeal and then they were rolling to a gentle stop alongside the island platform. The exodus started slowly, gathered momentum and reaching its peak, fell back like an ebb tide. By the time Mills was ready to leave the coach, the flow was down to a trickle.

No one tried to intercept him at the barrier, yet he knew they were there waiting for him in the concourse. If there had been more people about, the man standing by the Arrivals and Departures Board would not have been quite so conspicuous but as it was, he stood out like a sore thumb. Turning to the right, Mills strolled towards the cloakroom situated near Platform 1. He thought it was an odds-on certainty that at least one of the back-up men would be covering the main entrance.

A strong smell of disinfectant greeted him as he walked into the Men's Room and while he couldn't see any sign of the attendant, it was obvious from the damp tiles that he'd only just finished mopping over the floor. Satisfied that he had the place to himself, Mills entered the nearest cubicle and locked the door behind him before unzipping the holdall. The envelope lay on top of an oblong-shaped box and contained two keys and a parking ticket on which Walters had written OMD 117J – F35. The cardboard box wrapped in brown paper was something special and he opened it carefully.

When he left the cloakroom some ten minutes later, Mills was carrying a Colt Python .357 revolver in a shoulder holster. Made by Replica Limited, it was good enough at first sight to deceive a gunsmith.

*   *   *

Chesterman saw Mills draw level with W. H. Smith's where Hales was browsing through the paperbacks and was surprised when he turned back into the concourse. At first, it looked as though he was making for the nearest subway to the Underground but then, apparently changing his mind, he suddenly veered away. Johnson had switched positions and was no longer standing under the Arrivals and Departures Board, but a slight movement of his head suggested that Mills had spotted him in the small queue waiting for the stopping train to St Albans. Chesterman didn't like the idea much but he thought it best to play safe and move Hales up one place while Johnson dropped back to third man. Changing the batting order was going to be a risky business and he knew it would have to be done discreetly if they were to avoid tipping their hand for the second time running. By entering one of the phone booths at the far end of the hall, Mills presented him with just the opportunity he'd been waiting for.

Mills placed the holdall on the floor between his feet,

sorted out his loose change and then lifted the phone off the hook. Eleven thirty in the morning wasn't the best time in the world to get in touch with his solicitor but it was possible that Gilchrist had had the foresight to warn his secretary to expect a call from him.

A woman with a brisk, no nonsense manner answered and managed to say "Wells, Bull and Dixon" before the blips cut in. Ramming a tenpenny piece into the slot, he punched the button and asked to speak to Gilchrist.

The woman said, "Who shall I say is calling, please?"

"Mills," he said, "Edward Mills. Mr Gilchrist asked me to ring him."

It was a long way from the truth but it seemed to have the desired effect. The woman mellowed a little and told him to wait just one minute. It was all very polite but not particularly efficient because Gilchrist proved elusive. By the time somebody managed to locate him, six of the ten minutes Mills had paid for were gone.

Morris Gilchrist said, "Edward, you don't know how good it is to hear your voice again after all these years. How are you?"

"I'm in pretty good shape."

"I'm glad to hear it. Of course, I had heard a whisper that you'd made a remarkable recovery. By the way, where are you calling from?"

"St Pancras. I don't want to seem rude, Morris, but what have you got for me?"

"Your parents' house fetched thirty-two thousand. After legal fees and Capital Transfer Tax, your share amounts to a little over eight and a half. I'm afraid it's not as much as you might have expected but there were a number of other beneficiaries under the will."

Mills frowned at his reflection in the mirror. Either Gilchrist was being deliberately obtuse or else he'd misunderstood. "We're not on the same wavelength," he said curtly. "I want to know if your Enquiry Agent has been earning his fee?"

"He's found Boxall but, as your solicitor, I would advise you to avoid him like the plague. After all, you don't want to give the police the . . ."

The blips cut Gilchrist off in mid sentence. Feeding another coin into the box, Mills waited until the mechanism had stopped whirring and then said, "As my solicitor, there are just two things I want from you – Boxall's address and four hundred in cash, split down the middle between fives and tens."

"I'll have to go to the bank."

"You do that small thing, Morris, and we'll meet for a drink in your favourite pub at one o'clock. It's still The Silver Chalice, isn't it?"

"It is."

"Good. Now suppose you tell me where Boxall's living."

"28 Hadleigh Road, Ealing. But I think you'll be making a big mistake, Edward, if you try to see him."

Mills thought Gilchrist sounded weary, as if he knew his advice would be ignored. "I've already made my big mistake."

"Back in '64, I presume?"

"You're dead right," said Mills, "I should have caught a plane to Rio de Janeiro while the going was good." He put the phone down and left the box before Gilchrist had a chance to come back at him.

The concourse looked even more naked and as he strolled towards the Underground, Mills noticed that the passengers waiting for the stopping train to St Albans had been allowed through the gate on to the platform. Since the shadow had also disappeared along with the rest of the queue, he thought it likely that the surveillance team had been re-organised, which meant there was a new man up front. Deep in thought, he walked into the station, bought a ticket to Marble Arch from one of the vending machines in the booking hall and rode the escalator down to the Piccadilly Line.

Knowing something of the techniques employed by Special Branch, he drifted towards the far end of the platform, confident that the lead man would follow him into the same compartment. Unless they had changed their routine procedures, it was a safe bet that the back-up would be in the next coach but one. Out of the corner of his eye he saw the distant signal change from red to green; seconds later, a faint breeze of warm air ruffled the hair of the schoolgirl standing in front of him and then the train roared into the station.

There were a number of spare seats in the front compartment and turning left, he chose one just inside the doors. Facing him across the centre aisle was a mournful little man

13

with plump thighs who was holding hands with a girl in a shapeless maxi-skirt which looked as if it had been rescued from a jumble sale. A couple of French tourists, strap hanging inside the entrance, acted as a shield, making it difficult for anyone at the other end of the coach to keep a close eye on him. Although it was impossible to hear what they were saying, Mills had an idea they were lost, an impression which was reinforced when the taller of the two produced a map of the Underground system and opened it out. They were still trying to decide where they were going when he got off the train at Holborn.

A railway inspector, a man clutching an executive-style briefcase and two middle-aged women left the same coach slightly ahead of him. The businessman was in no great hurry to reach the exit and veering across the platform, he stopped in front of one of the information billboards, seemingly interested in the bus routes serving High Holborn. Mills walked on past him and followed the directional signs for the Central Line. It came as no great surprise to him when the businessman subsequently reappeared in time to scramble into the last carriage of the west-bound train to Ealing Broadway.

Special Branch were neither careless nor stupid and he had a feeling that the last-minute dash had been deliberate, a sort of diversion which was intended to hold his attention while they made the switch. Appearances were often deceptive but glancing round the compartment, he couldn't see anyone who was either young, fit or alert enough to be numbered with the opposition. It could be a sign that they had changed their tactics but the fact that they were no longer dogging his shadow didn't bother Mills. Once they saw him disappearing into the underground car park at Hyde Park, he figured they would be only too anxious to close the gap.

Every seat in the compartment was taken and people were even standing in both entrances. A trickle got out at Tottenham Court Road but there was a mass exodus of shoppers at Oxford Circus and by the time the train pulled out of Bond Street, the coach was best part empty. Marble Arch wasn't any too popular either, which made life difficult for both parties because there was not enough crowd cover for the opposition to remain inconspicuous, and Mills had to act as if he was blissfully unaware of their presence. Surrendering his ticket at the barrier, he walked out of the station and, crossing Oxford Street, turned into Park Lane.

Chesterman wasn't sure what to make of it. There had been moments, especially at Holborn, when he'd been convinced that Mills was playing with them like a fisherman, but now he appeared to be more relaxed. It could be a sign that he was under the mistaken impression that he'd given them the slip; on the other hand, knowing something of his reputation, Chesterman thought Mills might still have a few tricks up his sleeve. In his opinion, anyone who could hide eight hundred and fifty thousand dollars from the Fraud Squad was a man to be reckoned with.

A bus momentarily blocked Chesterman's view and when next he saw him, Mills was entering the pedestrian subway in Park Lane which led to the car park under Hyde Park. Suddenly everything began to make sense and he knew that the phone call from St Pancras and the game of cat and mouse on the Underground were simply the prelude to a meet. The bastard was going to slip through their fingers and there wasn't a damn thing they could do about it except wave him goodbye and take down the number of the car as it sailed past them. Mills wouldn't be lost for ever but that wasn't the point. Wray had said that he was to be kept under tight surveillance from the moment he stepped off the inter city, and they had made a balls of it. Angry with himself, Chesterman signalled Hales and Johnson to cover the exits while he went after the target.

Mills cut through the subway, lengthening his stride with every pace. He thought he still had a lead of thirty yards on the front man but even so, this wouldn't give him much time to find an ambush position. Entering the car park, he dumped the holdall into a wastebin and then ducked behind one of the supporting columns which separated one bay from the next.

The Special Branch man was coming fast, stepping out like a light infantryman at a hundred and sixty paces to the minute, a hunter who was about to become the hunted because this section of the car park was deserted and the quarry was lying in wait for him. Mills heard the footsteps falter, sensed that only the large concrete pillar was between them, and reached for the Colt Python in his shoulder holster. For a moment it seemed they had inadvertently arrived at an impasse but then he moved forward again and Mills stepped in behind him and pressed the barrel against his neck.

"Keep your hands down," he said softly.

"What is this?" Chesterman moistened his lips. "A hold up? Look, I'm not carrying much on me but you can have what I've got, only for Christ's sake don't do anything stupid."

"You missed your vocation, you should have been an actor."

"Look, why pick on me? I'm just an office manager, a glorified clerk."

"I've got news for you." Mills pushed a little harder, digging the barrel into his neck. "As of now, you're a messenger boy."

Chesterman breathed out. A messenger boy? Well, that was a relief; for a moment he had thought Mills might be crazy enough to squeeze the trigger. "What is this," he muttered, "some sort of joke?"

"You tell the Man that Mills has declared war on him and then see if he laughs."

"What the hell are you talking about?"

"A state of war. Just pass the word around and maybe it'll reach the right ears. Of course, I'm not looking for an unconditional surrender."

War? Unconditional surrender? Chesterman closed his eyes; Mills was crazy, mad as a hatter.

"We can always agree to an armistice. The terms would be one hundred and fifty thousand dollars at ten percent compound interest over ten years. We'll forget the odd thirty-six cents and call it a round three hundred and eighty-nine thousand and sixty-one dollars."

"Let me guess the rest," Chesterman said dryly. "You want it in sterling at the current exchange rate."

"You're catching on." Mills transferred the Colt to his left hand and stepped back. "You can turn round now," he said in a voice that was surprisingly mild.

Chesterman hesitated, wondered if he should stay put and then, on further reflection, decided it was best to humour him.

"Ever been had?"

Chesterman stared at the revolver which Mills was holding in the open palm of his hand and never saw the punch coming. His jaw, however, was in exactly the right position and he went down and out like a log.

Mills placed the gun beside him and then walked away, looking for Bay F35 where the Mini was parked.

2

THE SILVER CHALICE in Upper Thames Street had changed out of all recognition. The Victorian façade was still there but the interior had been gutted, the Snug, Lounge and Saloon bars merging into one big, impersonal, chrome-fitted, vinyl-upholstered, dimly lit room. Mills could remember when the place had an atmosphere but that was a long time ago. Probably the pub had been featured in one of the Sunday Colour Supplements which in turn had led to its discovery by far too many people. Glancing round the crowded, nouveau-art interior, he thought there was one journalist in town who had a lot to answer for.

Gilchrist had found a small corner table for two, close enough to one of the speakers to ensure that nobody would hear their conversation above the piped music. Diplomacy had always been his strong suit, an asset that had enabled him to become the senior partner in Wells, Bull and Dixon at the age of thirty-six. Wells and Bull were both deceased and marrying Dixon's insipid daughter had given him an advantage over the opposition, but even so, it had required all his tact and considerable powers of persuasion to hold the firm together after the old man had retired. There was an old saying that the Welsh were born orators and when it was most needed, Gilchrist had all the passionate eloquence of a Nye Bevan.

Gilchrist said, "I've taken the liberty of ordering lunch." He waved a well-manicured hand towards a plate of cold roast beef and salad, and flashed a smile, radiating the kind of warmth that women found irresistible. It was part of his stock-in-trade charm that had had the desired effect on Wendy Dixon, but she was the sort of gullible, homely girl who was an absolute pushover for someone like Morris. It was his good fortune that he'd been the first presentable man to

17

show any interest in her, an interest which had been and still was largely stimulated by the size of her bank balance.

"I thought a carafe of red wine but of course if you would prefer something else, Edward?"

"I'd like a lager."

"Certainly – draught or bottled?"

"Bottled," said Mills, "Carlsberg if they've got it."

Gilchrist raised a hand and snapped his fingers, summoning a blonde waitress who was got up like a Pearly Queen, one of the features of The Silver Chalice that visitors from overseas found quaint. Unfortunately, the girl had a marked Swedish accent which didn't do a lot for the Cockney image, and the pub had run out of Carlsberg. Mills took her word that their draught beer was very good and settled for a half of mild and bitter.

"This isn't your lucky day, is it, Edward?" Suddenly aware of the faux-pas, Gilchrist reached inside his jacket and produced a fat manilla envelope. "Maybe this will make up for it. Perhaps you wouldn't mind signing the attached receipt?" He smiled apologetically. "I'm afraid our accounts department is very meticulous about these things."

"I'm meticulous too," said Mills. "You don't mind if I count it, do you? I like to know what I'm signing for."

"It's all there."

"I'm sure it is." Mills ripped the envelope open and looked inside. "After all, you can't afford to be caught with your fingers in the till."

"I can see that you're still very bitter."

"Does that surprise you?"

Gilchrist shook his head. "No, but in your place, I think I'd try to bury the past and start a new life." He rested both elbows on the table and pressed his fingertips together as if in prayer. "Have you heard from your brother since he went to the States?"

"What do you think?"

Gilchrist wasn't surprised. Doctor Ralph Mills believed in looking after number one. He had been at the head of the queue to quit the National Health Service when the Labour Party announced their intention to phase out pay beds and had gone to New York, where rumour had it, he enjoyed a very lucrative practice.

"What about your sister, Barbara?"

18

"Her husband's just been transferred to Glasgow." Mills tucked the envelope into his breast pocket, signed the receipt and pushed it across the table. "Why all the questions, Morris?" he said quietly.

"I was wondering if you had somewhere to stay."

"I'll find a place."

"I have a flat in Moravian Place just off Cheyne Walk."

Mills raised his eyebrows. Cheyne Walk – the snob end of Chelsea? Morris was obviously doing better than he'd thought, and in more ways than one.

"Actually, it belongs to the firm but you're more than welcome to it. Incidentally, Wendy and I are off to the Algarve for a fortnight's holiday on Saturday."

"With the children?" The response was automatic, unthinking.

"No, they're still away at boarding school; they don't break up for another three weeks yet."

"Well, it's very kind of you to offer but . . ."

"No buts."

Gilchrist smiled at the Swedish waitress who placed a tankard of mild and bitter in front of Mills and returned his smile, lowering her eyelashes in a way that suggested she was interested.

"No buts," he repeated. "Here, take the keys; you'll be doing me a favour by keeping the squatters at bay. They're getting to be quite a problem these days."

He was pushing hard, like a door-to-door salesman anxious to close the deal before the customer asked too many awkward questions. Mills wondered if Gilchrist was trying to salve his conscience in some small way; perhaps, after all these years, the knowledge that he'd briefed a deadbeat of a QC still troubled him. Barristers, like doctors, rarely admit to having bungled a job but after the trial was over, even the QC's Junior had conceded that they should have made a much better showing in court.

"Well, what do you say, Edward?"

"You've talked me into it."

Mills was conscious of sounding ungrateful but Gilchrist didn't seem to notice. If anything, he appeared relieved that his offer had finally been accepted.

"Are you going anywhere this evening?" he asked between mouthfuls of cold roast beef and salad.

19

"I wasn't thinking of doing so."

"Good; well, I'll ask Elizabeth to drop in on her way home from the office, if that's all right with you?"

"Does she go with the flat?"

Gilchrist placed his knife and fork together on the plate and wiped a crumb from his lip. His mouth which until that moment had been set in anger, suddenly creased into a smile that was noticeably false.

"Certainly not," he said. "Elizabeth Eastgate is one of my colleagues; she's just passed her finals."

"Really?"

"Make no mistake, Elizabeth is very competent. I thought she could present our final statement together with a cheque for the remaining eight thousand one hundred and perhaps answer any points you may have regarding your mother's will."

"Why all the rush, Morris?"

"Well, there's no real hurry; I just thought you'd like to have the cheque now instead of waiting another fortnight."

Was it more than just a thoughtful suggestion? As politely as he knew how, was Gilchrist letting it be known that he didn't want anything more to do with him? Was everything to be wrapped up, cut and dried, before he and Wendy returned from the Algarve?

"Perhaps you're right," Mills said pensively. "I can certainly use the money. When can I expect to see your Elizabeth Eastgate?"

"About five thirty."

Mills reached for the tankard of beer and drank it thoughtfully. Wells, Bull and Dixon had looked after the family's affairs for as long as he could remember but that didn't mean the association had to go on for ever. After all, the estate had been wound up and the family was scattered, with Ralph in New York and Barbara in Glasgow. Possibly Morris was only anticipating events but all the same, he couldn't help feeling that Gilchrist had some ulterior motive for severing the connection.

"Have you seen Boxall?"

Mills lowered his tankard. "Not yet."

"Well, take my advice, think twice before you do."

The last counsel from solicitor to erstwhile client? Well, he could shove his advice, shove it right up as far as it would go. Boxall was the key, the guide dog who was going to lead him to the man, the bastard who'd set him up all those years ago.

Mills picked up his knife and fork and attacked the cold roast beef, cutting off a slice that was almost red raw like Sidney Boxall's face had been when the screws had found him lying unconscious in the shower room.

*   *   *

Chief Superintendent Wray stepped into the lift, closed the wrought-iron gate behind him and then pressed the button on the control panel. Much like an asthmatic old man, the lift wheezed him up to the sixth floor where, in marked contrast to the slow motion ascent, it suddenly came to an abrupt, spine-jarring halt. Not for the first time, Wray thought that the lift had a lot in common with the people who worked for the Department of Subversive Warfare. One moment you would be rubbing along quite happily working hand in glove with them and the next, they would pull the carpet out from under your feet. They were the twilight people, operating within parameters which overlapped the functions of the SIS and Special Branch; a charter that caused a lot of heart-burn on occasions, especially amongst the senior civil servants at both the Home and Foreign Office.

The War Department constable manning the desk outside the security area greeted Wray with a faint smile and then examined his identity card, recording the details in the Occurrence Book before issuing him with a Visitor's Pass. The buff-coloured form looked innocuous but it was the open sesame which took him through the gate and on down the narrow, gloomy corridor to Harper's room at the far end. For a large man, Wray was surprisingly light on his feet and the PA in the outer office didn't hear him until it was too late. From the sound of her voice, he got the impression that Miss Nightingale was more than a little annoyed at having to announce his arrival over the intercom.

In contrast with his PA, Harper didn't seem at all put out, but then few people ever knew what he was thinking.

He said, "Well, this is a pleasant surprise. It's good to see you again, Stanley."

"And you, Cedric."

"I must say you're looking very fit. Have you been dieting?"

21

Wray lowered himself into a leather armchair which creaked under his weight. "Does it look like it?" he grunted.

"You amaze me." Harper shook his head as if in disbelief. "I could have sworn that you'd lost at least half a stone."

"I only wish I could."

Wray was convinced that Harper always probed his weak spot to put him at a disadvantage. Of average height and weight, Harper looked as if he belonged in a track suit, which was damned unfair considering he'd been deskbound for the last fifteen years and rarely took any exercise apart from pottering about in his garden. If outward appearances were anything to go by, the pressures that went with the job had not left their mark on him. His hair was still brown, there were no worry lines in his face and judging from the set of his mouth which seemed permanently on the point of breaking out into a smile, his caustic sense of humour was as sharp as ever. Harper was one of the most youthful-looking men of fifty-two he'd come across and no stranger seeing them together would ever guess that they were the same age.

"Well now . . ."

Wray smiled fleetingly. Those two little words meant that Harper had had enough of the social pleasantries. "Edward James Mills," he said tersely.

"The SIS man? What about him?"

He was released from Leicester today, and the fun's already started."

"Fun?" echoed Harper. "What on earth are you talking about, Stanley?"

"He's sent you an ultimatum; either he gets three hundred and eighty-nine thousand and sixty-one dollars by way of compensation or else he's going to make trouble. Chesterman tells me that this figure is based on the original one hundred and fifty thousand Mills embezzled plus compound interest of ten percent over ten years."

"He's after a nest egg, is he?" said Harper. "Well, aside from the fact that Mills is obviously crazy, do you mind telling me how and why he got in touch with Sergeant Chesterman?"

"Because either your Department or the SIS wanted him placed under surveillance and the ball ended up in my court."

Wray was hoping for a positive reaction but Harper neither confirmed nor denied it. Taking out his pipe, Wray began to fill the bowl with Dunhill Standard Mixture from an old tobacco pouch. It was a favourite gambit, one that he employed whenever it was necessary to play for time.

"I think he knew that we were waiting for him at St Pancras," he said.

"And naturally he turned the tables on you."

Wray struck a match and held it over the bowl. Harper had always been quick to draw the correct deduction from any inference no matter how vague, but the sarcasm didn't become him.

"I'm afraid there's more to it than that, Cedric. Mills led Chesterman into a trap and held him up at gun point with a Colt Python .357 while he delivered his ultimatum. As it happened, it was a Replica but Chesterman didn't know that until he recovered consciousness and found the revolver lying by his side."

Harper picked up a pencil and drew a large question mark on the blotting pad in front of him. "It's all very dramatic, isn't it?" he said thoughtfully. "And it's not what you would expect of a rational man either. I mean, if I'd been Mills and wanted to reopen the case, I would have got in touch with the National Council for Civil Liberties."

"That isn't his style. Mills is the sort of man who thinks everyone is against him. Even tried to nail a prison officer called Patterson for victimisation while he was in Albany but of course he couldn't make it stick. Still, that doesn't mean he won't give us a few headaches now that he's loose."

"Us?" Harper said sharply. "He's your problem, not mine. I didn't ask for him to be kept under surveillance."

"Oh, come on," Wray said irritably, "thanks to Mills, two of your agents got the chop in Prague. Now don't try and tell me that you are not after his hide."

"It was an SIS operation, Stanley, and we just happened to catch a few of the brickbats. I've already told you, he's their man, not mine. I don't give a damn what happens to Mills."

The protest seemed a little too vehement to be wholly convincing. Determined to sit it out, Wray fixed his gaze on the high porthole window which was divided by strips of wood into a number of octagonal segments.

After several minutes of silence, Harper said, "What is it you find so interesting out there, Stanley?"

"Chesterman has a lump on his jaw the size of an egg and I think that entitles me to an explanation."

"Oh, do you?"

"And what's more, I'm not leaving here until I get one."

Harper studied him thoughtfully. Wray often gave the impression that he was good-natured and easy-going but there was a streak of obstinacy just below the surface, a trait which they had in common. Once his mind was made up, nothing could dissuade him. If Wray said that he intended to stay put until he got what he wanted, then, if necessary, he would sit it out until his pension came due.

"An explanation?" Harper shook his head. "I don't know what's going on either, but if it's any help, I can give you some background information, information that never came out at the trial. Naturally, it's for your ears only."

"Do I have to sign anything?"

"I wouldn't advise you to repeat anything you're about to hear. Anyway, you're already bound by the Official Secrets Acts."

"So?"

"So it all began back in 1964 with a Professor Yuri Kiktev, a fifty-four-year-old missile expert who was working on MIRVs."

"On what?" asked Wray.

"Multiple Independently Targeted Re-entry Vehicles – H Bombs from outer space, that sort of thing. Apparently, Kiktev had become infatuated with a young woman, a certain Larissa Fedorovna Pavlichenko of the Moscow State Ballet Company. Well, of course there's nothing unusual about that; after all, lots of middle-aged men keep a mistress, even in Russia, and in Kiktev's case it was perfectly understandable because to say the least, his wife is no oil painting. I daresay he could have got a divorce but that wasn't enough for Larissa Fedorovna Pavlichenko. You see, she had been on tour with the ballet company in 1960 and had seen how the other half lived. One can only assume that when it was announced that the Moscow State was to visit this country again in 1964, she told Kiktev that she intended to defect, because he, the poor besotted idiot, decided to go with her and got in touch with our Embassy in Moscow. Well, you can guess how the SIS reacted; this was the biggest thing that had happened to them since the Penkovsky affair. His asking price of one million dollars in Bearer Bonds seemed fair enough to the SIS considering what he had to offer, but

24

there was a slight problem. While the ballet company was performing in London, friend Kiktev would be attending a conference of Nuclear Physicists in Prague and somebody had to get him out of Czechoslovakia before La Pavlichenko went over the wall, which is where we came into the picture. The rest, Stanley, is history. The ballet tour went ahead but the Prague conference was conveniently postponed at the last minute. Dear, sweet Larissa defected on schedule, and Kiktev, who by a curious coincidence had a nervous break-down shortly afterwards, ended up in a nursing home. The Czech STB Intelligence Service raked in my two agents either before or after the event and Mills scooped a million dollars."

"In Geneva?"

"That's right."

"What was he doing in Switzerland?"

"You'd better ask the SIS."

Wray leaned forward and tapped his pipe over the glass ashtray on Harper's desk. "I think you're snowing me," he said quietly. "My guess is that you asked your Minister to have a few quiet words with the Home Secretary and that's how we got landed with this surveillance job."

"You can get out of it."

"How?" Wray said angrily. "Go on, tell me how?"

"Try informing the Assistant Commissioner that you need to double the manpower because Mills is on to you and then see what happens. Look, if somebody is using Special Branch as a stalking horse, you can bet it isn't the SIS or me. If you want my opinion, it's the Fraud Squad."

"You may have a point." Wray gave up, inspected his pipe to make sure it was out before slipping it into his pocket and then launched himself out of the chair. "They could be after the missing eight hundred and fifty thousand."

"They could indeed."

"Of course, if Mills should get in touch with your Depart-ment, you will let us know, won't you?"

"I wouldn't dream of holding anything back from you, Stanley. Anyway, as I told you, my people haven't the slightest interest in the man. Not any more."

It was a lie and they both knew it. Barely five minutes after Wray had left the building, Harper called Central Registry on the intercom and asked for the file on Edward James Mills.

3

MILLS GLANCED AT the number on the front gate to make sure that he had the right address and then got out of the car. Finding Hadleigh Road amongst the jigsaw of interlocking streets which formed a maze around St Catherine's Church had taken him the best part of half an hour and he wondered now if it had been worth the effort. Boxall's flat was supposed to be on the ground floor of the large Edwardian semi-detached but the To Let sign hanging in the window either made nonsense of Gilchrist's information or else his pigeon had left the coop within the last few days. Opening the front gate, he walked up the path and rang the bell.

The door was opened by a pleasant, dark-haired woman in a sleeveless cotton dress who looked as if she might be in her late thirties.

"Good afternoon," Mills said politely. "I'm sorry to trouble you but I wonder if you can help me?" He smiled and pointed to the hanging card in the downstairs window. "It's about the flat."

"Oh yes?" Her face brightened visibly. "Are you interested in taking it?"

"Well, no. Actually, I'm looking for a Mr Sidney Boxall. I was told that I would find him at this address."

"I'm afraid you've missed him; he left us on Monday. Is he a friend of yours?"

"Hardly. You see, I work for the United Finance Company and we're rather anxious to trace him. He didn't happen to leave a forwarding address by any chance, did he?"

"No."

The woman was suspicious now and obviously didn't trust him, which was understandable. Mills had met any number of petty thieves while he was in prison who managed to gain an entry by posing as a salesman or an official from the gas

26

board. He wished there was some way he could establish his identity and win her trust but he had nothing to show her except a brand new wallet. His eyes flickered thoughtfully; money always impressed people.

"That's awkward; Mr Boxall is three months behind with his hire purchase repayments." He took out his wallet and flipped it open, making sure that she caught a glimpse of the fat wad of notes while he went through the motions of looking for a calling card. "Did he take it with him?"

"What?"

"The twenty-six-inch Sony colour television set. He didn't leave it in the flat by any chance, Mrs . . . ?"

"Mrs Aston," she said. "No, he didn't and that's a fact."

"Wouldn't you know it?" Mills looked rueful. "The oldest dodge in the world, Mrs Aston, and we fell for it."

"A television set?" she repeated blankly.

"Yes; as a matter of fact he still owes three hundred and seventeen pounds fifty on it."

"I can't believe it, he was such a nice man." She nibbled her bottom lip and frowned. "Perhaps you'd better come inside, Mr . . . ?"

"Mills." He returned the wallet to his inside pocket and took her hand, shaking it firmly before his name had time to register. "It's very good of you," he said warmly, "and I promise I won't keep you long."

She smiled again, no longer suspicious but anxious to be helpful. "This was Mr Boxall's flat," she said, opening a door off the hall.

The flat consisted of an L-shaped bed-sitting room with an adjoining kitchenette which was just a shade bigger than a walk-in cupboard. A drop-leaf table and two upright chairs with padded seats filled the dining alcove so that, of necessity, the divan had been pushed against the wall at right angles to a wardrobe and chest of drawers in order to create a false impression of space. Directly opposite the bed, two easy chairs faced one another across a low coffee table in front of the gas fire.

"It looks very nice," he murmured appreciatively.

"Yes, we think it's comfortable."

"Did Mr Boxall give you any idea where he might be going?"

27

"Well, he said something about a friend finding him a temporary job in Torquay."

"When was this, Mrs Aston?"

"Oh, last Sunday evening about ten minutes after I'd told him he was wanted on the phone out there in the hall."

Boxall could have been telling her the truth. This was the peak holiday season when casual labour was in demand and it was possible that a friend had found him a job down in Devon, but all the same, it was a bit of a coincidence. Perhaps he was letting his imagination run wild but he couldn't help feeling that somebody had been anxious to get Boxall out of the way.

"Let's see," Mills said speculatively, "he was working for Sketchley Dry Cleaners, wasn't he?"

"No, no, that must have been some time ago. He's been with Swiftsure Radio Cabs in the High Street ever since I've known him."

Boxall had been a driver, one of the best in the business until the Caterham bank raid went sour. He thought somebody must have done a lot of hard grafting to get him a job with a reputable firm like Swiftsure Radio Cabs.

"Yes, well it would seem that either our records are out of date or else Mr Boxall deliberately tried to mislead us. Perhaps, with any luck, Swiftsure might be able to give us a lead." Mills smiled and edged his way towards the hall. "Anyway, that's not your problem."

"What do you think he did with the television set? I mean, I'm quite certain he never brought it home with him."

"He probably sold it for cash, that's the usual form."

"I would never have dreamt he could be so dishonest." She shook her head regretfully. "It just goes to show that you can't trust anybody these days."

"I'm afraid you can't." Mills gripped her limp hand again and shook it briefly. "You've been most helpful, Mrs Aston," he said warmly, "and I'm very grateful."

"It's kind of you to say so, but really, I haven't done anything." She opened the door for him. "It's been nice meeting you, Mr. Wills."

Mills didn't bother to correct her. She was still standing on the doorstep, arms folded across her chest apparently deep in thought when he pulled out from the kerb and drove off.

A white Cortina followed him as far as the first set of

traffic lights in Ealing Broadway where it was replaced by a Ford Transit. Mills thought he'd lost the van on Western Avenue but shortly after ditching the Mini in a side street off the Bayswater Road, he saw it again. The Ford Transit was then parked on a double yellow line opposite the Lancaster Gate entrance to Kensington Gardens and the driver seemed to be having trouble with the engine. He was also being harassed by an officious traffic warden.

*   *   *

Iain Gattis thought that Harper's office could do with a good face lift. The colourwash on the walls had gone from white through cream to a dull yellow and the ceiling was smudged with black from the fluorescent lighting. The Property Services Agency were supposed to ring the changes periodically but if memory served him correctly, the prints of Waterloo and Balaclava had looked pretty faded when Harper had briefed him shortly after he joined the Department in 1972. The grey-blue carpet was ex-RAF, part of the surplus accommodation store which had been thrown up as a result of the latest Defence cuts, but at least it was brand new.

"The card index on the IRA?" Harper initialled the file he'd been reading and tossed it into the Out-tray. "Is it up to date?"

"Apart from a couple of loose ends," Gattis said cautiously.

"What loose ends?"

"Farren and Rooney. There's a rumour circulating in Belfast that they've been sent over here to set up an active service unit."

There was no need for Gattis to elaborate. Farren and Rooney were high on the wanted list. Two of the most successful gunmen with the Provos, their victims included nine members of the Security Forces and five civilians, one of whom had been a senior civil servant with the Northern Ireland Office. Both men were known to have slipped over the border in September '75 when things had got too hot for them in Belfast, but although an informer claimed he'd seen Rooney in Dundalk towards the end of March, Farren had apparently vanished into thin air.

"What does the Army think?"

"As far as they're concerned, it's just one more unconfirmed report. They didn't even bother to include it in their monthly intelligence summary. However, for what it's worth, they're convinced that Farren and Rooney are not lying low in Ulster." Gattis scratched a spot on his chin. "I thought we might ask Dublin to keep their ears and eyes open. Of course, all we have on them is a rough description and a couple of Identikit likenesses but you never know, we might have a stroke of luck."

"I suppose it's worth a try." Harper's lack of enthusiasm was positively contagious. "Anyway, one of your assistants can deal with that problem, Iain. After all, it's not exactly urgent, is it?"

"Hardly."

"I'm glad we agree because I've got a much more important job for you. It's rather a delicate matter but as an ex-CID man, it should be right up your street." Harper glanced at his millboard his brow furrowing as if he had some difficulty in deciphering his own handwriting. "Have you ever been to the Isle of Wight?"

"Can't say that I have."

"Well, now's your chance. I want you to scout around Newport and see what you can dig up on Mr Frederick Patterson. He used to be a prison officer at Albany until he resigned from the service and opened a newsagents and tobacconists in Shanklin."

"What's he been up to?"

"Nothing," said Harper, "I'm merely interested to know if he's as hard as some people have alleged."

"Like who for instance?"

"Edward James Mills."

"The SIS man turned double agent?" Gattis shook his head. "Mills was before my time but from what I've heard, I wouldn't believe a word he said."

"Good, that means you're just the man to play the devil's advocate." Harper unclipped a sheet of paper from his scratch pad and pushed it across the desk. "These are just a few names and addresses; two of those mentioned are former colleagues, one of whom, by name of Usher, is still in the prison service. The third is a felon who did time with Mills. I'd rather you didn't approach that one unless it's unavoidable because he's certain to be biased."

"What sort of hat will I be wearing?" Gattis grinned. "Am I supposed to be a police officer or will I be going in blind?"

"No, I thought you could pass yourself off as a civil servant from the Positive Vetting Unit. You won't have any difficulty with the Governor of Albany because we've agreed between us that Patterson is to be one of the referees nominated by Sturgess."

"Who's he?"

"Actually, Sturgess doesn't exist but you'll say that he's about to join the security staff at Porton Down, the Chemical Warfare Research Establishment. I've concocted a potted life-history for him but you may have to embroider it a little if things get awkward."

Harper smiled in a way which implied he was quite sure Gattis was unlikely to find himself in deep water. Making light of any hidden pitfalls was part of his technique for instilling confidence.

Gattis sighed. "How long have I got?"

"It shouldn't take you more than a couple of days."

The Harper touch again. Gattis stared at the sheet of paper in his hand and thought it would take him that long to decipher the untidy scrawl.

"Do you have any other questions?"

"Only one. What has Mills got against Patterson?"

"Loss of remission," said Harper. "He's probably got a persecution complex, but I'd like to know what you think."

It was the classic iceberg situation; only one ninth of the hazard was showing and Harper was only giving the vaguest warning of the dangers below the surface.

*   *   *

They met on the staircase going in opposite directions; Mills heading towards Gilchrist's flat on the second floor, the girl on her way down to the lobby. As they came towards one another, he noticed that she was quite tall, had dark shoulder-length hair and a face that was attractive yet full of character. The chin was perhaps a little too heavy, squared off like a man's, but the natural curve of her mouth softened the features and somehow made them seem all the more striking. By the time they drew level, he was also aware that the denim skirt and blouse lent a subtle emphasis to a very trim figure.

31

Mills side-stepped to his left to leave her more room and she smiled a thank you in the way that one stranger greets another. And then the penny dropped.

"Miss Eastgate?" he said tentatively.

She stopped and turned about to face him. "Mr Mills, I presume?"

Like Stanley meeting Livingstone, he thought, except that she's much better looking.

"Yes. I'm sorry you didn't find me at home."

"There's no need to apologise, I was early." Her smile was warm and friendly.

"Only you see Morris said that you'd be here about five thirty so I nipped round the corner to get an evening paper."

She hadn't asked for an explanation but he'd given her one just the same. This was the first time that he'd been close to an attractive woman in over ten years and he felt out of his depth.

"Anyway, I'm glad we bumped into one another."

"Yes." She hesitated for a moment as if unsure what to say next. "Actually, I pushed the envelope through your letter box. The cheque is attached to our final statement of account which is quite straightforward." Her forehead creased in a frown. "I mean it's simple to understand."

"I'm sure it is. Won't you come in for a drink?"

"It's a little early, isn't it?"

"I think we've got some instant coffee."

"Well, that's very kind of you but if you don't mind, I think I'd better give it a miss. I've got my car and I'd like to avoid the worst of the rush hour."

"Can't you spare a couple of minutes? I've come up against a problem and I'd appreciate your advice."

"Is it anything to do with conveyancing? You see, that's really my field."

She was quick off the mark, eager to put him off yet careful not to seem impolite.

"No, but Morris said you would be able to answer any queries I might have."

"Oh, did he?"

There was a stony expression on her face which matched the tone of voice. Something told him that Gilchrist was going to get a piece of her mind in the very near future.

"Well, I'll certainly do my best but you may want a second opinion."

"I doubt it," said Mills.

She made one last attempt to wriggle out of it, glancing pointedly at her wristwatch to give the impression that she had another engagement. Vexed that he refused to take the hint, she then gave up the struggle and followed him upstairs.

Mills opened the door, picked up the envelope from the mat and left it with the *Evening News* on the hall table. The flat looked as if it had been designed by the man who was responsible for the film sets at Pinewood. There were no dividing walls, just one big living area which embraced the hall, living room, dining nook and kitchenette. Lebensraum, spacious gracious living, had been the basic theme but in achieving it, the architect had created a home that had all the warmth and intimacy of an empty theatre. Elizabeth Eastgate took one look at the apartment and raised her eyebrows expressively.

"Think twice before you make any comment." Mills smiled at her. "Morris lent it to me."

"Oh?"

"Well, I suppose the flat really belongs to Wells, Bull and Dixon."

Her lips pursed fleetingly but long enough to make it obvious that this was the first she'd heard about it.

"Instant coffee?" said Mills.

"No thank you."

"A drink then?" He glanced across at a teak and chromium trolley laden with bottles and glasses. "I think Morris has provided just about everything. Sherry, gin, vodka, whisky, brandy?"

"I'm afraid it's still too early for me. Look, I don't want to rush you but you said something about wanting my advice." She bit her lip but looked embarrassed. "I'm sorry," she muttered, "that was very rude of me."

"You don't owe me an apology."

She sat down in an armchair, prim and erect like a schoolmistress, her knees close together. The skirt was mid length but it couldn't conceal the fact that she had nice legs.

He smiled at her as warmly as he knew how. "I got you up here under false pretences. I only want to know the name and address of your Private Enquiry Agent."

"I didn't know we had one."

"Morris hired somebody to find Boxall, didn't he?"

"I've no idea and I'm afraid I've never heard of Boxall either. Look, Wells, Bull and Dixon are a very big partnership and regrettable as it may seem to you, we do rather tend to work in separate compartments."

The explanation carried a ring of truth and he knew that she wasn't trying to be evasive. Elizabeth Eastgate might be a competent solicitor but she would never make a good poker player even if she lived to be a hundred.

"Finding this man Boxall obviously means a great deal to you," she said quietly.

"You could say that."

"Why?"

It was a good question and one that was difficult to answer. Boxall had shared the same cell with him at Durham until somebody had worked him over, giving him a facial as he lay unconscious on the duckboards. So far so good, he thought; now try explaining to Elizabeth Eastgate that you were framed and then see what happens. Just watch the expression of disbelief appear on her face when you tell her that Boxall and the two eye witnesses who fingered you for the job were lying in their teeth and that the potato embedded with four bloodstained razor blades found inside your mattress had been a deliberate plant.

"I got seven years for grand larceny but that wasn't enough for the man. He wanted me kept inside long enough to become a vegetable. I'd still be doing time in Leicester if I hadn't contracted TB."

Mills saw that he'd misjudged her reaction. There was no expression of disbelief; she merely looked wary, the way people do when they're confronted with something they can't quite understand.

"Yes, well . . ." Elizabeth Eastgate stood up and sidled towards the hall. "I'll ask around; perhaps the office manager knows the name and address of this private detective."

"There's no need for all that. I can ask Morris."

She was only a few paces from the door now and her relief was evident. "He won't be in the office tomorrow."

"Oh?"

"Because his wife insisted that he should help with the packing."

34

The Yale lock was stiff and she couldn't turn it; reaching past her, Mills opened the door.

"They're off to the Algarve on Saturday for a fortnight's holiday," she said brightly. "It's all a bit sudden but Morris decided that Wendy needed a break."

Mills shrugged. 'That's typical of Morris, he always does things on the spur of the moment."

"I wouldn't have said so but then you obviously know him better than I do." Her lips parted in a nervous smile. "Well . . . it's been nice meeting you," she said faintly.

Before he knew what was happening, Elizabeth Eastgate shook his hand and fled. Halfway down the first flight of steps she turned round and called out something about telephoning him in the morning, and then she was gone, one very worried young woman. Mills thought that she would have been even more alarmed if he'd voiced his growing suspicions about the flat.

The flat was all wrong, from the pile of LPs by the hi-fi which looked as if they'd been a job lot in an auction to the drinks on the teak and chromium trolley, carelessly arranged to make it seem that the apartment was often in use. Wells, Bull and Dixon didn't own the lease and neither did Gilchrist. He knew on which side his bread was buttered and it would be more than his life was worth to keep a woman on the side. Morris wasn't doing him a favour; he'd practically forced the keys on him because he was working hand in glove with Special Branch. It would certainly explain how they came to be waiting for him in Hadleigh Road.

Mills retrieved the *Evening News* from the hall table and wandered back into the living room. The woman who was featured on the front page hadn't changed all that much; her face was perhaps a little thinner so that she looked even more shrewish, if such a thing were possible. Although Pavlichenko's reappearance in London was something he hadn't bargained for, it might produce a chain reaction, forcing the man in the shadows to move against him, to come out into the open. Until that happened, he would have to keep up the pressure and stay one jump ahead.

Mills tossed the newspaper aside. Walters wouldn't like it but it wouldn't hurt him to wait another hour or so for his two hundred; right now, laundering the flat was more important than paying off an ex con. Sorting through the pile of LPs, he looked out Sibelius' Fourth Symphony and put it on the record player, turning the volume up full blast.

*　　　*　　　*

Chesterman hooked one leg over the arm of the office chair and stared at the telephone. Wray should have left Acton station by now and in another five minutes he would be turning into Broadmead Avenue, heading towards his home. There had been a time when Chesterman too had a place in the suburbs to go home to, but that was before the afternoon he'd been fool enough to arrive home early and unexpected.

He thought how sad it was that you could live under the same roof with a woman for more than twelve years and never really know her. Looking back, he supposed Margaret must always have been a free and easy little bitch only he'd been too wrapped up in his work to notice it. There was no telling how many men had shared her bed while his back was turned but in all probability they would have stayed together, rubbing along quite happily, if she hadn't been stupid enough to get herself caught at it.

Chesterman glanced at his wristwatch, visualised Wray opening his front door, lifted the phone off the hook and dialled.

The number rang twice before it was answered and then a familiar voice said, "Yes? Who's calling?"

"Can't you guess?" Chesterman said dryly.

"You're not still in the office, are you?" Wray said irritably. "I thought I told you to get off home."

Chesterman touched the swelling on his jaw and winced. Life was bloody unfair; he got rebuked for being conscientious while the bastard who'd assaulted him was allowed to go scot free because somebody very high up had ruled that he was untouchable.

"I was just about to when Johnson phoned in to say that Mills had had a visitor, a Miss Eastgate from Wells, Bull and Dixon. It seems they must have run into one another on the staircase so he's not too sure what passed between them before they entered the flat. Anyway, it appears Mills is anxious to trace Boxall and wanted to know how he could get in touch with Gilchrist's private detective."

"And?"

Chesterman smiled to himself. The Chief Superintendent never believed in using two words where one would do. Sometimes a grunt was all the prompting he gave a subordinate.

"Miss Eastgate said she only handled conveyancing and didn't know who the firm had hired but would try and find out. Johnson thinks she would have promised him the moon if it meant she could escape from the flat. I gather Mills was acting a bit paranoiac."

"Oh yes? What's he doing now?"

"I understand he's got the record player going full blast. Johnson thinks it's something by Sibelius."

Wray muttered something under his breath and then lapsed into silence. The seconds ticked away and stretched into a minute. Chesterman was beginning to wonder if they'd been cut off when he suddenly cleared his throat, making a noise like a dumper truck tipping a load of gravel.

"I think he may be on to us, George."

"That's what I thought."

"You'd better leave a message for Johnson's relief that I want to see him first thing in the morning. I only hope to God that Mills hasn't laundered the flat."

"I could check it out."

"No, we'll leave it to the relief man. However, there is one favour you can do me, Sergeant."

"Name it."

"Don't come in tomorrow. Take a rest day, that's an order – got it?" Wray put the phone down before he had a chance to protest.

Chesterman frowned. What good was a rest day to him, cooped up in his digs in Hammersmith with no one to talk to and nothing to do? Glancing at the *Evening Standard* which lay open on the desk in front of him, he wondered if there was a film worth seeing.

The entertainment section began on page twenty but he didn't get that far. A photograph in the Londoner's Diary caught his eye. There was a short paragraph underneath to the effect that Larissa Fedorovna Pavlichenko, the world famous ballerina, had just flown in from New York to begin rehearsals for a short season at London Coliseum. He stared at it. First Mills and now Pavlichenko. He wondered if there might be some connection.

4

MILLS STEPPED OFF the escalator at Waterloo, turned to the right and headed towards the waiting room beyond the ticket offices. The peak evening period was over and the station was beginning to unwind, with the arrivals and departures becoming less and less frequent. A mechanical sweeper was describing figure of eights at the far end of the hall near the shopping arcade but despite the flurry of activity on Platform 8 where mail was being loaded on to the 1920 to Portsmouth Harbour, there were only a few passengers hanging about in front of the information board and the terminus looked curiously deserted.

There was no sign of the tail who'd fastened on to him the moment he'd left the flat in Moravian Place to walk to Knightsbridge Underground, but that didn't mean the watchdogs had given up their chase. In all probability, Special Branch were ringing the changes more often and hanging well back so that they were harder to spot. Whatever their tactics, he was in no hurry to shake them off; wheeling left in front of the ticket offices, he strolled towards the row of pay phones under the archway.

Gilchrist had a convenient morality. When it suited him, there was no more zealous guardian of the special relationship between solicitor and client but if things got a little rough, it seemed he wasn't above betraying a confidence. Some people would call it enlightened self-interest but Mills thought it was about time Morris learned the facts of life. No bare-back rider could straddle two horses pulling in opposite directions. Ducking under one of the plastic bone-domes, he picked up the telephone and dialled Gilchrist's home number.

If Gilchrist was surprised to hear the coins go down in the box, he was careful not to show it. No one could have been more affable or charming and it was easy to get the impression that he was pleased to hear from him again.

Mills said, "I think it's time you and I had a heart to heart talk."

"You sound a little upset," Gilchrist said cheerfully. "Is something the matter?"

"I'm plagued with bugs."

"What?"

"And they're not the insect kind either."

"Have you been drinking?"

"Don't be coy with me," Mills said angrily. "You know damn well what I'm talking about."

"Really? Well, I'm afraid you've called at a very inconvenient moment, Edward. We're expecting people to dinner."

Gilchrist was on the run, groping no doubt for any excuse to terminate their conversation so that he could get in touch with Special Branch. A perfect set-up had gone bust and they were the only people who could tell him how to handle it.

"You set me up, Morris. I don't like that."

"You must be drunk. Ring me at the office tomorrow when you've had a chance to sober up."

"You've got the day off – remember?"

"That's right, so I have. Obviously you can't take a hint, so perhaps I'd better make myself clear. I don't want to have anything more to do with you."

"Your wife might come to the same conclusion about you, Morris."

"What the hell are you talking about?"

Gilchrist was bluffing. For all his assumed anger, he couldn't disguise the note of alarm in his voice. One more nudge and Mills knew that he would collapse like a pricked balloon.

"I'm talking about the flat in Moravian Place and Elizabeth Eastgate. I can make it seem as though they go hand in hand. How do you suppose Wendy will react to that little time bomb, Morris?"

"Are you threatening me?"

"What do you think?" Mills said icily.

"I think we should put our cards on the table."

The sudden about-face was almost breath-taking. Gilchrist hadn't merely collapsed, he'd run up the white flag and was suing for peace at any price.

"When?"

39

"Well, tonight is out of the question. You'd better drop by tomorrow morning; Wendy has an appointment with her hairdresser at eleven."

"I'll try to bear that in mind."

"You'd be well advised to; I don't like people who try to play games with me."

"Neither do I," said Mills. "You pull one more trick and I'll break you in two." He slammed the phone down and left the booth, angry with himself for having allowed Gilchrist to rattle him.

There were quite a few taxis waiting in the rank outside the station but he ignored them and walked out into Waterloo Road. There was a lot to be said in favour of taking a bus, especially if you boarded it between stops. Jumping one just as the traffic lights were changing to green was a good way to catch Special Branch off balance. Mills thought Ray Walters wouldn't be very happy with him if he arrived with a tail.

*　　　*　　　*

Gordon Liddell folded the *Evening News* in three and dropped it into the wastepaper bin by the dressing table in his room at the Grosvenor House Hotel. Even though Larissa Fedorovna Pavlichenko might still be in the sack trying to catch up on the jet lag, he thought it was time he called on her and renewed their acquaintance. The CIA man stared at his reflection in the mirror and wondered if she would recognise him after all these years. He still wore his dark hair short but there was a lot of grey coming through and he hadn't needed gold-framed glasses back in '66 when she'd arrived in the States hotfoot from London, disillusioned with the British and ready to fall in love with the dollar. His face hadn't lost that lean and hungry look but not even the conservative suits which he picked up from Jerry Ward's on Madison and 34th whenever he was in New York, could disguise the spare tyre around his midriff.

Pavlichenko might be the darling of every ballet fan from Boston to San Francisco but to the CIA she was just one big pain in the ass. The 'ifs' and 'buts' had always made history in a perverse sort of way. If that conference in Prague hadn't been postponed for a lousy fortnight and if she had stayed cool instead of losing her head, things would have been a whole lot different. If she hadn't jumped the gun, the SIS might have gotten Kiktev out of Czechoslovakia, conference or no conference. In which case, the UK economy being what it was, the State Department would only have had to mention the IMF for the British Government to see the light and pass the Russian on, meek as a lamb. And if State had then known from Kiktev what they learned years later, namely the problems the Russians were having with their Multiple Re-entry Vehicles, then the Strategic Arms Limitation Talks would have begun on an entirely different footing. If the scientists and the Pentagon had been able to pick Kiktev's brains, billions of taxpayers' dollars could have been saved. If, if, if – the list was endless. Larissa Fedorovna Pavlichenko was back in London, back in the country that had granted her political asylum in 1964 and subsequently had been unable to keep her in the life-style to which she had rapidly become accustomed.

Liddell thought it would be very interesting to see what would happen if Mills attempted to get in touch with her now that he was out of jail. Edward James Mills – now, there was a real enigma. A leg man for the SIS, an insignificant courier whom most people believed had leaked the news that Kiktev intended to defect. Double agents came in all shapes and sizes but Mills was in a class of his own. He'd been clever enough to avoid being charged with treason but stupid enough to get seven years for theft. A double agent? Or maybe just a fall guy . . .

Liddell frowned. First things first, he told himself, talk to Pavlichenko, give her the list of names for Mills, brief her so that she knows what to do if he does try to get in touch, and then make a deal with Harper at the Department of Subversive Warfare. He took the sheet of paper bearing the list of names out of his pocket and stared at it. Ingold, Quarry and Thurston – a trio of senior British Civil Servants whose influence he suspected was often prejudicial to American interests. One of them was possibly a traitor, and if he was right about that, Mills could be just the man to smoke him out.

Larissa Pavlichenko's flat in Alford Street was within easy walking distance of the Grosvenor House Hotel; Liddell pocketed the list, glanced at his wristwatch, saw that it was almost eight o'clock and wondered where he could get a bunch of flowers for the lady when all the shops were closed.

*   *   *

Ray Walters's flat was in Sheldon Court, one of a number of tower blocks that had changed the appearance of the Old Kent Road out of all recognition. The prefabricated concrete, steel and glass structures which had replaced the ugly terraced houses and now dominated the skyline might have every modern convenience, but they had destroyed the old community spirit, creating in its place a climate where mindless violence and vandalism were accepted with a kind of oriental fatalism.

Mills wondered if the planners ever came back to look at their blue-print Utopias; broken glass littered the forecourt and the up-and-over, steel-grey garage doors had been sprayed with paint in psychedelic patterns. Most of the overhead lights in the lobby had been smashed and the artists had been busy with their felt-tipped pens in the stairwell. The graffiti embraced a wide spectrum from 'Arsenal rules – OK?' to a graphic illustration of how someone called Martha obliged her various boyfriends. The lift which took him up to the eleventh floor had also been daubed but somebody had tried to remove the more offensive slogans; the face-clean had not been wholly successful for beneath the smears, it was still possible to see what some people thought about the West Indians.

Walters answered the door with a bright welcoming smile and ushered him into the sitting room. Mills had never set foot inside the place before but Walters had described the flat to him in such detail when they had shared the same cell block at Leicester that he had formed a very clear and accurate picture of it. The room faced north-east and he could see now why Ray disliked the view and why the three-piece suite in beige-coloured vinyl had been carefully arranged in a semi-circle around the television, well away from the large picture windows which overlooked the freight yards at the Bricklayers' Arms and the bend in the river at Southwark Park.

Walter said, "This is the wife, Sheila. You've heard me talk about her often enough."

Mills nodded and smiled at the blonde who was curled up

42

in an armchair with a gin and tonic. The pink tank top and matching flares she was wearing didn't leave much to the imagination; the lurex was stretched so tightly across her thighs that the outline of her pants showed through the slinky material.

"And this is Stan, my younger brother." Walters rubbed his hands together as if washing them under a running tap. "The future welterweight champion, isn't that right, Stan?"

"You can bet on it," said Stan.

Younger brother seemed as if he was ready to step into the ring. Legs braced apart, he flexed his hands and rocked up and down on his toes. Except for the scar tissue above the right eyebrow, he had the open, innocent-looking face of a choirboy.

"A drink." Walters snapped his fingers. "Get the man a drink, Sheila, we've got business to discuss."

"Have we?" Mills reached into his hip pocket and tossed a wad of notes on to the settee. "I thought we'd already discussed your fee, Ray. In case you've forgotten, it's two hundred split down the middle between fives and tens."

"That was before the cost of living went up." Younger brother smiled. "You know how it is with inflation."

"No, I don't. Suppose you enlighten me?"

"Well, there's a matter of Value Added Tax," said Walters. "Customs and Excise want their share of the cake."

"And just how big is their slice?"

"Two grand."

"Two thousand?" Mills turned his head, following Walters as he moved round behind him. "Are you out of your mind? I don't have that kind of money."

"Ray thinks you have." Sheila inspected the silver lacquer on her fingernails. "What about all those lovely Bearer Bonds you've got tucked away?"

He supposed it was only natural for Walters to assume that he had cashed the missing Bearer Bonds; after all, everyone else did – the Fraud Squad, the SIS and Special Branch.

"You don't want to believe everything you read in the papers," he said.

"It was just a rumour, was it?" Walters clucked his tongue and frowned. "And I thought we were such good friends. You know something, Stan? I think he's holding out on me. Maybe we should persuade him to see reason."

The cue was obvious but younger brother was much too fast for him and he took a vicious jab under the heart. Mills felt his legs start to buckle and lurching forward, he walked into a left hook which caught him high up on the right side of the jaw. A looping right smashed into his mouth, splitting the bottom lip open as he fell back and collapsed on to the settee. Leaning over him, younger brother reached inside his jacket and removed the wallet.

"Now, there's a thing," Walters said cheerfully, "you've got blood all over your chin. Anybody would think you'd been in a fight."

"You've got a great sense of humour," Mills said sourly.

"No more than you, old son. I mean, we all know you're sitting on eight hundred and fifty grand's worth of Bearer Bonds."

The future welterweight champion was standing with his legs apart, counting the money he'd found in the wallet, his lips mouthing the running total.

"Suppose we have a drink and talk it over?" Walters placed a hand on his shoulder and squeezed it gently. "What do you say?"

Mills eyed the heavy glass ashtray on the occasional table which lay within reach of Sheila. "I could use a Scotch," he said quietly.

"That's more like it." Walters gave his shoulder another friendly squeeze and then moved away. "I knew you would see it my way."

Younger brother was still busy counting when Mills lashed out and kicked him in the groin. His mouth opened, giving voice to a scream that ranged in octaves from base to falsetto before he sank down on to his knees, his forehead eventually touching the carpet like a Moslem praying towards Mecca. Walters was slow to react and before he was able to defend himself, Mills had dived across the room, grabbed the ashtray and smashed it into his skull. Reeling sideways, he toppled over and fell like an axed tree, clashing heads with Sheila with a sickening crack. The glass spun from her fingers, emptied the remains of the gin and tonic over her legs, and then rolled across the carpet.

The future welterweight champion was still on his hands and knees moaning softly long after Mills had retrieved his money and walked out of the apartment. As far as he could tell, no one in Sheldon Court seemed very curious about the disturbance on the eleventh floor.

*   *   *

Morris Gilchrist opened the french windows and stepped out on to the patio. The sun was below the horizon now, the last rays of light fast disappearing from the evening sky so that he was no longer able to see the wicker gate at the bottom of the garden. Everything was so peaceful and quiet that only the reflected orange-yellow glare from the standard lamps above the Kingston bypass, way over to the left, succeeded in destroying the illusion that his house in Wimbledon was far, far removed from the centre of London. A faint breeze ruffled the leaves of the plane tree beyond the lily pond and his nostrils twitched, savouring the aroma of a newly-mown lawn that he had watered earlier in the evening.

Persuading Wendy to take a holiday in the middle of Wimbledon fortnight had been fraught with difficulty but more than ever now, he was glad that he had managed to win her round. He had known Edward Mills for a very long time but not, it seemed, as well as Temple did. The Intelligence man hadn't been exaggerating after all; Edward was dangerous, a man so disturbed that he was capable of almost anything. He certainly wasn't exactly predictable, not after the way he had behaved on the telephone, and maybe Temple was right, maybe he should have been detained in Broadmoor. Knowing what he did now, sending Elizabeth Eastgate to see him had been stupid and irresponsible, especially as the final account could just as easily have been sent through the post.

He thought Temple was a strange man too, but then, if only half of what he'd heard was true, so were most people who lived in the shadowy world of Intelligence. They had bumped into one another some eighteen months ago. Gilchrist frowned; no, bumped into was wrong, it implied an element of chance and Temple was not the sort of man who left anything to chance. Temple had known which was his favourite restaurant and had lain in wait for him. His suggestion that Mills was not the only rotten apple in the barrel had seemed ludicrous at first until he remembered that Philby had been the third man in the Burgess-Maclean affair.

Gilchrist took a thin cigar from the silver case he kept in

45

his breast pocket and lit it carefully, shielding the match against the faint breeze. Another Philby behind Mills? Well, it was by no means impossible. Edward had only been the equivalent of a Third Secretary when he'd been temporarily attached to the Embassy in Bonn and it was most unlikely that news of Kiktev's intention to defect would have reached his ears in the normal course of events. Of course he only had Temple's word that Mills had been a junior officer in the SIS, but until he was arrested and charged with theft, Gilchrist had always been under the impression that Edward was in the Diplomatic Service.

Still, Temple's credentials had been impeccable. And the man had certainly opened his eyes and made him see things in a different light, dispelling any reservations he had about the sanctity of the special relationship between client and solicitor. Temple had made him see that it was his duty to keep the Intelligence Service informed of any developments and he had been glad to co-operate because no matter how dated and naive it might seem, he liked to think that he was a staunch patriot.

After Temple had made the initial approach, they had continued to see one another about once a month, always meeting secretly at a different time and place. This air of conspiracy, the fact that no one, not even Wendy, knew about Temple, and the cloak and dagger aspect of being given an unlisted telephone number which connected him with an answering service, fascinated Gilchrist and he felt that somehow he was 'in the know', part of the establishment which protected the establishment.

There were times, however, when Gilchrist thought the various Intelligence agencies were snarled in a web of their own making. Security was all very well but it was carrying things a bit far when someone like Chief Superintendent Wray gave the impression that he'd never heard of Temple when he was, in fact, the man who'd put him in touch with Special Branch in the first place.

Gilchrist flicked his cigar, spilling ash on to the patio. So much for Special Branch; for all their air of innate superiority, they hadn't been too clever and thanks to their inefficiency, Mills was now gunning for him. Temple had every right to be angry with them and he'd made some pretty acid comments about their heavy-handedness on the phone just now when he'd learned that Mills had already tumbled to the fact that the flat was bugged. The next twelve hours or so were going to be pretty unpleasant, possibly even dangerous. Thinking it over, Gilchrist was glad that he had listened to Temple and accepted his offer of police protection. Apart from asking 'V' Division to have the house visited by one of their Panda cars at irregular intervals during the night, Temple had also arranged for two security men to be present when Mills arrived in the morning. What were their names now? Ayres and Ormskirk? – no, that was wrong, it was Ayres and Ormerod.

A light came on in the master bedroom and he guessed that Wendy was turning in, having an early night. Well, that was understandable, they had a long day ahead of them tomorrow and he for one, wouldn't be sorry when they took off from Heathrow for the Algarve. Turning on his heel, Gilchrist walked back inside the house and locked the french windows behind him.

Some twenty minutes after he too had retired to bed, two men entered the garden and picked the lock on the wooden summer house which was partially hidden from the house by a large clump of rhododendrons.

5

HE WAS FLOATING amid clouds of cotton wool, weightless as an astronaut in space. The room was much smaller than he remembered it and somebody had switched the furniture, swapping the heavy oak desk for a three-ply wardrobe with a walnut overlay. The carpet too was different, haircord instead of Persian and the shelves had disappeared along with the hand-tooled, leather-bound volumes. There was no Lake Geneva out there beyond the window, only a granite, cube-shaped building with narrow apertures, each protected by a grille much like a prison cell. There was no gentle lapping of water against the fibreglass hull of the power boat that had been moored by the jetty, only a harsh grinding squeal which touched a raw nerve and set his teeth on edge. And it appeared the seasons were also interchangeable, winter becoming summer in a trice so that his body temperature fluctuated wildly from extreme sub-normal to fever point.

A shaft of light streaming in through a gap in the window curtains played on his face and Mills woke up, bathed in sweat, his heart pounding like a trip hammer. The nightmare never varied because it was based on reality, the reality of waking up late one afternoon and wondering what the hell he was doing in a small back room of a seedy apartment house which backed on to the railway marshalling yards in Geneva, the reality of suddenly discovering that three days were missing from his life which he couldn't account for. Gilchrist and the psychiatrist whom the QC proposed to call as an expert witness were both of the opinion that he'd been suffering from amnesia, a sort of mental black-out induced by overstrain. Counsel had argued that it was their only line of defence and he'd allowed himself to be talked into it.

Mills kicked the bedclothes aside, swung his feet out on

to the floor and sat on the edge of the divan, rubbing sleep from his eyes. Joachim Ziegler . . . Christ, that much revered old physicist had a lot to answer for. Saintly looking he might be, but he had gone into the witness box and lied his head off. 'Yes, the accused had called at his house on the Quai Gustave Ador and yes, they had spoken at length about his old friend Professor Yuri Kiktev, and yes, the date in question on that occasion had been Thursday the fifth of June 1964. But no, there had not been a subsequent meeting on Wednesday the eighteenth of June. How could there have been, when he was delivering a series of lectures in Paris from the thirteenth to the twentieth inclusive? And no, he had never seen a briefcase containing Bearer Bonds to the value of one million dollars.' An unbiased witness, according to the prosecution, and the court had accepted his testimony because he was Joachim Ziegler the distinguished scientist and philosopher and it was ridiculous to suppose that a Nobel Prize winner would commit perjury.

Ziegler was an honourable man, but so was Brutus, and like Brutus, he too had been involved in a conspiracy. No matter what other people thought, there had been a second meeting. He'd sat there in the study across the desk from Ziegler drinking coffee while the old man examined the Bearer Bonds; sat there watching the power boat bobbing up and down on the choppy surface of the lake while the good doctor listed them so that when they met in Prague a week later he could tell his friend Kiktev that the SIS intended to honour their end of the bargain. He recalled asking Ziegler what had happened to his previous housekeeper and the old man saying that she was away on holiday and that the new woman was just somebody the agency had found as a stand-in until she returned. He had total recall right up to the moment the cup and saucer had slipped through his fingers and the room had started to revolve, but nobody had believed him then and nobody was going to believe him now.

Originally, their second meeting was to have been on the twenty-first of June but subsequently it had been moved forward to the eighteenth. Moved forward to the eighteenth because that was the one free day in Ziegler's lecture tour when he could make the round trip to Geneva from Paris without anyone being the wiser. At least, that was his theory, but Mills couldn't prove it; the man in the shadows who'd set him up had made damn sure that there was no incriminating signal on record. There was also one other major stumbling block. Ziegler might have been, like Bertrand Russell, an active campaigner for Nuclear Disarmament, but that didn't make him either a fellow traveller or a communist. Just why he had been drawn into the conspiracy was something only Ziegler could explain and the chances were that he would carry that secret with him to the grave, if he wasn't already dead. Back in March there had been a small paragraph in the *Daily Express* to the effect that he'd been admitted to a clinic in Kandersteg with a terminal heart disease.

The man in the shadows had held all the trump cards up to now, but his luck couldn't last for ever. Or could it? Mills shook his head; once started on that train of thought, he knew it was only a question of time before he threw in the towel and gave up the fight. Brooding wouldn't get him anywhere but leaning on Gilchrist might well step up the pressure. He had two hours to kill, two hours before he confronted Morris. Running a hand over the stubble on his chin, he decided it was time he shaved and took a shower; he was halfway to the bathroom when the telephone rang.

A very business-like woman from Wells, Bull and Dixon said, "Mr Mills?"

"Yes." He thought Gilchrist had his staff well trained, clocking in on time even though Morris himself never showed up at the office much before ten. "Yes, that's me."

"One moment please, I have a call for you."

There was a faint click from the switchboard as she plugged in the extension and then Elizabeth Eastgate came on the line and wished him good morning. Like the switchboard operator, she was also very brisk, very efficient and very cool.

Before he had a chance to reply, she said, "Concerning a Mr Boxall, I've had a word with our office manager and I'm afraid he's unable to throw any light on the subject."

"I see."

"I've also checked the duplicate of our final statement and it appears we haven't raised any charges for a private investigator."

No charges? Well, Elizabeth Eastgate wasn't telling him anything he hadn't already suspected. It was beginning to look an odds on certainty that Special Branch had found

Boxall and Morris hadn't billed him because he didn't want anything on record.

"Thank you."

"What?"

"For taking so much trouble." Mills ran his tongue over the split in his bottom lip and winced. "Actually, I shall be seeing Mr Gilchrist later this morning."

"I doubt if he'll be able to help you."

"Oh, why's that?"

"I've already spoken to him."

Elizabeth Eastgate sounded embarrassed and he thought it probable she was mentally kicking herself for ever getting involved.

"He said that although you had asked him to trace Mr Boxall, he had declined to do so."

"And naturally you believed him?"

"Is there any reason why I shouldn't?"

Her voice was icy, chilling to the bone like an easterly wind moving in behind a cold front.

"Do you have a pen handy?"

"A pen?" she echoed faintly. "Look, Mr Mills, I think perhaps it would be best if you spoke to Mr Gilchrist after all."

"And I think you ought to have a word with Mrs Aston."

"Who?"

"Mrs Aston; her address is 28 Hadleigh Road, Ealing. I don't know her telephone number but you can get it from Directory Enquiries. Ask her if she's ever heard of a Mr Sidney Boxall, and if she has, ask yourself who told me where I could find him."

There was a longish pause before Elizabeth Eastgate said, "Would you mind repeating that address please?"

Suddenly, Mills had a feeling that he was about to gain a useful ally. And he needed one badly.

*   *   *

Iain Gattis wished he could have conducted the interview in slightly less formal surroundings. The small office which the Governor of Albany Prison had put at his disposal was too functional and it was difficult to put a man at his ease when they were obliged to face one another across a narrow table seated on hard-bottomed tubular steel chairs. Harper's

51

brief for checking up on Patterson was all very well as far as it went, but it didn't tell him much about Usher except that he'd joined the prison service after being demobbed from the army in 1953 and had known Patterson for a good many years.

Usher wasn't the most communicative of men. In twenty minutes of yes and no answers to his questions, Gattis had established that he was married with two children, a boy and girl aged twelve and nine respectively, was a keen gardener and enjoyed the occasional round of golf.

Gattis looked at the notes he'd made and frowned. Clearly they were getting nowhere fast and since the oblique approach was not paying any dividends, he might just as well come straight to the point.

"I suppose you know why I'm here?" he said abruptly.

"It's something to do with Mr Patterson, isn't it?" Usher met his gaze impassively. "And positive vetting."

"That's right; he's been nominated as a referee and I'd like to know something about him. What sort of man is he?"

"I'd say he was loyal, hard working, reliable and honest – one of the best."

Gattis closed his eyes in exasperation. He should have known that Usher would come up with all the hackneyed old adjectives, giving him the sort of thumbnail sketch that was a fat lot of use to anyone.

"Listen," he said patiently, "you're not telling me anything I couldn't get from his next-door neighbour. Now, you may not realise it, but when someone is up for positive vetting, you can often get an insight into his character from the sort of man he nominates as a referee."

"You don't have to worry about Mr Patterson, Mr Gattis."

"I don't?"

"No, he's as straight as a die."

"That's funny. I heard he was something of a left winger."

"Like hell he is." Usher's face clouded in anger. "Fred served in the Commandos during the war, took part in the D-Day landings and was awarded the Military Medal for bravery, or didn't they tell you that?"

"And that was the time when most people thought the sun shone out of every Russian's arse and Stalin was good old Uncle Joe, right?"

52

"How many more times do I have to tell you that he's not a communist or a fellow traveller?"

Gattis rubbed his jaw, concealing a smile of satisfaction. The abrasive approach was beginning to pay off; Usher was opening up, ready to tell him everything he wanted to know.

"Look, Fred's never had any truck with these people, he reckons they're traitors. He'd like to put them up against a wall." Usher checked himself and frowned. "I'm making him sound like a fascist when he isn't. He's a fair man."

"Is that how the prisoners saw him?"

"Yes, hard but fair. They knew where they stood with him."

"He treated everyone alike, did he? Even someone who'd sold his country short?"

Usher looked thoughtful. "You're referring to Mills, aren't you?" he said quietly.

"Well, he was in Albany, wasn't he?"

"Yes, and he lost all his remission, but that was nothing to do with Fred. Mills had a chip on his shoulder and he was a difficult prisoner. I'll tell you something else; curious as it may seem to you, none of the inmates had any time for him. They gave him a rough ride, that's why he was transferred to Durham."

There was no stopping Usher now, he was flowing like a river in full spate. Listening to him, Gattis knew that Harper had been right all along. There was no mystery, no conspiracy, no victimisation by the staff; Mills was just a nut with a persecution complex. It was as simple as that.

*   *   *

Gilchrist depressed the play button on the Grundig, and Mills said, 'You pull one more trick and I'll break you in two.' There was a sharp clatter as the phone went down and, stopping the tape, he rewound it to the same starting point. Although Temple already knew the gist of the recorded telephone conversation, he thought Ayres and Ormerod might want to hear it for themselves when they arrived.

Gilchrist stared at the digital twenty-four-hour clock on his desk and frowned. Twenty past ten, forty minutes to go before Mills arrived. Surely they ought to be here by now, surely Temple wasn't going to let him down on the last minute? Twenty past ten; Wendy was going to be late for her hair appointment if she didn't get a move on. Twenty past ten, and

Mrs Yelf, their daily woman, was still thumping and banging about with the vacuum cleaner on the upstairs landing, making enough noise to wake the dead. Of the two, it was hard to decide who was the most disorganised but he fancied that Wendy had a slight edge on Mrs Yelf.

The melodic chimes of the front-door bell interrupted his train of thought and he walked out into the hall, calling out to Mrs Yelf that he would answer it. It was a waste of breath; Armageddon couldn't stop Mrs Yelf once she started Hoovering. Removing the security chain, he released the trip lock and opened the front door.

The taller of the two men said, "Mr Gilchrist?" He flashed his warrant card and smiled cheerfully. "My name's Ormerod and this is my colleague, Mr Ayres. I believe you're expecting us."

The accent placed him from the Midlands but there was a faint brogue and he remembered Temple saying that until recently, Ormerod had been working under cover amongst the Irish community in Birmingham.

"Yes, yes, do come in." Gilchrist moved aside. "If you'd like to go into the study, it's the first door on your left."

"You have a very nice house," Ayres said quietly.

"Yes, we think so too." He closed the door behind them and then followed both men into the study. "Of course we were lucky to buy it when we did, before house prices went through the ceiling."

"Quite," said Ormerod. "Where is Mrs Gilchrist, sir?"

"Getting herself ready; she has an appointment with her hairdresser at eleven."

"Oh, I see." His eyebrows met in a brief frown. "Do you have a daily woman then, sir?" He jerked a thumb towards the sound of the vacuum cleaner.

"Yes, a Mrs Yelf – she's here most days from nine to three thirty." The frown was back again and Gilchrist felt vaguely uneasy. "Why, is something the matter?"

"Well, let's say that Mr Temple forgot to mention her."

"And that could make things awkward?"

"It could be a little embarrassing if she's still here when Mills arrives." Ormerod cupped a hand over his mouth but was too late to stifle a wide yawn. "Sorry about that," he said sheepishly, "I'm afraid we were up most of the night."

"Oh?"

54

"Mr Temple wasn't happy when he heard how 'V' Division proposed to cover the house – seems their Panda cars were fully committed so we got landed with the job instead."

Gilchrist nodded. If they had been prowling round the house all night it would explain why they needed a shave and why their suits were rumpled.

"Perhaps you would ask Mrs Gilchrist if she could spare us a few minutes of her time, sir?"

"You want to see her?"

"Yes; we won't keep her long."

Wendy? Why should they want to have a few words with his wife? She wasn't involved, and surely it would be best if she wasn't there to witness what could be an unpleasant scene with Edward. He wondered if he should make this point to Ormerod but on reflection, decided that Temple's men knew what they were doing.

"I'll go and fetch her then," he said lamely.

"If you wouldn't mind, sir." Ayres opened the study door and smiled. "It's just a formality."

The man who called himself Ormerod waited until Gilchrist had left the room and then sat down at the desk, eyeing the Grundig which was hooked into the telephone.

"What do you think, Rooney?" he asked softly.

"I think he's beginning to smell a rat."

"So do I."

Ormerod depressed the play button, and Mills said, 'You pull one more trick and I'll break you in two.' There was a sharp clatter and then an intermittent purring tone before a curiously neutral voice announced, 'This is an answering service. Please wait for the bleeps to finish before leaving your message.' The cue followed but for some reason he couldn't understand, the tape ran silently for several moments before Gilchrist said, 'This is Morris. I'm afraid we have a problem, Mr Temple . . .'

Ormerod switched off the Grundig and stood up. "Tricky," he muttered.

"No problem," said Rooney. "Look, Farren, we can go through his tapes and wipe out anything that incriminates Temple."

"And us."

"And us," he agreed quietly. Rooney saw the door open and fell silent.

55

Gilchrist said, "This is my wife. Wendy, this is Mr Ormerod and Mr Ayres."

Rooney shook her hand and smiled warmly. He thought Wendy Gilchrist ought to go on a diet; she wasn't bad looking but her waist and legs were too thick for his taste and she was beginning to acquire a double chin. She knew how to dress though, and he reckoned the two-piece suit in navy blue silk must have cost Gilchrist a small fortune.

Farren said, "It's good of you to see us, Mrs Gilchrist."

Wendy glanced at her jewelled wristwatch and frowned. "Yes, well I hope you won't make me late for my appointment."

"That's why we wanted to see you."

"Oh?"

"I'm afraid you'll have to cancel it," Farren said calmly.

"Cancel it, Mr Ormerod?" she echoed. "Why should I?"

"Because I say so."

"Because you say so?" Her face started to turn red. "Who are these people, Morris?" she said furiously. "Just don't stand there, do something, tell them they can't come into my house and order me around like a servant. Who do they think they are?"

Rooney took a handkerchief out of his pocket and moved towards her. "Let's be reasonable, Mrs Gilchrist," he said pleasantly, "it's not much to ask, is it?"

"Reasonable? My God, you got a nerve. Who do ..."

Her voice was still rising when Rooney forced the handkerchief into her mouth, choking her off in mid sentence. Pinioning both arms to her sides, he then forced her down on to the floor.

Gilchrist said, "My God, what's going on? Have you people gone stark raving mad?"

"Now there's no need to get excited, Morris; Ayres isn't going to hurt her." Farren reached inside his jacket, showed him the Police Positive and then shoved the revolver into Gilchrist's stomach. "Not if you behave yourself."

Gilchrist collapsed into a chair. This wasn't happening, this wasn't real, surely to God he was dreaming. Mrs Yelf was still vacuuming upstairs, wasn't she? And what sort of organisation was Temple running anyway? He was in SIS, wasn't he? It was a self-induced hallucination, he was tired, overworked, under a strain ... Yes, that must be it ... His eyes

56

slowly focussed on Wendy and he saw that Ayres had tied her ankles with a length of cord. Watching his wife being trussed up like a chicken, Gilchrist knew it was for real after all.

He saw the man called Ormerod point to the telephone. "Cancel it," he said tersely.

"Cancel what?"

"Your wife's appointment at the hairdressers."

Gilchrist stretched out a trembling hand and lifted the phone off the hook. He wondered what Ayres and Ormerod proposed to do about Mrs Yelf.

*   *   *

Mills turned into the cul-de-sac, a narrow unmade-up lane which led to the large neo-Georgian house where the Gilchrists lived in splendid isolation backing on to Wimbledon Common and well away from any neighbours. Despite the passage of time, everything was pretty much as he remembered it except for the flowering cherry trees in the left-hand corner of the front garden. They had gone, uprooted to make room for a second garage. He supposed that was Wendy's doing because Morris had always been a conservative at heart and liked things to remain the same.

The house and grounds, extending to half an acre, were his pride and joy. Morris might not know a damn thing about gardening but it was evident that he was a first rate foreman. No weeds or grass seedlings were allowed to despoil the wide sweeping gravel drive, the lawn compared favourably with the standard set by the groundsmen at the All England Club and the flower beds looked as if they were a show piece for *Homes and Gardens.* Like an advert in a glossy magazine, Mills thought it was just a shade too perfect, too neat and tidy to be real. Even the bell button was marked 'push' and when he did so, melodic chimes echoed in the hall.

The door was opened by Gilchrist, but he was a different man from the one he'd met yesterday. The old Welsh bounce and confidence had gone and his eyes were lacklustre. If he didn't know him better, Mills would have said that he'd been hitting the bottle.

"Oh, it's you," he muttered thickly, "you'd better come in."

He stepped to one side and waved a hand much like a policeman on point duty controlling the flow of traffic. The door to the inner hall was ajar and Mills could hear a radio playing in the kitchen.

"I thought Wendy was going to have her hair done?"

"What?"

"Both garages are closed."

"Yes, yes, so they are." Gilchrist licked his lips. "I must have put the car away after taking her to the hairdressers."

Must have? It was unlike Morris to be absent-minded, he wasn't given to wandering around in a daze. Maybe he had been drinking after all?

"Perhaps you'd like to go into the study, Edward. You know where it is – nothing's changed."

Mills nodded, pushed the door open and walked into the inner hall. The music faded out on the radio giving way to the jingle which preceded the news bulletin, but he didn't catch the headlines, nor did he see Rooney emerge from the cloakroom behind him. The rabbit punch chopped into his neck and suddenly he was falling into a dark, bottomless pit.

6

THE REGULAR 'plunk poink' noise sounded familiar but he couldn't place it until there was a roar of applause and the umpire said, 'Advantage Miss Wade'. Mills opened both eyes slowly. He thought someone had put the television set in a funny position because it was above his head and the picture was distorted, the tennis players elongated as if he were seeing their image in a trick mirror. Miss Wade smoothed her dark hair and then crouched, shifting her weight from one foot to the other, lips slightly parted, forehead creased in a tense frown as she waited to receive service. Somewhere out of camera, her opponent served and the ball came in hard and fast, straight down the centre line, and she moved across court, stretching her backhand to meet it.

Mills turned his head and stared at the shaggy carpet in front of his nose; raising his eyes, he saw there was a dressing table and stool in the far corner. It was a bedroom then, and he was lying flat on the floor and the television set was built into an L-shaped range of fitted cupboards, shelves and chests of drawers that hugged two walls. There was another burst of applause, less enthusiastic than before, and the umpire called 'deuce'. Turning on to his left side, Mills pushed himself up from the floor and staggered to his feet, his legs feeling as if they were made of cotton wool.

Wendy Gilchrist was lying on the king-size double bed staring up at the ceiling. The navy-blue skirt had been raised above her plump thighs, the jacket unbuttoned and the slip torn down the front and peeled open like a banana. Both shoulder straps on the white bra had been ripped off and the garment pushed above her heavy breasts. There was an ecstatic burst of applause behind him but he was barely conscious of it and he didn't hear the umpire or Dan Maskell murmuring that it was Virginia Wade's second game point.

59

He was too mesmerised by the gag in Wendy Gilchrist's mouth and the knitted tie around her throat that was very similar to the one he was wearing. Similar? Mills fingered his shirt and found it unbuttoned at the neck. It was more than similar; somebody had used his tie to strangle Wendy Gilchrist. His hands were caked in something too and he noticed that there were dark brown stains on his clothing, except for the shirt front where they showed up bright red. Blood? Christ, he was covered in blood. The crowd clapped and cheered and this time he heard the umpire say. 'Game to Miss Wade. Miss Wade leads by five games to two and by one set to love.'

'Do something,' said a small voice, 'don't just stand there as though you were paralysed from head to foot. Do something . . . Like what? Like cleaning yourself up.' Much like a sleepwalker, he felt his way to the en-suite bathroom.

Everything was pampas green with gold taps; the bidet, the pedestal washbasin and the triangular bath. Removing his jacket, Mills draped it over the linen basket and rolled up his sleeves. He ran the hot water until it was almost scalding and then washed and rinsed his hands over and over again, using a nailbrush and finally a pumicestone to remove the more persistent stains. No surgeon scrubbing up before an operation could have been more thorough, but it was only when he was drying his hands on a tiny face towel that he began to question how and why he'd been covered in blood. Morris, he thought, yes, where the hell is Morris?

He tried both single bedrooms, the second bathroom, the children's playroom, the linen and airing cupboards and finally, the guest room above the study. The Gilchrists weren't in the habit of inviting people to stay overnight if they could avoid it, but this was one occasion when the room was occupied. The woman was lying on one of the twin beds under the window, her face turned towards the door, her eyes fixed in a glassy stare. She was wearing a floral patterned short-sleeve pinafore and she was very dead; strangled like Wendy Gilchrist, except that the killer had used a pair of tights which he'd tied in a large floppy bow behind her right ear, as if seeking to make her death even more obscene. Numbed by the discovery, Mills backed out of the room, closed the door quietly behind him and went downstairs.

The study looked as if it had been hit by ꞁ bomb. The

contents of every drawer in Gilchrist's executive desk had been emptied on to the floor so that it was almost impossible to see the Axminster carpet beneath the scattered files and personal letters. The telephone lead had been ripped out of the socket and the Grundig festooned with yards and yards of magnetic tape like tinsel on a Christmas tree. A small occasional table was lying on its side in the hall as if somebody had blundered into it.

The door to the kitchen was open and he could see the work-tops and the split-level hob and oven unit but not the breakfast bar in the corner under the large picture window facing the garden. The bloodstains on the bright yellow Marley floor caught his eye and he knew then what to expect.

Gilchrist was lying face down close to the breakfast nook, his head pointing towards the utility room. He'd been gagged and his wrists were roped behind his back but unlike Wendy and the woman in the guest room, the killer had neglected to tie his ankles. Neglected? Mills frowned; perhaps neglected was the wrong word, maybe it had been a deliberate oversight. The police would take one look at the trail of bloodstains and assume that Morris had been trying to escape when the killer had caught up with him and attacked him with the carving knife that was lying under the table, stabbing him repeatedly in the chest and back until he was dead. The killer? Why did he think only one man had been involved? He'd been jumped from behind and that meant that somebody else must have been holding the two women hostage while Morris answered the door. Motive? The police wouldn't have to look far for a motive, not when they saw the two women upstairs. No evidence of sexual assault? So what? The rapist had panicked, lost his head and killed them. The disturbance in the study? Forget it; don't look for a logical explanation when you're dealing with a homicidal maniac.

A sudden click startled him and his eyes darted towards the electric clock on the wall above the breakfast table. Ten minutes to three; a gap of almost four hours then since Morris had let him into the house. The rabbit punch had left him out cold for the best part of four hours. It was Geneva all over again, only worse, much worse. This time they would put him away for good.

His hands began to shake and he could feel a familiar tightness constricting his chest. The whole right side was

61

hard and unyielding as if the surgeon who had stitched him up after the lobectomy had forgotten to remove some piece of armour plating. Psychosomatic, so the experts said, induced by hyper-tension. Well, he was tense all right . . .

What was it he'd said to Elizabeth Eastgate on the telephone? 'I shall be seeing Mr Gilchrist later this morning.' Now, that had been brilliant, really brilliant, because that meant Special Branch had known all along exactly where they could find him. They were probably sitting outside the house right now, waiting and wondering what the hell he was doing. If that was the case, they must have seen the intruders leave, unless the killers went out through the garden on to Wimbledon Common. No, that couldn't be right; Special Branch would cover the back as well as the front of the house. Or would they? Gilchrist had been their man so they didn't have to keep a close watch on the house because sooner or later, he would tell them everything that had happened.

Mills looked at his hands and decided he could use a drink. If nothing else, it would calm his nerves, might even help him to think more clearly. Hurrying into the dining room, he opened the sideboard, found a bottle of Johnnie Walker and poured himself a large whisky. The tightness in his chest began to ease.

One thing was quite certain; he couldn't return to the flat because that was the first place they would look for him. Perhaps he could go to Glasgow, look up his sister Barbara and ask her to help him? It wasn't a bad idea except that running to Glasgow wouldn't solve anything, not when the man he wanted to expose was here, somewhere in London. What about Elizabeth Eastgate then? If she had spoken to Mrs Aston, she might be inclined to think there was something in his story after all, might even be prepared to help him. Christ, he needed someone to help him, especially someone like Elizabeth Eastgate. All he needed now was her address. Mills finished the whisky, left the glass on the sideboard and returned to the study.

It took him less than five minutes to find Gilchrist's address book amongst the litter on the floor. Whatever his faults, Morris had always been a thorough man and judging by the number of names, it seemed he'd listed even the most casual of acquaintances. Glancing down the Es, Mills saw that Elizabeth Eastgate resided at 21 Frogmore Gardens in

Ravenscourt Park; he was about to make a note of her address when it occurred to him to hold on to the book on the million to one chance that it might give him a lead.

The address book might or might not prove useful, but he wouldn't get very far in his present state. Morris, however, was roughly the same height and not so much heavier that he couldn't find at least one suit in the wardrobe to fit him. The prospect of facing the unpleasant sight of Wendy Gilchrist's half-naked and dead body made him shudder.

The television was still on and Harry Carpenter was bringing viewers up to date with a run-down on the matches that had been played on the outside courts. The camera cut from the studio to Number One Court for a Men's Doubles, focussing on Newcombe and Roche who were taking a breather, before switching to the electric scoreboard which showed they were ahead by two games to one in the opening set. Mills turned the set off and opened the wardrobe. There were no less than ten suits hanging on the rail and he settled for a two-piece grey pinstripe.

Draping the suit over a chair, he collected his jacket from the bathroom and went through the pockets. The wallet was still there but it was empty except for an out-of-date driving licence. There ought to have been a handful of loose change in his trousers but that had gone too along with the key to the flat. Neat, thought Mills, very neat; the man had set him up and then boxed him in. He didn't have the means to stay on the run. He could get away from the house all right but it was a long walk back to London.

He needed money and fast. The Gilchrists then? Morris hadn't been the sort of man who'd gone through life using a credit card. Despite marrying well and enjoying a lucrative practice, he'd never broken the habit of paying for everything with cash. The feeling of euphoria was short lived, evaporating the moment he saw Wendy's handbag lying beside the king-size double bed, its contents scattered over the carpet. He knew then that Morris's wallet would be the same, picked clean.

Changing rapidly, he rolled and tied the discarded suit and bloodstained shirt in a bundle and then went downstairs again. They had probably taken the keys to both cars, but he'd learned a trick in the SIS worth two of that.

*   *   *

63

Johnson opened the ashtray in the facia and stubbed out his cigarette. Hales had never said that he objected to him smoking in the car but then he didn't have to. Words were unnecessary; one look at the expression on his face was enough for him to know how Hales felt about the habit. It was all very well for Hales to boast that it wouldn't bother him in the least if the manufacturers never made another cigarette; giving them up hadn't been a hardship for him because he'd never been addicted. It would be a different story though if Wrigleys stopped making spearmint; Hales was a three-packet-a-day man and his jaws never stopped moving, just like a cow chewing the cud.

Johnson cleared his throat and pointed to the clock in the dashboard. "It's almost three thirty."

"So it is." Hales shifted a wad of chewing gum from one cheek to the other. "I could do with a cup of tea."

"I don't like it."

"All right, if you've gone off tea, have a coffee instead."

"I was referring to Mills. What the hell is he up to?"

"Search me." Hales shrugged his shoulders. "Maybe they're still talking over old times."

"After four and a half hours? I always knew one of us should have watched the back of the house. He's probably skipped off over the common."

"No chance; we would have heard about it."

Johnson stared at the radio. He thought Hales was almost certainly right. Gilchrist was to offer him a lift to the station and if Mills had turned him down and left by the back way, Gilchrist would have immediately telephoned Wray.

"Look, if you think the radio's on the blink, why don't you call up control?"

"Maybe that's not such a bad idea." Johnson reached for the handset and squeezed the pressel switch. "Zero," he said, "this is Tango One."

Control said, "Roger Tango One. Send your message."

"Negative, no message; this is a radio check."

"Roger. I read you loud and clear Tango One. Use correct procedure in future. Zero out."

"That put you in your place," said Hales.

"Better safe than sorry."

Johnson watched Hales unwrap another piece of gum

64

and reached for the packet of Silk Cut in the glove compartment. "About the Gilchrists?" he said abruptly.

"What about them?"

"I thought they were leaving for the Algarve today?"

"That's right; they're booked on the 1630 flight out of Heathrow."

"Well, it's 1530 now. They're cutting it a bit fine, aren't they?"

"Fifty, fifty-five minutes; it won't take him that long to get to London Airport." Hales frowned. "Hang on a minute," he said thoughtfully, "Gilchrist will have to check in with British Airways at least half an hour before the flight departure time."

"Yes, that's what I was thinking." Johnson struck a match and lit his cigarette. "Perhaps I ought to give him a ring." He jerked his thumb, pointing to one of the houses opposite. "I could ask to use their telephone."

"Well, I don't suppose it'll do any harm." Hales leaned forward and peered through the windscreen, trying to read the registration number on the Morris Marina as it left the cul-de-sac and turned up the hill. "UWW 521R," he muttered. "That's Mrs Gilchrist's car. And guess who's driving?"

"Mills?"

"If it isn't, he's got a double."

"You'd better get after him."

"Don't worry," said Hales, "I intend to." He reached forward to turn the ignition key and then noticed that Johnson was about to scramble out of the car. "What the hell . . ."

"I'm going to phone the house – something's wrong."

"What about Mills?"

"You don't need me to hold your hand, do you?"

"Do I hell."

Hales fired the engine into life, selected first gear and stabbed his foot down on the accelerator. Waiting until Johnson had slammed the door behind him, he then let in the clutch viciously. Hales was a good driver, one of the best, and he pushed the car up to fifty within the space of three hundred yards and was doing close on sixty when he rounded the corner at the top of the hill. Unfortunately his best was not good enough; Mills had such a head start on him that by the time Hales reached the Kingston bypass, the Marina was nowhere to be seen.

7

THE WOMAN HAD been very pleasant about allowing him to use her telephone, refusing his offer to pay for the call, but Johnson found himself wishing he'd picked someone who was less inquisitive. It had been a mistake to telephone Wray after he'd been unable to raise the Gilchrists and the operator had confirmed that their number was unobtainable. A mistake because it had only aroused her curiosity. Johnson had never met anyone quite like her; she had been effusive, charming, clever and subtle enough to pry into his business without being obvious. He reckoned that nobody would have escaped from Colditz had she been the Commandant.

Crossing Copse Hill Road, he quickened his stride, anxious to reach the cul-de-sac where the Gilchrists lived. The Post Office had promised to send an engineer round to the house but he had a strong premonition that there was more to it than a simple fault on the line.

There was a battered-looking Zodiac parked outside the drive and a man was standing on the doorstep gazing up at the house as if puzzled to know why he couldn't get an answer. Hearing footsteps on the gravel, the man turned about and stared at Johnson.

"What's the matter?" Johnson asked cheerfully. "Aren't you having any luck?"

"No, I can't raise a peep out of them." The man jerked a thumb towards the second garage. "I know they're off to the Algarve but they wouldn't leave the doors open like that. Anyway, that's where Mrs Gilchrist keeps her Marina." His eyebrows met in a frown. "It would be just like her to pop round to the High Street to do some last minute shopping."

"Yes?"

"But if that's the case, her husband ought to be at home."

"Perhaps he's in the garden?"

"No, I've looked there, tried the back door too but there was no answer." The man shook his head. "I can't understand where my wife's got to, it's not like her to be late. I mean, she's always home by four or four fifteen at the latest; she knows the kids will be wanting their tea."

Johnson rubbed his jaw. It wasn't difficult to put two and two together and come up with the right answer. The Gilchrists were obviously the sort of people who would employ a daily woman and when the man returned from work to find his wife wasn't at home, he'd jumped into his car and driven straight round to the house to collect her.

"Why don't you try the door again while I take a look round the back?" Johnson produced his warrant card and smiled briefly. "I don't suppose there's anything to be worried about, it's probably a false alarm."

"What is?"

"The phone call; one of the neighbours noticed a man behaving suspiciously and thought he might be a burglar. It happens all the time, Mr ... ?"

"Yelf, Ron Yelf." The man swallowed nervously. "You want me to ring the bell again?"

"That's right; you keep your finger on it while I nip round the back." Johnson grinned. "If there is an intruder, he won't know whether he's coming or going."

"Him and me both," said Yelf.

The door to the utility room was locked just as he'd been told it was; moving round to the kitchen, Johnson pressed his nose against the window and peered inside. The dining nook lay in shadow and it was some moments before he saw that there was a body lying face down on the floor close to the breakfast table.

*   *   *

Mills wondered how much longer his luck would last. Special Branch had obviously seen him driving off in Wendy's car and while it was sometimes difficult to be sure how the opposition would react, he thought it was highly likely that in this instance they would have gone straight round to the house to have a few words with Morris. If that were so, the Operations Room at Scotland Yard would have swung into action some five or ten minutes later. From then on it was anybody's guess how long it would be before his description and the registration number of the Marina had been disseminated to every patrol car and policeman on the beat.

It had been apparent from the start that he would have to ditch the Marina as soon as possible, but that was easier said than done. Once he abandoned the car, he would be reduced to walking and he didn't fancy his chances on foot, at least not clear across London to where Elizabeth Eastgate lived in Ravenscourt Park. He really had no choice but to stick with the car and sweat it out.

Although he'd made good time on the A3 as far as Wandsworth, he'd hit the beginning of the weekend rush hour at Clapham Common when the lights had been against him all the way to the Elephant and Castle where he was now snarled up in a traffic jam. Like a man on a treadmill, he was going nowhere fast. Tightening his grip on the steering wheel, Mills stared at the lorry in front of him and willed it to move on.

The lights were still at red when he heard the 'blee bah' note of a police siren in the distance. It was hard to place the direction at first, but as the car drew nearer, it became evident that it was coming towards him. A minute later, blue light flashing and hazard blinkers showing, the Rover 3500 shot past him, weaving in and out of the traffic like a demented snake. It wasn't until a motorist behind him blasted an angry warning on his horn that Mills realised that the lorry had moved off. With a sigh of relief, he shifted into gear, released the handbrake and let in the clutch.

Crawling past the Metropolitan Tabernacle, he waited for a break in the oncoming traffic and then turned right into the New Kent Road. A mile beyond the flyover into the Old Kent Road, he left the A2 and parked the Marina in Kingslake Street, within easy walking distance of Sheldon Court. Mills didn't think Ray Walters would be exactly overjoyed to see him again, especially as he was going to tap him for a small loan.

Sheldon Court never had, never would be an oasis of peace and quiet. Some sort of eight-a-side football match was in progress on the grassed area behind the garages and, judging by the raucous shouts of dissent punctuated by four-letter words, it was pretty obvious to Mills that the referee's decision was a long way from being final. A very frightened thirteen-year-old girl fleeing from two other girls, one black, one white, raced across the forecourt and disappeared through the swing doors well ahead of him but only just in front of her pursuers. By this time he entered the lobby, all three were nowhere to be seen. Mills stepped into the other lift and pressed the button for the eleventh floor.

Sheila Walters answered the door, took one look at him and then tried to slam it in his face. Although she showed great presence of mind, his foot was already inside and she didn't have enough weight to resist the shoulder charge. The impact knocked her off balance and staggering back into the hall, she sat down heavily on her rump, her tinted glasses coming adrift to reveal a swollen cheek and an eye that was black and blue. For a slim woman, Mills thought she had a surprisingly loud voice and her screams of rage provoked an instant reaction from Walters who charged out of the living room like a runaway carthorse. Mills stretched out a leg, watched him take off in a swallow dive and closed his eyes in mock sympathy a second before Walters ploughed into the wall.

Mills said, "I thought you'd be pleased to see me again, Ray."

Walters groaned, muttered an expletive under his breath and then slowly got to his feet. A pink strip of Elastoplast concealed the gash in his skull made by the ashtray, his right eye was still closed and there was a lump the size of a pigeon's egg on his forehead.

"How's that brother of yours, the future welterweight champion?"

"He'll live." Walters hugged his stomach and shot him a baleful glare. "Now piss off and leave us alone."

"Lend me five pounds and I will."

"What?"

"I reckon I can get by on a fiver." Mills smiled. "It's not much to ask, is it?"

"Me lend you money? Shit, you've got to be joking."

"You can make it back ten times over." He could see that Walters was interested; it showed in the way his one good eye narrowed speculatively. "Of course, you'll have to look out for the fuzz."

"Don't listen to him." Sheila Walters climbed to her feet and rubbed her bruised backside. "Don't listen to him, Ray, we've had enough trouble with them already." She turned on Mills, her face twisted in anger. "They were here last night after you'd gone."

"Who were?"

"Who do you think?" she snarled. "The bloody bogeymen, that's who."

It seemed he'd underestimated Special Branch, and that was a big mistake. Until now, he'd been under the illusion that he'd shaken them off after leaving Waterloo Station but it was evident the evasive tactics hadn't worked and they'd stuck to him like glue.

"What happened?" he asked softly.

"Nothing," said Walters, "they asked us not to press charges."

"Asked?" Sheila's voice rose in fury. "Christ, they didn't ask, they bloody well told us – one squawk out of you lot and your sodding feet won't touch the ground."

It figured. Special Branch had been anxious to keep CID out of it because they were convinced that sooner or later he would lead them to the missing Bearer Bonds. Well, that was yesterday and everything had changed since then, and now Special Branch would simply back off and call it a day, leaving the way clear for CID to pick up the pieces.

Mills pointed to Sheila. "Are you going to let her do all the talking, Ray?"

"Why not? You haven't said anything that's worth listening to yet."

"There's a car in Kingslake Street which is going begging. I wouldn't advise you to unload it on anyone but it's got a good set of tyres and you can flog the radio too."

"A fiver you said?"

"That's right; a fiver will buy you the make and the registration number."

Walters hesitated for a moment and then reached into his pocket, "Four oncers," he said, holding up the notes, "that's all it's worth; take it or leave it."

Whatever twinge of conscience he might have had evaporated very rapidly. He'd got on with Walters well enough when they'd been on the inside but there was no common bond between them now. Mills thought it was funny how you saw people in a different light in a different environment.

70

"Do you have a telephone, Ray?"

"A telephone?" Sheila said bitingly. "Whatever next? Your friend wants a lot for his money, doesn't he?"

Walters ignored her and pointed a finger towards the door. "Behind you," he said, "on the hall table."

"The car you want is a Marina." Mills plucked the money out of his hand and backed away. "The number is UWW 521R." Still keeping his eye on Walters, he knocked the telephone over on to the floor and then stamped on it, smashing the handset. "Sorry about that," he said casually, "but we can't have you chatting up the local Nick while I'm still in the neighbourhood."

Walters was equally indifferent. "You needn't have bothered," he said, "the GPO disconnected the bloody thing three months ago."

*   *   *

Gordon Liddell collected a visitor's pass from the War Department constable and moved through the gate into the security area where Miss Nightingale was waiting for him. Compared with the CIA's huge complex at Langley, Virginia or the KGB's mausoleum in Dzerzhinsky Square, the Department of Subversive Warfare was housed in a rabbit hutch. If big was not necessarily beautiful, he thought being small wasn't so goddamned marvellous either. Harper's organisation had never been involved in a fiasco like the Bay of Pigs but on the other hand, neither had it pulled off a coup on the scale of the CIA's intervention in the Dominican Republic, for the simple reason that it was the pygmy amongst the giants of the Intelligence world. The Department of Subversive Warfare was the direct descendent of the wartime SOE, the vigorous father siring an ailing son whose survival was continually in doubt, given the present economic and political climate.

Glancing sideways at his escort, it occurred to Liddell that Harper's PA was living embodiment of everything the firm stood for. Ten years had come and gone but as far as he could see, Miss Nightingale hadn't changed. She was still well groomed and neatly turned out in a two-piece that obviously suited her conservative taste and pocket but, as always, she reminded him of a proud yet impoverished

71

gentlewoman who found it difficult to make ends meet, just as the Department of Subversive Warfare did.

Hard times or not, the moment Liddell stepped inside Harper's office, it was evident to him that the man had lost none of his charm. Whether it was genuine or not, he greeted him warmly. Accepting his invitation, Liddell sat down in the leather armchair reserved for visitors but remembering previous visits, declined the offer of a cup of coffee. Although the carpet was new, he observed that the office had lost none of its Dickensian gloom and the pigeons were still out there crapping all over the porthole windows.

Harper said, "It's been a long time, Gordon."

"Ten years."

"Really? Is it as long as that? When last I heard, you were in Vietnam."

"I left there in '71."

Harper stroked his chin and looked thoughtful. "And what have you been doing with yourself since then?"

"Driving a desk in Langley. And you?"

"Oh, this and that."

"There's a story going round Washington that you burnt your fingers over Angola. Any truth in it?"

Harper supposed it was almost inevitable that Washington should assume he'd been responsible for recruiting the mercenaries, but it rankled all the same. His knowledge of the Angolan business had been strictly limited to what he'd read in the newspapers and seen on television, but he doubted if Liddell would believe it.

"You ought to know me better than that, Gordon. Anyway, you didn't come here just to talk about Angola, did you?"

"No. As a matter of fact, I'm interested in what you have to say about Edward Mills."

"We're on the subject of ancient history now, are we?"

"Well, history has always fascinated me; it has a habit of repeating itself." Liddell removed his gold-framed glasses and polished them with a handkerchief. "You see, I think we may have another Dreyfus."

Harper thought the 'we' was significant; it implied the American had a proprietary interest in Mills.

"You're wrong, Gordon," he said firmly, "totally and completely wrong. Mills is no Dreyfus."

"He engineered the whole thing, did he, Cedric? Shopped

72

Kiktev to the KGB, fingered your people in Prague and then stole a million dollars' worth of Bearer Bonds? Is that how you see the conspiracy?"

"Conspiracy?" Harper shook his head. "There was no conspiracy, only a chain of events that enabled Mills to steal a million. Look, Kiktev may have been a brilliant scientist but he was also a flamboyant and conceited extrovert. Discretion? He didn't even know the meaning of the word. I believe he was convinced that a man of his stature had nothing to fear from the KGB because as far as they were concerned, he was one of the great untouchables in the Soviet Union. Naive? Certainly; just look at the way he got in touch with our Secret Intelligence Service. The KGB aren't fools; they knew what was in the wind. Persuading the Czechs to postpone the Prague conference was their way of bringing the whole sorry affair out into the open."

"It won't wash, Cedric." Liddell pinched his nose between index finger and thumb to show that he thought the explanation stank. "Somebody tipped them off and it wasn't Larissa Fedorovna Pavlichenko."

"Oh, but it was. Not intentionally perhaps, but when she defected, the KGB had all the proof they needed."

"And your two? – Martin Strougal and Gustav Benes – did she blow their cover too? Is that how they got stiffed in Prague?"

Strougal and Benes – their names were an echo from the past. Strougal, the former RAF bomber pilot who'd collected a DFC and bar, and Benes, the wireless operator who'd managed to evade the Gestapo after Jan Kubis and Josef Gabchick had assassinated Reinhard Heydrich in May 1942. Strougal and Benes, part of the legacy his Department had inherited from SOE; Strougal and Benes, two middle-aged Czechs who should have been put out to grass long before their number came up in '64.

"No, you can put them down to Kiktev; he was anxious to save his hide. Anyway it was enough to keep him out of a forced labour camp."

"But not out of a mental hospital."

"Even so, he wasn't harshly treated, at least not by their standards, Gordon."

"Which is more than you can say for Mills."

"Mills was sentenced to seven years' imprisonment for

theft. Entirely through his own efforts, he managed to stretch it into double figures." Harper stifled a yawn. "That may be contrary to what you've heard, but it still happens to be true."

"I'm a gambling man and I play a lot of poker." Liddell smiled. "So don't try to fool me, I can read you like a book."

"Japanese style, I presume."

"What?"

"Upside down and back to front," said Harper.

"Oh, very funny." Liddell creased his mouth in what passed for a smile. "I always knew you British had a sense of humour but when are you people going to stop burying your heads in the sand? Do you figure all your troubles will simply disappear just because you can't see them? Whether you like it or not, you've got a rotten apple in the barrel, and his name isn't Mills."

Harper glanced at the telephone, wondered if he should tell Liddell about the call he'd received from Gattis earlier that afternoon and then decided it would serve no useful purpose.

"The SIS held a very thorough enquiry, Gordon, and they were satisfied that there was no third, fourth or fifth man."

"I'm not interested in their conclusions; in fact, I'll forget the whole damn business if you can explain to me why our State Department suddenly developed cold feet over Angola."

Harper felt his jaw drop. Were they back on Angola again? Liddell had lost him. Try as he might, he couldn't see the connection between Mills and Angola.

"I'm not with you," he said faintly.

"For God's sake," Liddell exploded angrily, "don't give me that crap. You must know that Washington encouraged the South Africans to intervene against the MPLA only to do a smart about-face just when they had the Cubans on the run. And you know why too. All right, so it is an election year but domestic politics wasn't the only reason why our State Department changed its mind. I don't know why we Americans should attach so much importance to British opinion – I mean, you people have lost an Empire and gained nothing in return, your economy is in a mess and you don't have any military muscle. But it seems to me we're always looking over our shoulder, hoping whatever it is that we're trying to do will meet with your approval."

"So?"

74

"So I'm saying there is at least one man, possibly even a cell of two or three, in your Foreign and Commonwealth Office who for the past ten to fifteen years has been able to influence successive British governments in a way that has been harmful to the long-term interests of your country and therefore of mine."

Harper rested both elbows on the desk and cupped his chin in both palms. Apparently, Liddell had mounted his favourite hobby horse and now was determined to ride it.

The lecture lasted all of twenty minutes. By the time Liddell was finished, he'd analysed Soviet policy in Africa, touched upon every difference of opinion that had arisen between the U.S. and British governments over Laos, Cambodia, Vietnam and the Middle East and demonstrated that the West was losing out all down the line. He also half convinced Harper that there might after all be something to his theory about the ultimate culprit being in the British Foreign and Commonwealth Office.

"You know," Harper said thoughtfully, "I still don't understand why you're so interested in Mills."

"You don't?" Liddell unfolded a piece of paper and placed it on the desk. "There are three names on that list, names I have given to Larissa Fedorovna Pavlichenko. Point Mills in the right direction and he could be a useful weapon."

"Assuming I can find him, you want me to steer Mills towards La Pavlichenko, is that the idea?"

"Yes."

Harper glanced at the list and raised his eyebrows.

"All right," he said quietly, "you've got yourself a deal."

8

MILLS SAT DOWN on a bench and stretched out his legs. He'd lost count of the number of times he'd strolled round the park in the last half hour while he waited for Elizabeth Eastgate to return home from work, but a few people were already beginning to shoot him some very odd looks.

Mills glanced at his wristwatch again and wondered where she had got to. Ten past six. He doubted if the train journey from Holborn to Ravenscourt Park would take her more than thirty minutes on the Underground. On the other hand, if she had taken her car to work she could be snarled up in the rush-hour traffic. He thought that was unlikely however, because he had a hunch that the MGB parked outside 21 Frogmore Gardens was hers. Perhaps she had a date then? Perhaps she'd even gone away for the weekend? Perhaps . . . if . . . maybe . . . the permutations were endless.

He desperately hoped Elizabeth Eastgate would return home soon because he was anxious to give his side of the Gilchrist murders before she heard the news some other way. The evening papers weren't carrying the story yet but there was a chance that it would make the Stop Press in later editions. The police, of course, wouldn't release any details until the next of kin had been informed and somebody would have to break the news to the Gilchrists' children away at their boarding schools. In fact, it was an even bet that the BBC would be the first to break the news.

He realised now that he should have listened to Morris, taken his advice, put the lost years behind him and made a new life. But soft options had always been an anathema to him. Now three people had died because he'd refused to let it rest. It was, however, a little late in the day to have second thoughts.

A District Line train pulled out of Ravenscourt Park and

clattered over the steel girder bridge heading towards Stamford Bridge. Shielding his eyes against the sun, he watched the tiny figures leave the island platform on the embankment. The minutes ticked away and the stream of passengers leaving the station became a trickle and then, just when it seemed that Elizabeth Eastgate was not even amongst the last of the stragglers, she appeared on the steps looking cool and elegant in a green cotton dress. Entering the park, she followed the winding asphalt path for a short distance before branching off across the grass to take a short cut to Frogmore Gardens. Mills waited until she was inside the house and then left the bench.

He hadn't the faintest idea what he was going to say to her, but he would cross that bridge when he came to it. The first and most important step was to persuade her to invite him inside. Two little girls playing hopscotch on the pavement outside the next door house gave him a brief, inquisitive look, decided he wasn't worth bothering about and went back to their game. Mills pushed the front gate open, walked up the path and rang the bell.

Elizabeth Eastgate was patently surprised to see him.

"Mr Mills," she said faintly. "What on earth ... ? How did you know where to find me?"

"Morris told me."

"Mr Gilchrist?"

"Yes." Mills, improvising wildly, reached his jacket for the address book. "He asked me to give you this. He said it was important you should have it."

It sounded a cockeyed story even to his ears and it was evident that she didn't know what to make of it. Her eyebrows narrowed in a small frown of bewilderment and then rose expressively.

"I don't understand; why should Morris want me to have his address book?"

"I'm afraid it's a rather long story. Perhaps ... ?" Mills left the question hanging in the air and gestured, waving a hand towards the hall in the hope that she would invite him inside.

"Yes, well ..." She hesitated, and for a moment it seemed she was going to ignore the hint. "Well, in that case I suppose you'd better come in."

It wasn't exactly a gracious invitation but at least he'd cleared the first hurdle.

"I must say I find his behaviour a little strange." She opened a door off the hall and showed him into the living room.

"You've spoken to Mrs Aston then?"

"Mrs Aston?" she repeated blankly. And then the penny dropped. "Well, yes. You were quite right. About Mr Boxall, I mean. And I admit that it seems very odd. After all, why should Morris lie to me? It isn't as if he'd done anything wrong?"

"Morris is dead," he told her, his nervousness making him abrupt.

"What?" She swallowed. "What did you say?"

"Morris is dead – murdered."

"I don't believe it."

"They killed him and Wendy and some other woman."

"They?"

Total disbelief showed in her voice and he knew that they had reached the crunch point. If she didn't believe him he was sunk. He winced slightly as the muscles on the right side of his chest went into spasm and he felt he was going to suffocate. Psychosomatic, hyper-tension – the doctors always had a soothing explanation.

Elizabeth Eastgate was staring at him. "Did you see the killers then?"

"No."

"They why did you say 'they' killed him and Wendy and some other woman?"

Suddenly she was very calm, neither believing nor disbelieving, simply the cool, astute solicitor probing for the truth.

"Because I assumed there had to be more than one."

"Why?"

The simple question was always the most difficult to answer. How was he going to make her understand unless he started with Ziegler and went on from there?

"It's a very complicated story and I'm not sure I can give you a brief explanation."

"There's no hurry," she said quietly. "I'm not going anywhere."

He started from the beginning because he felt that that was the only way he could tell it and make sense. He put it across badly, jumping backwards and forwards in time whenever he remembered some point of detail which previously he'd omitted; on several occasions he almost lost the thread of what he was saying and would have dried up altogether if Elizabeth Eastgate hadn't been there to prompt him with a shrewd question at the right moment. The longer he continued, the more it seemed to him that his story lacked all credibility, but by that stage he was past caring whether it sounded wholly improbable or not, and he stumbled on until reaching the end, his voice finally tailed off and died in a mumble.

Mills waited for her to say something but the long silence dragged on, condemning him it seemed more eloquently than mere words ever could. "I guess I didn't make a very good witness," he said at last.

"You were rather incoherent."

"And totally unconvincing?"

"I didn't say that." She turned her back on him and moved towards the sideboard. "In fact, strange as it may seem, I believe you precisely because you did make such a poor witness. A liar, a man with something to hide, would have been much more plausible."

He thought it was a somewhat negative reason for accepting his story but it was certainly better than outright rejection.

"Would you like a drink?" She was crouching in front of the sideboard, the green cotton dress way above her knees, unaware that she was showing a lot of thigh. "I'm afraid I can only offer you a glass of sherry."

"No," said Mills, wiping his mouth, "no, it's very kind of you but I ought to be going."

"Going?" She frowned. "Where to? You can't get back to the flat in Moravian Place, you said so yourself. And you don't have any money."

"Well, I was hoping . . ."

"That I would lend you some? I've only got fifteen pounds in my purse and the banks are closed until Monday."

Mills swore under his breath. Friday, it had to be bloody Friday.

"You can stay here." Elizabeth stood up and smoothed her dress. "I'll make up a bed in the spare room."

"No, that wouldn't do."

"Why ever not?"

"Because the police may come looking for me. I should have thought of that possibility before. You see, they know that we're acquainted."

"Nonsense; how would they know that?"

"The flat was bugged."

"Oh. Well, that does tend to make things a bit awkward."

A bit awkward? That was a masterly understatement.

"Still, we can face that problem when we come to it."

"What are you trying to do? Get yourself struck off?"

"I'm the only solicitor here," she said calmly, "and I know what I'm doing."

Mills saw the faint smile on her lips and wondered if she did.

*   *   *

Harper thought the pub in Shepherd Market was a long way off the beaten track for Wray but at least it had character and atmosphere, which was more than could be said for the Master at Arms where they occasionally met for a drink. The fact that the Special Branch man had chosen Shepherd Market instead of his usual haunt suggested he was anxious to avoid his colleagues. As Harper threaded his way between the tables towards the corner nook where Wray was ensconced with a whisky and soda, he thought his old friend seemed a very worried man. Apparently lost in thought, Wray only became aware of him when he pulled out a chair and sat down.

Harper said, "I got your message, Stanley."

"I can see that."

Wray was sucking on an empty pipe. He sounded tense and on edge. Usually he liked to give the impression that he was good-natured and easy-going but, for once, he made no attempt to disguise his feelings.

He sighed and pushed a glass of whisky towards Harper. "Yours," he grunted. "Help yourself to water."

"I have a feeling you're not exactly pleased with life, Stanley."

"I'm not."

"Who's trodden on your corns then?"

"It's no joking matter, Cedric." Wray toyed with his pipe, tapping the stem against the ashtray in a cadence slow enough

80

for a funeral march. "In fact, I'm not sure I should be talking to you."

"It's like that, is it?" Harper said guardedly. If Special Branch were going to ask for help, he needed to know what was in it for his own Department.

"I could lose my pension if word got out."

"Well, in that case, perhaps you hadn't better say anything."

"It concerns Mills." Wray filled his pipe, jabbed it between his teeth and struck a match. "Of course I'm aware that he has no connection with your Department but I think you ought to know that he's wanted for murder."

"What?" Suddenly conscious that other people were close enough to overhear their conversation, Harper leaned forward and lowered his voice. "Who did he kill? One of your men?"

"No, it was his solicitor, a man called Gilchrist. He also murdered Gilchrist's wife and a Mrs Yelf. I believe she was their daily woman."

"When did this happen?"

"Some time between eleven o'clock and a quarter to four this afternoon when Johnson saw him leave the house in Mrs Gilchrist's car."

"Johnson?" queried Harper.

"One of my men. I had two of them watching the house; the other one took off after Mills but lost him on the Kingston bypass. Johnson telephoned me a few minutes before he made a 999 call. I don't have too many details because he's still there at the house helping the local CID with their enquiries."

"I suppose there's no doubt in your mind?"

"That Mills did it?" Wray drew on his pipe. "Everything points to him and certainly Mills has become progressively more violent. Apart from giving Chesterman a lump on his jaw, he turned very nasty with a former prison mate. I don't know what the man had done to annoy him, but he gave Walters a right hammering yesterday evening – did his wife and brother over too."

Harper reached for his whisky and drank it thoughtfully. It seemed the prison psychiatrist had been right after all; Mills was hard, embittered, violent and dangerous. Hardly the innocent fall guy he'd always claimed to be. So much for Gordon Liddell and his Dreyfus theory.

"You realise that we'll have to leave Mills alone now? I mean, the ball is with CID."

"Quite."

"However, there are a couple of things that still bother me about this case."

"Oh?" Harper looked up from his drink. "Such as?" he asked sharply.

"Well, Gilchrist – I never really understood how he came to be involved. You see, he approached his local Crime Prevention Officer some weeks ago, ostensibly because he was worried about Mills, and 'V' Division put him in touch with us. But somehow, he gave me the impression that he'd been very close to somebody in your lot or the SIS before I came on the scene. There was nothing I could put my finger on; it was just a feeling I had. Of course, it might have been my imagination."

Harper thought his tone of voice implied otherwise. Wray was a shrewd judge of character and few people were able to put one over on him. Then too, he wasn't the sort of man who'd express reservations about Gilchrist unless he had good reason.

"It certainly wasn't us," Harper said, "I haven't given Gilchrist a thought since the trial."

Wray shrugged. "And there's Boxall. I take it you've heard of him?"

"Wasn't he in Durham with Mills?"

"Yes. Anyway, Mills sent word to Gilchrist asking him to engage a private detective on his behalf because he was anxious to trace Boxall. Gilchrist didn't like the idea and that's why he saw the local Crime Prevention Officer. To cut a long story short, the Home Office decided to place Mills under surveillance and we were told to find Boxall so that Gilchrist could string him along." Wray examined his pipe, saw that it had gone out, and struck another match. "I put Chesterman on to it and he telephoned round the various Divisions until he ran him to ground in Ealing. That's when it transpired that somebody claiming to be in the Serious Crimes Squad had been asking after Boxall too – a man with an Irish accent."

"Did this somebody give a name?"

"Yes, but it didn't belong to him."

"Curious," muttered Harper, "very curious."

"It gets better. Boxall vanished into thin air four days before Mills was released from Leicester."

Harper frowned. It was beginning to look as if he owed Liddell an apology. Maybe the American's theory wasn't so far-fetched after all.

"Perhaps, with hindsight, we ought to have kept an eye on Boxall."

"It's always easy to be wise after the event, Stanley."

"So people keep telling me. However, it doesn't matter now; everyone's out looking for Mills and he won't get far. Apart from a sister in Glasgow, there's no one he can turn to, unless . . ."

"Unless what?"

"It's just possible that Elizabeth Eastgate might be prepared to help him. She's a solicitor, one of Gilchrist's associates, and that's all I'm going to tell you."

"All, Stanley?"

"Well, except for the fact that she lives at 21 Frogmore Gardens in Ravenscourt Park."

"Does CID know about her?"

"Not yet, but it can only be a question of time before they start asking Johnson some very awkward questions. At a guess, I'd say you could count on eight hours."

There was no need for Wray to spell it out, the hint had been broad enough; there never had been, never would be any love lost between CID and Special Branch. Provided he was prepared to risk it, there was a fair chance that he could grab Mills before CID laid their hands on him. Boxall; in the end of course, everything hinged on Boxall. Harper knew only too well that if there was a simple explanation for his disappearance, he would stand to lose far more than his pension. A simple explanation? Wray hadn't offered one; he'd merely thought it very odd that Boxall should have vanished into thin air, and that ought to be good enough for him. After all, they had known each other for a very long time and he'd come to respect Wray's sound judgment and intuitive hunches over the years.

Eight hours? They would be pressed for time but they could do it if he pulled out all the stops. Harper pulled at his lip wondering whom he should send. Elizabeth Eastgate would have to be handled with kid gloves but he could probably leave her quite safely to Harry Vincent; Vincent could sell a television set to a blind man if he had mind to. Drew? His lips met in a thin line; Drew was a bit of a hard nose but he'd always worked with Vincent and he'd be useful if Mills was there and turned ugly. Gattis was returning from the Isle of Wight on the 1551 from Ryde Pier Head, so he'd be available too. The duty officer would have to run all three to ground, alert the motor pool and warn the staff of the safe house at Goring-on-Thames to expect a guest. But that shouldn't take more than an hour and with any luck, they would be available for briefing around eight p.m. He seemed to recall that Muriel, his wife, had invited some people to dinner, but it couldn't be helped; it wouldn't be the first or the last time she'd have to cope without him.

"I can see I've given you plenty to think about."

Harper looked up with a smile. "Let me get you another drink," he said.

"No thanks, one's enough for me. Besides, I ought to be getting along, you've obviously got a lot on your mind."

"Yes, as a matter of fact, I have. I was thinking that if . . ."

"No." Wray wagged an admonishing finger. "No, I don't want to hear it, Cedric, I'm likely to be in enough trouble as it is. Just do me a favour and forget we ever met this evening."

9

HARRY VINCENT tossed his notes into the pending tray and frowned. Perhaps, at forty-two, it really was time he asked Harper for an administrative job. Maybe Drew was right, maybe he was becoming too cautious and too set in his ways. But there was a bad smell to this particular assignment and he had a nasty feeling that they could end up in the proverbial shit unless they were very careful. The photographs of the house in Frogmore Gardens, arranged in sequence on his desk, were still damp to the touch and that was a bad sign. A sense of urgency was all very well but a lot of things could go off at half cock when a job was organised in a hurry.

"I don't like it," he muttered.

Drew leaned across him and stubbed out his cigarette in the ashtray. "What's the matter now, Harry? Something wrong with the photographs?"

"Well, you've got to admit they're a rush job."

"And that's bad?" Drew shook his head. "You're getting to be an old woman. Look, our people used a Post Office detector van to take those pictures and you couldn't ask for a better decoy vehicle than that." He smiled broadly. "I bet the licence dodgers had a heart attack when they saw it cruising round the neighbourhood. But why should you care?"

"I worry because we're rushing our fences."

"So what? That's Harper's problem, not yours." Drew pushed his cuff back and tapped the face of his wristwatch. "Time's getting on," he said pointedly, "and I've got a date, remember."

Vincent suppressed a smile. That would be the trim little number from the American Embassy in Grosvenor Square, the honey blonde with the impeccable New England background and the private income, the latest in a long line of conquests but one who was obviously destined to be rather more durable than the others. Drew was rising thirty now and ready to settle down with the right woman, the overriding consideration being that this certain someone should have plenty of money.

"You'll have to cancel it then," he said mildly.

"Why the hell should I? We're not lifting Mills this side of midnight."

"Maybe we aren't, but I'm not taking any chances." Vincent marked one of the photographs with a biro and handed it to Drew. "Anyway, that's where I want you, come one thirty," he said. "In the garden, watching the back of the house, ready to grab Mills as he slides down the drainpipe."

"Assuming he's there, Harry."

"Let's not be too pessimistic." Vincent pointed to the cross he'd marked. "How long do you think you'll need to get into position?"

"Ten, maybe fifteen minutes. You can drop me off in Latimer Road and I'll cut through the alleyway between the two rows of houses. The fence at the bottom of her garden is about five foot; climbing over it should be a doddle."

A doddle? Well, that was more than could be said for the rest of the operation. What if Mills went to ground inside the house and Elizabeth Eastgate asked if he had a search warrant? What if the CID turned up to make their pinch while he and Drew were still in the neighbourhood? Just thinking about the possibilities was enough to give a man ulcers.

"You've gone all silent again, Harry."

"I was waiting to see if you had any questions."

"Oh yes?"

It was evident from his sceptical tone that Drew didn't believe him; hiding his annoyance, Vincent said, "All right, if everything's so crystal clear, you'd better go down to the Armoury and sign for the Webley."

"Sign for it?" Drew's voice rose in astonishment. "Why should anybody want my signature for a bloody air pistol?"

"Because it's an air pistol with a difference – it puts people to sleep."

*   *   *

86

Elizabeth Eastgate turned over yet another page in the address book and without looking up, crushed her cigarette in the ashtray, grinding the stub as if she was milling corn. Mills thought she was probably on the Ws by now but as far as he could tell from her facial expressions, most of the names were unfamiliar. On a number of occasions she had inclined her head and smiled in a way that suggested she'd recognised a mutual acquaintance amongst the friends and associates of Morris Gilchrist, but there had been no frowning look of bewilderment to show that she had stumbled upon someone who seemed out of place.

It stood to reason that Gilchrist had been in touch with some shadowy figure in one of the security services over a considerable period of time and had been given a number to contact in case of an emergency. Knowing how thorough Morris had been in life, he'd thought there was a fair chance that at least the dialling code had been recorded in the address book, but it was beginning to look as if Gilchrist had been too well briefed.

Had he been wise to mention this possibility to Elizabeth Eastgate before asking her to go through the address book? Maybe she was now thinking that he'd been trying to cover his tracks, preparing her for the fact that there was not one shred of evidence to back up his story? Usually, it was possible to read her thoughts but looking at her now, curled up in the armchair with both legs tucked under her rump, it was hard to know what was going on in her mind. Moments later when she closed the book with a definite snap and a wall of silence grew between them, he began to wonder if the gesture held some special significance.

"Well, what do you think?" His voice sounded a little cracked as though there was a rasp in his throat. "I mean, how does it look to you?"

"The address book?" She leaned forward and scratched an itch on her shin. "It seems pretty straightforward and above board to me, but then I hardly know any of the names on the list. Morris moved in a different circle and we rarely met outside the office."

In her own inimitable fashion she was letting him know that it had been a waste of time. Forget the damn book, he thought, it's just another blind alley.

"About Geneva?" she said diffidently.

87

Geneva? Mills frowned. Surely to God she didn't want him to go over the same old ground again?

"I've already told you what happened."

"I know why you went there but not who sent you."

Mills rubbed his chin. It wasn't the same old ground and it was possible that she might put her finger on something he'd missed.

"It started in Bonn."

"Yes, so you said."

He smiled. This was the legal mind cutting through the dross, urging him to get to the point.

"I was supernumerary to establishment and awaiting posting, so I was the natural choice when head office asked for a leg man with field experience. I returned to London on Friday the thirtieth of May and was briefed by Ollenshaw, the Deputy Controller of the Russian Section, who told me to establish contact with Doctor Joachim Ziegler in Geneva. The operation was to be codenamed Pond Jump for some obscure reason."

"Why couldn't they have used a local man?"

Although the answer stuck out a mile, it was the sort of question an outsider would think pertinent.

"Because there was a good chance the KGB would know him. That's not to say that they didn't have my photograph on record in Dzerzhinsky Square, but for the Pond Jump thing Ollenshaw was banking on the fact that I would be in and out of the country before the Swiss Section could get a line on me. Anyway, I returned from Geneva late on the fifth of June and reported to Ollenshaw the following morning. Ten days later, after the Treasury had completed their paperwork, I flew out to New York, checked in at The Pickwick Arms on East 51st Street and subsequently collected one million dollars' worth of Bearer Bonds from Hanson and Baldwin, the Wall Street brokers. There was plenty of time as I wasn't due to see Ziegler again until the 21st. I was booked on BOAC departing Kennedy on Tuesday the seventeenth of June at 1600 hours local time when I found the coded telegram waiting for me at the hotel. My meeting with Ziegler had been moved forward. The rest you know. I switched to Pan Am, flew to Frankfurt, arriving there early on the eighteenth, where there was another message waiting for me at the airport. I then dialled the number I'd been given and was connected to an answering service. There was nothing unusual about that, it was a gimmick I'd come across before and I thought I recognised the voice on the other end of the line."

"So?"

"So I caught a Swissair flight to Geneva and walked into the sucker trap, taking the Bonds with me. I surfaced again three days later, the Bonds didn't."

"What about the coded telegram? Wasn't that proof of the change of plan?"

"I burnt it – that's standard operating procedure."

A thumb crept towards her mouth and she nibbled at the nail, her forehead creased in a frown. "Did Ollenshaw know that you were friendly with Janet Rayner?"

Delicate, he thought, oh, very delicate. Elizabeth Eastgate had missed her real vocation; she should have gone into the Diplomatic instead of reading Law. Friendly with Janet Rayner? Well, that was putting it mildly. She was just down from Cambridge and theirs had been a real crash, bang, wallop affair while it lasted . . . before he'd discovered that she was regarded as the FO's personal bicycle, the sporty type whom a lot of people working in Carlton House had ridden at one time or another.

"Ollenshaw didn't miss much," he said quietly.

"So he'd know that you were no longer seeing her?"

It was easy to see which way her mind was working. The man in the shadows had arranged that the title deeds to the villa in Juan les Pins should be sent to Janet Rayner, knowing that she would ring him up to say what she thought of somebody who had the impertinence to use her flat as a forwarding address.

"I should think so."

"Then it has to be Ollenshaw."

Q.E.D. The solution to the problem, except that it didn't jell with the facts.

"You're wrong," he said. "Ollenshaw was cleared by the Board of Inquiry. They were very thorough."

"I seem to recall that Harold Macmillan was assured that there was no third man in the Burgess-Maclean affair."

It wasn't a valid point. The SIS had burnt their fingers over Philby and they'd taken the lesson to heart. They'd probed into every aspect, even re-opening the inquiry when the title deeds had turned up, and they had got nowhere. No, that wasn't strictly true; the title deeds and that eminently respectable notary in Avignon who was supposed to have acted on his behalf, had finally nailed him to the cross.

"I know what you're thinking, but there was no cover up. You can take my word for it."

"I still believe Ollenshaw was behind it." She smiled. "Call it womanly intuition if you like, Edward."

He hated to disillusion her, especially since the use of his first name was obviously a portent of a closer relationship.

"I thought so too at one time," he said morosely. "Unfortunately, Ollenshaw was killed in a car crash back in '73."

*　　　*　　　*

Alone now in his Notting Hill flat, Farren ripped open a can of Heineken and refilled the glass, his eyes never leaving the television screen. The camera panned Gilchrist's house from left to right and then zeroed in on the Press Liaison Officer, a tall, lean, hungry-looking man with straight black hair, who was standing in the drive reading a prepared statement in a flat monotone from the piece of paper in his hand. Farren thought the house on film was not as he remembered it; the camera somehow distorted the image, making the frontage seem much larger than it was. The study, for instance – surely the windows had been much smaller and narrower too?

Farren placed the glass of beer on the arm of his chair and fished out a packet of cigarettes. Why was he watching the BBC anyway? The events were still fresh in his mind and he was unlikely to forget what had happened in a hurry. The look of terror on Gilchrist's face when he saw the carving knife and realised that Rooney was going to kill him. And Rooney, ice cool and detached, the suggestion of a smile on his lips, a man who enjoyed his work. A man? This twenty-four-year-old former errand boy and butcher's assistant for whom killing had become a way of life? No, Rooney wasn't a man, simply a machine, a child-like psychopathic gunman who was surely destined for a padded cell when the shooting stopped and the politicians no longer had any use for his kind.

They had worked together and lived in each other's pockets for seven years and he didn't like this new arrangement of being separated from Rooney both before and after a job. Maybe Temple had a point, perhaps it did make for better security but all the same, he wished they were still under the same roof so that he could keep an eye on him. Rooney had become too confident, too contemptuous of the opposition, and that was always dangerous.

A voice with a Northern Ireland accent intruded upon his thoughts and then he heard the unmistakable tinkle of broken glass as the gang of workmen swept the jagged shards and bits of plaster into the gutter. Glancing up at the screen, Farren recognised the familiar sight of the Europa Hotel in Belfast, the most popular target in town. How many times did that make it? – eight, nine, or was it now in double figures? He shook his head, unable to compute the total, and not caring much either. The purpose of terror is to terrify; Lenin had said it and if Lenin was right, why bother to telephone a warning to the manager that you'd just planted a bomb in his hotel? Because the Europa Hotel was something special and it would look bad if a member of the Press Corps or some visiting European businessman was carried feet first out of the lobby with a blanket over his face? It didn't make a lot of sense, but of course he'd never had much respect for the people who played around with gelignite. They usually went for the soft target and thought themselves no end of heroes if they killed or maimed half a dozen innocent bystanders in a single blast. Dangerous? Only if they were handling jelly that was beginning to weep, otherwise the risk of being caught red-handed was negligible ninety-nine times out of a hundred. Lying in ambush, waiting to nail a member of the Security Forces with an Armalite M16 rifle was a different proposition altogether. To be successful in that field, you really did need a cool head and steady nerves.

Belfast had faded from the screen and now here was a replay of the cool, efficient Miss Chris Evert in action, destroying her opponent with practised ease. A very attractive young lady to be sure but he was in no mood to watch her. Launching himself from the armchair, Farren crossed the room in a few strides and plunged the screen into darkness.

Tomorrow. Tomorrow morning he would go to the drop on Hampstead Heath and see if Temple had left a message for them in the dead letter box. Temple, the faceless man in the background who pulled the strings and made the puppets dance. Surely Temple could afford to let them go now? After all, Mills was no longer a threat and they had disposed of Boxall, so what was there left to fear except fear itself? Farren cocked his head on one side and smiled inanely. Nothing to fear but fear itself; that was good, very good. Who was it who'd coined the phrase? Roosevelt? He seemed to recall his tutor at Queens saying it was Roosevelt.

Farren sniffed acrid smoke and whirled about, his nostrils twitching like a rabbit's. A thin plume drew his eye to the neat round hole in the carpet where a cigarette lay smouldering. He supposed it must have slipped through his fingers while he was watching the news on television, a logical if somewhat obvious deduction except that he could not recall having lit it. Nor could he remember knocking the glass on to the floor, but there it was all the same, lying on its side in a puddle of beer.

And he'd thought Rooney was slipping. Shit, it was he who was losing touch with reality and needed a baby-sitter instead of the other way round. Well, that only went to show how far they'd come in the space of seven years, because it seemed to him that their respective positions had been reversed with Rooney now the guiding mentor and tutor.

Rooney? Farren smashed a clenched fist against his forehead. Christ, he wasn't slipping, he was cracking up. What on earth had come over him? Rooney and Farren didn't exist; they were Ayres and Ormerod. Ayres and Ormerod, Ayres and Ormerod, Ayres and Ormerod; he whispered the names to himself over and over again as if repeating a catechism he'd learned in Sunday School.

10

A LARGE GREY tabby cat rose on all fours, arched its back
like a bow, stretched both front legs to their full extent and
then, having limbered up, leapt from the roof of the garden
shed to land silently on the grass verge. Yellow eyes regarded
Drew with an unblinking stare until suddenly losing interest
in him, the cat turned away and padded off down the alleyway, its tail erect as an aerial. A few minutes later, the still-
ness of the night was disturbed by a loud clatter as a dustbin
lid fell off and rolled across a back yard. Somewhere over in
Latimer Road a dog woke up long enough to bark three or
four times in a half-hearted manner.

Drew crouched in the shadows and waited, thankful that
Vincent had insisted he allow himself plenty of time to get
into position. Cats and dogs had always been the bane of his
life and there were marks on his body to prove it. In Beirut
he'd had to undergo a painful course of injections against
rabies because some mangy, flea-bitten mongrel had bitten
him on the leg, and on another occasion in Paris, while breaking into a flat, he'd accidently trodden on a Siamese cat before
his eyes had become accustomed to the pitch darkness. Apart
from lacerating his thumb, the cat had yowled its head off,
forcing him to beat an undignified retreat. Beirut, Paris, and
now London; you could be quite certain that no matter where
you went, some bloody four-footed animal would queer the
pitch at just the wrong moment.

Queer the pitch? That had usually been the case, but it
seemed luck was on his side this time because there were no
lights showing in any of the houses which backed on to the
alleyway. Satisfied that everybody had slept through the
noise, he left the shadows and moved to the fence, testing
it first to make sure it would bear his weight before levering
himself up and over.

The garden wasn't all that big but evidently it was too much for Elizabeth Eastgate to cope with. The grass, which had been left to grow ankle high, was beginning to seed itself and the flower beds were choked with bindweed. The rose bushes needed dead-heading too and the privet hedges, though affording privacy from the neighbours, had been allowed to get out of hand. Keeping a wary eye on the bedroom windows, Drew made his way across the lawn towards the coal bunker near the back door where he would be within easy striking distance of the drainpipe.

He was just getting into position when Vincent's car turned into Frogmore Gardens and pulled up outside the house.

*   *   *

Mills sat up in bed, groped for the light switch and then had second thoughts about it. There was probably an innocent explanation for the sudden clatter which had aroused him from a troubled sleep, but he wasn't so sure about the car. At two o'clock in the morning in a quiet back street like Frogmore Gardens it almost certainly meant he was in trouble. Throwing the covers aside, he rolled out of bed and grabbed his clothes off the chair.

The odds were stacked against him but if he was quick enough, there was just a chance that he might be able to slip through the net. Although the police were bound to catch up with him sooner or later, it seemed that making a break for it was the best way to help Elizabeth. Even in the short time he'd known her, she'd come to mean a lot to him. Of course, she would have her work cut out explaining the rumpled bed in the spare room, but while they were bound to suspect that she'd been harbouring a wanted criminal, they would have a hard time proving it.

Drawing back the curtains, he raised the sash-cord window, climbed out on to the sill and then slowly turned about. The drainpipe was only some three feet away and he managed to bridge the gap easily enough, finding a toe hold with his right foot on one of the supporting brackets until he was able to take a firm grip on the pipe with both hands. Leaning out into space and planting his feet against the wall, he then descended to the ground, applying in reverse a technique he'd acquired in the SIS.

Drew raised the Webley air pistol, dwelt in the aim until

Mills had both feet on the ground, and then squeezed the trigger. The range was less than ten feet and the tranquillising dart thumped into his neck just below the left ear. There was a moment of frozen immobility before his legs began to buckle at the knees and catching Mills under the armpits, Drew was able to arrest his fall.

A few seconds later, Vincent rang the front doorbell.

*   *   *

Vincent looked up at the house, saw that it was still in darkness and rang the bell again, keeping his finger on the button until eventually a light appeared on the landing. Some three or four minutes later, a second light came on in the hall and a muffled voice spoke to him through the letter box.

Vincent said, "Miss Eastgate?"

"Yes."

"I'm a police officer. I apologise for disturbing you at this hour but it is important."

He heard her trip the latch and then she opened the door as far as the security chain would allow.

"A police officer?" she queried suspiciously.

Although her face was quite expressionless, it was evident that she was weighing him up and was none too impressed with his appearance. His dark hair was curling over the collar and he knew that his sideboards needed a trim. His suit was rumpled too, but there was nothing unusual about that; Harper had always maintained that he could easily pass for a rag and bone man.

"Do you have some means of identification?"

What was it Harper had said? I want you to handle Miss Eastgate, Harry, because I know you have the savoir faire to sell a television set to a blind man? Well, so far he hadn't even managed to get a foot inside the door, which only went to prove that Harper wasn't infallible. He supposed he ought to be grateful that she hadn't asked to see a search warrant yet; at least producing the right ID Card wasn't a problem, not when you had a team of forgers working for the Department of Subversive Warfare. Flipping open his wallet, he held it out, close enough for her to see the photograph on the card but not the detail.

"May I come in now?" he asked politely.

"Yes – yes, of course." She slipped the chain off the hook,

stepped to one side and then closed the door behind him. "Is something wrong?"

"Didn't you see the news on television?"

"I didn't watch it last night."

"Mr and Mrs Gilchrist were murdered yesterday afternoon."

"Murdered?" she echoed faintly.

A hand stole towards her throat and closed the neckline of the pale blue housecoat. Watching her reaction, Vincent wasn't sure whether the wide-eyed expression of horror and disbelief was genuine or not.

"Wendy and Morris? Do you know who did it?"

"Let's say we're anxious to question a Mr Edward Mills. We know he had an appointment to see Mr Gilchrist yesterday morning."

"Oh?"

It seemed a perfectly natural exclamation but Vincent had a feeling that she was fishing for information, trying to discover how much he knew, which was a little awkward because Harper hadn't been able to tell him much about the case.

"And a witness reported that he'd seen a man answering to his description leave their house in Wimbledon."

"Yes?"

Vincent had to admire her. She was very cool, questioning him in a way that made him feel he was in the witness box.

"He was driving a car which belong to Mrs Gilchrist."

"Look, I know this may sound silly to you but I don't understand..." She paused to brush a lock of hair from her forehead, a gesture which Vincent thought was deliberately intended to emphasise her air of bewilderment. "I mean, how can I help you?"

"We think Mills may have come to see you." There was a wary expression in her eyes now and it was obvious that she was rattled. "He was here, wasn't he, Miss Eastgate?"

"What?"

"Do you mind if I take a look around?"

"Do you have a search warrant?"

"No, but I can get one if you insist." Vincent clucked his tongue and looked annoyed. "I'm disappointed in you, Miss Eastgate," he said coldly. "A solicitor has a duty to uphold the law, but you're behaving as if you had something to hide."

"I think you're treading on very dangerous ground."

"Really? Well, I think you're the one who has most to lose."

Vincent shifted his gaze, looking over her shoulder at the staircase to underline the point. "Don't you think it's time we did each other a good turn? You'll find that I'm not the sort of man to forget a favour."

He could see that she'd help him now before it was too late. And he had a hunch that she would meet him more than half way if he'd forget her earlier prevarication.

"As a matter of fact, he did come to see me. He had one or two queries regarding the will. You see, his mother died a year ago and we wound up the estate. He was only here for an hour or so."

"Then you won't mind if I look around?"

"No," she whispered, "no, of course not. Where would you like to start?"

"How about upstairs?" He smiled fleetingly. "We could always try the spare bedroom."

Her face was like an open book now and he could read her thoughts. She wasn't worried; she'd probably looked in on Mills, saw that he'd disappeared and just had time to pull the bedclothes up before answering the door. But that made her an accessory and she knew it, which was all to the good because it was always easier to manipulate somebody who felt they were in the wrong. There was a very good chance that the CID would call on Elizabeth Eastgate in the near future and naturally Harper was anxious that she shouldn't let the cat out of the bag.

*　　　*　　　*

Drew loosened his tie and unbuttoned the shirt at the neck. His face was bathed in perspiration and his legs still felt as if they didn't belong to him but at least he was no longer breathing like a grampus. Carrying Mills in a fireman's lift had been no joke and there had been moments when he'd wondered if he was going to make it to the car. Mills had seemed like a ton weight and easing him into the back seat had been difficult with his arms and legs flapping all over the place like some animated doll.

He glanced at the electric clock in the facia and frowned. What the hell was Vincent playing at? For God's sake, they didn't have all night – didn't he realise that time was running on and every minute counted? The way he was acting, anyone would think he was anxious to be on hand when the police showed up. As if in answer to his silent prayer, a beam of light suddenly appeared in the porchway as Vincent left the house and walked towards the Hillman Hunter. Leaning across the driver's seat, Drew snatched at the lever and threw the door open. Ducking his head under the sill, Vincent got into the car.

"Don't hurry yourself, will you?" Drew snarled.

Vincent leaned over the seat and raised the blanket covering Mills. "How's he doing?" he asked sourly.

"Resting. There was enough pentothal in that dart to keep an elephant quiet."

"You should have put him in the boot."

"My name isn't Hercules and I can do without a rupture."

Vincent was tempted to inform Drew that he'd missed an opportunity to do the opposite sex a favour, but on reflection, decided they'd had enough aggro for one night.

"Did Elizabeth Eastgate give you any trouble?"

It seemed the olive branch was being offered and he was glad he'd held his tongue.

"No." Vincent turned the ignition key and cranked the engine into life. "No – in fact, you could say she was very co-operative."

Leaving Frogmore Gardens, he followed the Uxbridge Road to the disused warehouse in South Acton where Gattis was waiting for them with an ambulance.

*　　　*　　　*

Harper rolled over on to his back where he lay immobile for several minutes before turning on to his right hip when an arm then fell out of bed to hang limply over the side, lifeless as a flag drooping from the masthead. The numbness which started in the fingers, moved swiftly upwards to deaden all feeling below the wrist and, stirring restlessly, he opened his eyes and gradually became aware of the chink of grey light showing through the gap in the curtains. The dawn chorus and Muriel grinding her teeth in a fitful sleep were far more effective than any alarm clock, and he was wide awake when the telephone rang.

Lifting the receiver off the hook, he answered the call in a low monotone, and said, "Is that you, Gattis?"

"No, sir," said a breezy voice, "it's me – Spencer – the duty officer."

98

Harper stared at the alarm clock on the bedside table. A quarter to five? Surely Gattis ought to have arrived at the safe house by now?

"I wonder if I could ask you to use the other means?"

His mind elsewhere, it was some moments before Harper realised that Spencer was referring to the secure link and then he reacted in an unusually curt manner. "All right," he said testily, "call me back in three minutes."

Replacing the phone, he slipped out of bed, grabbed his silk dressing gown from the hook and crept downstairs in his bare feet. A strong aroma of cigar smoke hung around in the study and drawing back the curtains, he opened a window to let in some fresh air.

The number of butts in the ashtray on his desk were a visible reminder of the long hours he'd spent waiting for a call from Gattis. There were times when he wondered how Muriel could be so long-suffering. He'd lost count of the numerous occasions he'd arrived home late for one of their dinner parties or had disturbed her in the middle of the night, and yet she never complained. Perhaps they ought to take a short holiday abroad once this business with Mills was over? He was still musing on how he could make it up to her when Spencer rang through on the green line. Greeting him briefly, Harper reached under the desk and tripped the switch on the black, oblong-shaped box at his feet. A split second later the red warning light came on to show that the scrambler was functioning.

Spencer said, "I thought you'd like to hear the text of an intercept we've just received from the monitoring station at Harrogate."

"Oh yes?"

"It seems they've been eavesdropping on our American friends in Grosvenor Square."

Harper thought he detected a note of disdain in his voice. Spencer was under thirty but somewhat straight-laced and pompous, the sort of man who felt compelled to make it clear that, in his opinion, spying on one's closest ally was quite beyond the pale.

"That's exactly what I asked them to do."

"Oh." Spencer cleared his throat noisily to cover his embarrassment. "Oh, I see. Well, the message is addressed personal for Liddell and reads as follows: For your eyes only.

Have received information from reliable source that Kiktev collapsed and died as a result of a massive brain haemorrhage on Sunday two zero June. Source unable to say why no official announcement as yet. Your guess as good as mine."

"What was the precedence?"

"Flash," said Spencer.

A flash message? Well, you couldn't go higher than that but all the same, one had to bear in mind that the CIA was apt to cry wolf at the least provocation.

"Do you want it brought forward on Monday?"

"No," said Harper, "just mark it 'Seen' and leave the rest to Miss Nightingale."

Dropping the phone on Spencer, he leaned back in the chair and clasped both hands behind his head. First Ziegler and then Kiktev; the one struck down with a coronary early in April and now the other succumbing to a massive brain haemorrhage. Ziegler and Kiktev carrying their secrets with them to the grave, still cheating everyone in death as they had in life.

The telephone rang again and this time it was Gattis calling from the safe house at Goring-on-Thames to say that the merchandise had arrived safely.

11

ALTHOUGH THE HOUSE was in the same postal district as Goring-on-Thames, it was quite separate from the town and lay on the opposite bank of the river, in total isolation. A large country residence with lawns on three sides which sloped down to the water's edge, it had been designed and built at the turn of the century as a weekend retreat for Josiah Handlemann, a merchant banker in the City of London. Changing hands on three occasions between 1908 and 1931, it was finally acquired by a stockbroker who remained in residence until the outbreak of World War II when the house was requisitioned by the Ministry of Public Works and Buildings as a repository for the Tate Gallery. Much to the relief of the last owner, it was subsequently purchased by the Ministry of Agriculture, Food and Fisheries who retained it until 1962 when the property was transferred to the Department of Subversive Warfare.

There was a neat little sign outside the lodge gates which showed that the house was now occupied by Number 3 Statistical Survey Unit, but the occasional guests of the Department, especially those who were unfortunate enough to be confined in the basement, knew otherwise. The rooms below ground level were quite unique, but only in England, for much the same facilities existed in the underground chambers of Dzerzhinsky Square. Apart from the fact that the passage of time could be artificially controlled by ultra-violet light in conjunction with a dimming system, the other refinements included a cell block, two interviewing rooms and a studio for the directing staff which was equipped with video cameras, monitoring screens and a digital display computer as well as the usual office furniture.

The lay-out of the basement was such that it was possible to adapt the scenery to meet almost any requirement, and a

101

team of stage hands had worked through the night to alter the appearance of one of the two interview rooms and the connecting passageway to the cell block. Watching his reaction on the monitoring screen in the studio, Harper was satisfied that Mills had been conditioned to accept that he was being held for questioning in a police station. His only worry was a vague feeling that Gattis might be unwilling to exploit the situation they had created. Vincent and Drew had no inhibitions where brain-washing was concerned but Gattis was a different kettle of fish.

"You know Iain," Harper said casually, "I get the impression you're worried about something."

"I am. I think we've got ourselves into one hell of a mess."

"What makes you say that?"

Gattis shook his head in disbelief. How Harper could be so bland when they'd kidnapped a wanted man was quite beyond his understanding. "Three people have been murdered and the police are looking for Mills."

"What if they are? If this idea of mine doesn't work out, we'll simply turn him loose and then they'll be able to pick him up. Nothing could be simpler."

"I know it's a little late in the day to have second thoughts, but what if he points the finger at us?"

"Do you really think that with his record, anyone will pay any attention to Mills?"

"Aren't you forgetting Miss Eastgate?"

Harper caught Vincent's eye and smiled. "Why don't you put Iain in the picture, Harry?" he said. "After all, you're the only one here who knows her well enough to have formed an opinion."

Vincent thought it was typical of Harper to bend the truth, to stretch a brief acquaintance into a close friendship, but it was justified in this instance. Gattis had the wind up and somebody had to put his mind at ease because it was too late to find a replacement for him.

"She thinks Mills is innocent, that he didn't kill anyone, that he's not a double agent, and she doesn't believe he stole those Bearer Bonds either. There were no witnesses to what happened last night and she's agreed not to say anything to the police." Vincent smiled wryly. "For what it's worth, I even managed to persuade her that we're on his side."

"You see, Iain," Harper said cheerfully, "I told you there was nothing to worry about."

"I'd be a lot happier if I knew what we are trying to achieve."

Harper pointed to a metal object lying on the table in front of him. "Do you know what that is?" he asked.

"Yes, it's a hand grenade, a drill model painted white."

"Indeed it is. To prepare the 36 grenade for use, you have to strip and clean it, carry out a striker test to make sure the mechanism is functioning and then prime it. That's what we are going to do with Mills."

"You're planning to use him as a weapon?"

"That's right." Harper weighed the grenade in his hand. "I asked the Quartermaster to produce this drill model in order to remind everybody of our final objective. It really is very apt."

"Is it?"

"Oh yes. It may interest you to learn that in the First World War the prototype of this grenade was known as the Mills Bomb."

"All right, sir," Gattis said quietly, "you've made your point. When do I start?"

"Now," said Harper. "I think we've kept him waiting long enough."

*   *   *

Mills had a strong feeling, almost a conviction, that something was wrong but he couldn't put his finger on it. The police constable in the interview room whose hands were clasped behind his back, whose feet were planted eighteen inches astride like a soldier standing properly at ease on a parade ground, could be an actor dressed up to look the part. On the other hand, there had been nothing phoney about the cell they had put him in. He recalled that breakfast had consisted of a slice of bacon, a spoonful of lukewarm baked beans and a piece of rock-hard fried bread, exactly the sort of fare you would expect to be served up in a police canteen. As far as he could see, there was nothing wrong with the interview room either. Sellotaped to the walls were the usual official posters ranging from 'Don't take your car for a drink' to 'Watch out, there's a thief about', and the small table and tubular steel chairs were definitely Government issue. The only thing that really prevented him from accepting the situation was the fact that for the second time within the space of twenty-four hours, there was a blank period which he couldn't account for. It began just as he was climbing down the drainpipe at the back of Elizabeth Eastgate's house, and no psychiatrist would ever convince him that it was simply a case of amnesia.

The door opened inwards and a man, neatly attired in a grey worsted suit, walked into the interview room. The newcomer had brown eyes, reddish brown hair and was about five foot nine. At a rough guess, Mills thought his age was somewhere between thirty-two and thirty-four and that he weighed around eleven and a half stone.

"Edward James Mills?"

"That's me."

Gattis signalled the police constable to withdraw and then sat down at the table. "I'm Detective Sergeant Garrett," he said crisply.

"Garrett," said Mills, "that's an easy name to remember."

"But you can call me Iain."

"We're going to have a friendly chat, are we?"

"Well, I'm hoping we can help each other."

"Pull the other leg," said Mills, "it's got bells on. Look, if you think you can make it stick, go ahead and charge me with murder, but you'll be drawing the old age pension before I make a voluntary statement."

"We seem to be talking at cross purposes." Gattis smiled in a conciliatory manner. "I'm attached to the Fraud Squad. CID have agreed that I can interview you first."

"I don't remember seeing your face before."

"Ten years is a long time, Edward; I was a police constable when they sent you down."

"Maybe you should go back to pounding a beat in Edinburgh."

Gattis wondered if it was just a lucky guess or whether, after four years in London, his accent was still so pronounced that Mills had been able to place it accurately.

"Do I laugh now or is the punch line still to come?"

"The joke is that somebody made you a Detective Sergeant." Mills rested both elbows on the table and leaned forward, hunching his shoulders. "I said my piece at the trial – what makes you think I'm going to change my story now?"

"You know what?" Gattis snapped his fingers. "That's exactly the point I made to my guv'nor. This may come as a surprise, but I think you were set up to carry the can."

"You must be the only man who does."

"Mind you, I'm not saying there was a miscarriage of justice."

"No, I suppose that would be too much to hope for," Mills said dryly.

"I've read the transcript over and over again and I reckon you had an accomplice, somebody who knew the Prague conference was going to be postponed and realised that here was an opportunity to grab a million dollars."

"Oh, so you're implying that I didn't shop Kiktev to the KGB?"

"No, of course you didn't; the whole operation was organised much too hastily for that kind of refinement. I mean, if you'd had more time to plan things, it stands to reason you would have come up with a much more solid story to explain those missing three days in Geneva. Still, I've got to hand it to you, Edward – the SIS couldn't break you, could they? You just sat tight and refused to account for the lost time."

"You've got it wrong; I didn't refuse to co-operate."

"No, I was forgetting, you were suffering from amnesia. However, in your place, I think I would have changed my story once the title deeds to the French villa and that numbered bank account came to light. But then, you may have been advised otherwise. Your QC was a bit of a deadbeat, wasn't he?"

Gattis waited for some kind of reaction but the question failed to strike a responsive chord. Taking out a packet of Rothmans, he removed the cellophane wrapper and offered Mills a cigarette.

"I don't smoke. I gave it up a long time ago."

"I wish I could." Gattis lit up and leaned back in his chair, savouring the pleasure of his first cigarette that day. "That girl you used to know – Janet Rayner," he said idly. "Ever hear from her?"

Mills shook his head.

"She's in Canada now, living in Vancouver and married to a dentist."

"How do you know?"

"Oh, we've kept tabs on her." Gattis mentally crossed his fingers and hoped that Harper's information was correct. "Obviously your accomplice knew everything there was to know about your love life, Edward. Using her to set you up was a shrewd move on his part, but then he didn't put a foot wrong from the start to finish, did he?"

The question didn't call for an answer; he'd been through it all before and knew that it was merely the beginning of a long narrative. Garrett – if that really was his name – would take him through the whole damn case, step by step, going over and over the same old ground. He would start with the letters of instruction to the notary in Avignon, all of which bore his fingerprints and signature and then go on to the numbered account.

As if prompted by telepathy, Gattis said, "About those letters . . ."

                    *   *   *

Harper wrinkled his nose in disgust and pushed the cup and saucer to one side. It was questionable whether the coffee had been drinkable in the first place but it was stone cold now and the grey-coloured skin which had congealed on the surface made him feel distinctly queasy. Vincent, his eyes on the studio monitor, reached for an ashtray and then swore under his breath as he realised that he'd dunked his cigarette into the coffee.

"Do you think it's sinking in?"

Vincent glanced at the stub floating on the surface and wondered what had prompted Harper to ask such a banal question.

"I was referring to Mills," Harper said dryly.

"Oh, I see." Vincent looked up at the television screen again and frowned. "It's hard to tell whether he's paying much attention to Gattis or not."

"I'm sure there's a look of concentration on his face."

"Yes, sir." Vincent thought it was wishful thinking on Harper's part but he was not prepared to say so.

"He's going back into the past, groping for an explanation, which is all to the good because it means he'll be very receptive."

"I hope you're right."

"I know I am," said Harper, "I can feel it in my bones. We'll take a fifteen-minute break after Gattis has finished with him and then you and Drew can take over as Detective Chief Superintendent Viner and Detective Inspector Donaldson. How does that suit you, Harry?"

"I'm not very happy about it," said Vincent. "I only wish Wray had been more forthcoming."

"You've got enough to go on and if you play it carefully, I'm certain Mills will fill in the relevant details."

'I doubt it. You heard what he said to Gattis about drawing the old age pension before he would make a statement."

"I think he'll change his mind."

Vincent chewed his bottom lip and looked thoughtful. "Well, if he does, you can bet he'll ask for a solicitor to be present."

"Which brings us to Miss Eastgate."

"I suppose so."

"And we know that she's willing to co-operate, don't we, Harry?"

"Yes, sir."

Somehow Vincent managed to project a note of conviction into his voice that was wholly at variance with his innermost thoughts.

*　　*　　*

A collision seemed on the cards but at the very last minute the radio-controlled power boat heeled over to starboard to narrowly miss the catamaran which lay becalmed in the centre of the pond. Watching the enthralled expressions on their faces, Farren was hard put to decide whether it was the father or his nine-year-old son who was getting the most pleasure from playing with the toy. On balance, he thought it was probably the father, if only because he was hogging the radio direction unit.

Farren switched his gaze to the clump of trees above the hollow in the far distance. There had been no message waiting for him in the dead letter box and the more he thought about it, the more it became obvious that Temple was unlikely to put in an appearance in broad daylight. Temple was a night creature, a man who needed the dark to preserve the secrecy of his identity. How did that old saying go? Tomorrow is another day? Well, tomorrow was going to be a whole lot better than today if he had anything to do with it. His mind suddenly made up, Farren turned his back on the pond and set off at a brisk pace across Hampstead Heath towards Spaniards Road.

The telephone kiosk near Jack Straw's Castle was occupied by a teenage blonde who looked as if she intended to stay there all day. Although he kept staring pointedly in her direction and even went so far as to tap on the glass, nothing would budge her and he spent a restless twenty minutes walking up and down the pavement, chain-smoking one cigarette after another, before she deigned to leave the call box. Her cloying perfume was everywhere and so overpowering that he was tempted to wedge the door open, but caution prevailed and he decided not to risk it. Lifting the phone off the hook, he dialled the number of Temple's answering service.

Farren supposed he ought to have guessed that the man would stay one jump ahead of everybody else but it was still a shock to discover that the line had been disconnected.

*　　　*　　　*

Mills thought that somebody must have had a few words with the police constable and put him wise. There had been a slight hiatus with Detective Sergeant Garrett before he twigged that his presence was no longer required, but he'd been quick off the mark this time, taking just one look at the two men before leaving the interview room unobtrusively. Mills wished he could follow the constable's example because if physical appearances were anything to go by, the atmosphere was about to become unpleasant. Of the two plain-clothes officers, it was a toss up as to who looked the more menacing; the tall, burly man with the unruly hair and long sideburns or his fair-haired companion with the cold steel eyes.

Vincent said, "I'm Detective Chief Superintendent Viner and this is Detective Inspector Donaldson. We'd like to have a few words with you."

"Is this going to be a one way conversation," said Mills, "or do I get to ask a few questions too?"

"Why not, it's still a free country."

"Try telling that to Special Branch or the Fraud Squad."

"Oh, we're not like them, are we, Mike?"

"No," said Drew, "we're completely different."

"So who are you?"

"CID," said Vincent, "from 'V' Division at Kingston on Thames."

"And just where are we now?"

"Wimbledon Police Station."

"I'll take your word for it."

"You know what?" said Drew. "We've got ourselves a regular doubting Thomas."

"You've got somebody who's going to sue you for assault and battery."

"Well, that makes a change; usually it's wrongful arrest." Drew stopped pacing up and down the room and leaned over Mills, thrusting his face close to his. "Nobody laid a finger on you, friend," he said coldly. "You simply fell off the drainpipe and banged your head against the wall. The doctor prescribed a sedative because he thought you were all shook up."

There was no bruise on his head but he could remember a painful sensation in his neck as if he'd been stung by a wasp and then he'd fainted. Fainted? No, he hadn't fainted and he hadn't fallen off the drainpipe either; the bastards had taken him out with a tranquillising dart fired from an air gun. And if this was a police station, where were all the other offenders? Even a select suburb like Wimbledon had its quota of drunks, especially on a Friday night, and yet he was the only prisoner who'd had breakfast brought in on a tray. A police station? Bullshit. This was an Interrogation Centre.

"What made you do it, Edward?"

Mills looked up quickly. "Do what?" he asked.

"Kill Mr and Mrs Gilchrist and the domestic help." Vincent smiled knowingly. "Of course we realise you had a grudge against Morris Gilchrist, but what harm had Mrs Yelf ever done you?"

"We're down to brass tacks now, are we?"

"You bet we are."

Mills pointed to the telephone at Vincent's elbow. "Is that thing for decoration or does it actually work?"

"You want to call a solicitor?"

"Yes."

"It figures." Vincent lifted the receiver off the hook and

109

handed it to him. "Dial 9 first," he said. "That'll by-pass the exchange and give you an outside line."

Vincent knew that it would do nothing of the kind. The figure nine would set the computer working and thereafter the area code and subscriber's telephone number would be flashed on to the digital display in the control studio. What happened after that was up to Harper but usually the engaged tone followed automatically and the directing staff then checked out the name and address of the other party.

"That's odd."

"What is?"

"The number's ringing but there's no answer." Mills put the phone down and smiled at Vincent. "Does that surprise you?" he asked softly.

"No, why should it?" Vincent wished Harper had said that he intended to ring the changes instead of leaving him in the dark. "I daresay she's out shopping. After all, it is Saturday morning."

"She?"

As soon as the words came out of his mouth Vincent knew that he'd blundered. Mills was a lot sharper than he'd thought and had pounced on his mistake.

"Miss Eastgate," he said reluctantly. "Of course I'm only guessing, but she is a solicitor and you were at her house last night."

"Congratulations," said Mills, "you've just scored a bull's-eye."

"Maybe you'll have better luck next time."

"Yes?"

It was evident that Mills didn't think so and that could mean that he was on to them.

"Why not give it another five minutes and then try again?"

Harper could hear every word of their conversation and he would have to bail them out somehow because Mills looked as if he was determined to sit tight and say nothing. Vincent supposed he could always broaden the scope of the interview in an effort to break through the barrier but on the other hand, he was reluctant to bring up the subject of the SIS inquiry at this stage in case the ploy went off at half cock. Drew was trying to catch his eye, silently urging him to do something to break the deadlock, but there was nothing he could do except wait it out and hope for the best.

Mills glanced at his wristwatch, saw that the five minutes was up and reached for the telephone. He thought it likely that they would vary the routine this time and give him an engaged tone but that wouldn't stop him from calling their bluff.

Contrary to his expectation, the number rang out, and then a voice said, "98264."

"Elizabeth?" Mills stared into space. "Is that really you?"

"Yes, who's calling?"

"It's me – Edward."

"Edward." He thought she sounded breathless as if she'd run through the house to answer the telephone. "Are you all right? I mean, where are you?"

"Wimbledon Police Station. I'm being held for questioning."

"Oh?"

"And I need help."

"Yes, yes, I can see that. Would you like me to get in touch with one of my colleagues?"

Her voice was neutral and he didn't know whether she was reluctant to become involved or whether she was trying to warn him that she thought the police might be listening to their conversation.

"I'd sooner you handled it," he said carefully.

"All right, Edward, I'll do what I can."

"Good. How soon can you get here?"

"Give me an hour."

Mills thanked her and rang off. Nothing made sense to him any more. The right side of his chest suddenly felt hard and unyielding and that too was a bad sign.

"Well now," Vincent said cheerfully, "I think it's time we took a break for lunch."

*   *   *

Liddell wasn't in the best of moods as he boarded the 1205 Swissair flight from Heathrow to Geneva. For one thing, he had wasted the best part of two hours trying to contact Harper, and for another, he had a feeling that he was off on a wild goose chase. He had never made any secret of the fact that he reckoned Kiktev was the key to the whole affair and that Ziegler had found a way to protect his old friend as best he could after the débâcle of the Prague conference,

111

but it had never been more than an interesting point for discussion and he'd never expected anyone to take his theory seriously. But someone had, and that was the trouble.

The signal he'd received had been somewhat vague but he supposed the CIA had assumed that the British would be monitoring the American Embassy, and reading between the lines, it became obvious that his people back at Langley expected him to look up Ziegler's lawyer in Geneva. What was it he'd said to the Director back in '68 after he'd talked to Larissa Pavlichenko? *If I'm right and Ziegler has written a letter of explanation, you can bet it won't come to light until after Kiktev is dead.* Well, that would certainly teach him to keep his mouth shut in future.

12

HARPER POURED HIMSELF a large whisky, added half a dozen cubes from the ice bucket and then, glass in hand, strolled across the morning room to stand in the bay window where he could keep an eye on the lodge gates at the bottom of the drive. It was a little early in the day for him to be drinking but on this occasion he felt in need of a sharpener. Indoctrinating Mills was proving much more difficult than he'd anticipated and he was counting on Elizabeth Eastgate to tip the balance. Counting? His lips met in a sour grimace; hoping would be more accurate because it was quite possible that she might refuse to take part in the deception. It was only with great reluctance that she had agreed to come down to Goring-on-Thames and after listening to her subsequent conversation with Mills on the telephone, he'd wondered if she could be trusted not to let the cat out of the bag.

He thought Gattis could well be right; they were getting themselves into a hell of a mess and he had only himself to blame. Lifting Mills had been a calculated risk, one that he'd taken on the basis of his previous knowledge of the affair and in the light of what Liddell and Wray had told him, but he hadn't foreseen the extent to which Elizabeth Eastgate would become involved. It was fortunate that the police hadn't got around to questioning her yet, but he doubted if that happy state of affairs would last for much longer. By now, some constable had probably found the car which Mills had abandoned, and 'V' Division, having been in touch with the Glasgow Police, would know that he hadn't sought refuge with his sister. Even if Special Branch were not forthcoming, it was only a question of time before CID discovered that Elizabeth Eastgate had been in touch with Mills.

A horn sounded twice, summoning one of the porters from the lodge to open the wrought-iron gates, and then a few moments later an MGB cruised through the entrance and drove up to the house. A fairly tall girl with dark shoulder-length hair got out of the car. Leaving his glass on the window seat, Harper went out into the hall, ready to greet Elizabeth Eastgate when the security guard let her into the house.

As soon as she walked into the hall, Harper was convinced that Vincent should consult an eye specialist. Clearly, he needed to wear glasses. In describing her, Vincent had led him to believe that she was not bad-looking, a description which, as he could now see for himself, was wholly inadequate for such a strikingly attractive young woman whose firm handshake suggested she was not lacking in character either.

"It's good of you to come all the way out here." Harper smiled warmly. "Believe me, Miss Eastgate, I'm very grateful."

"And Edward Mills? Will he be grateful too?"

The question was barbed and while her voice was far from strident, her attitude was definitely hostile.

"Perhaps not at first but I think he will be in the long run."

His frank reply took the wind out of her sails, just as he knew it would, because it was the last thing she'd expected.

"Well, at least that's an honest answer," she said hesitantly.

"It was no more than your question deserved." Harper placed a hand under one elbow and steered her into the morning room. "I've ordered soup, ham sandwiches and coffee – I hope that's all right?"

"Actually, I'm not hungry."

"Oh, I'm sure you can manage one sandwich, they're quite dainty."

His tone implied that the staff had gone to a lot of trouble just to please her and that they would be upset if she refused to have one.

"Now, what can I offer you to drink in the meantime?" Harper peered at the row of bottles and mineral waters lined up on the sideboard. "There's gin, whisky, brandy, sherry, lager . . ."

"I'd like a dry sherry, if you have that."

"How about Tio Pepe – not too dry for you?"

"Tio Pepe will be fine."

"Good. Do please take a chair, Miss Eastgate."

"I can see you're a very persuasive man, Mr Harper."

"Oh, do you think so?" Harper placed a glass of sherry on

114

an occasional table within reach of her armchair. "I never seem to have much luck with my bank manager whenever I want to increase my overdraft. Still, that's neither here nor there."

"I agree."

The social chit-chat was over. In a cool but polite way, she had made it clear that he was trying to avoid the main issue and that it was time he stopped beating about the bush.

"Yes, I suppose I do owe you an explanation." Harper fetched his glass of whisky from the window seat and then sat down in a high wing-back chair facing Elizabeth Eastgate. "I assume Mills must have told you his version of the Kiktev affair. I also assume you wouldn't be here unless you believed him."

"Quite."

"And you do want to help him, don't you?"

"Yes, of course I do, but I have a feeling that you and I may not agree what's best for Edward. I don't know who you work for, Mr Harper, but obviously you're not connected with the police, and I think there is something rather sinister about this house."

"Don't tell me you're frightened, Miss Eastgate?"

"Let's say I'm uneasy. I'm not used to dealing with people who gain admittance to my house under false pretences, people who seem to think they can take the law into their own hands and get away with it."

Harper thought that if this was how Elizabeth Eastgate reacted when she was afraid, he'd hate to be around when she was really angry.

"I must apologise for the way we behaved but I'm afraid we had no choice."

"I find that hard to believe."

"Well, I don't expect you to approve of our methods, but what do you suppose would have happened to Mills if we hadn't intervened?" Harper smiled at her over the rim of his glass. "He would have been arrested and charged with murder and you must know that the CID have a very good case. Now, I admire the police but they have their job to do. If they are satisfied that they have enough evidence to obtain a conviction, they're not going to waste their time looking elsewhere for another suspect. You can find Mills the best QC in London but don't tell me he'll try to demolish the case for the prosecution by investigating an alternative theory."

"But you will?"

"Yes."

"How?"

They had arrived at the moment of truth and he knew he would need all his powers of persuasion. What he had in mind would demean both her personal and professional integrity and, if the worst came to the worst, it could easily put her career at risk. It was a lot to ask but he thought Elizabeth Eastgate would agree to co-operate because, ridiculous as it might seem, it was evident that she was more than a little in love with Mills. Ridiculous? Well, there was an age difference of fourteen years between them and they had known one another for less than forty-eight hours. But neither of these observations was really pertinent when measured against the risks she'd already taken on his behalf. Anyone in her position who was prepared to help Mills evade arrest, had to be in love with him. It was a comforting thought to hang on to because if she did refuse to go along with him, it was also highly unlikely that she would agree to sign the relevant sections of the Official Secrets Acts, and then the fat really would be in the fire.

"As a matter of interest," said Harper, "what do you know about psychological indoctrination?"

It was a debatable point but, in his opinion, psychological indoctrination sounded much more reassuring than brainwashing.

*   *   *

The window was a slit which measured some twelve by eighteen inches and was recessed into the wall like a peephole in a concrete pillbox. Although the daylight seemed natural, Mills couldn't be sure whether it was artificial or not because the window pane was out of his reach. The stratus clouds in the sky looked very convincing except he'd heard that the army, using ultra-violet and infra-red, were able to fake whatever weather conditions they liked in their indoor training theatres. Jumping up and down to see what lay beyond the window had got him nowhere and the bed, which was the only item of furniture in the cell, had been bolted to the floor in the far corner.

If this really was a police station, he thought Elizabeth

Eastgate ought to have arrived long ago. Wimbledon wasn't all that far removed from Ravenscourt Park and yet, according to his wristwatch, more than two hours had passed since he'd spoken to her on the telephone. On the other hand, it was perfectly possible that the police were giving her the run-around, leading Elizabeth to believe that he'd been transferred to another station. He remembered Boxall swearing that this had happened to him after the Caterham bank robbery and that his solicitor had spent three days looking for him, but one had to bear in mind that Sidney had always been inclined to spin a tall story.

A key turned in the lock, the bolt was drawn back and then the door opened outwards and his friendly neighbourhood policeman walked into the cell.

The constable said, "Your solicitor's arrived."

"Never."

"What do you mean, never? She's waiting for you in the interview room."

Mills pushed himself off the bed and followed the uniformed constable out into the corridor. As before, the passageway was deserted but as they passed the stairwell, he heard a low murmur of voices punctuated by heavy footsteps overhead which seemed to indicate that the two to ten shift was reporting for duty.

Elizabeth Eastgate greeted him with a quick, nervous smile, her face very pale. The police constable muttered something about their legal right to privacy and left them.

Mills pulled out a chair and sat down. "It's good to see you again," he said.

"Thank you, Edward."

"Don't look so sceptical, Elizabeth. I really do mean it." He reached under the table, took one of her hands and squeezed it affectionately.

"How have they been treating you, Edward?"

"As well as can be expected."

"You haven't made a statement under caution, have you?"

"No. Why should I? They haven't charged me with anything yet."

"They will."

He was slow to grasp the implication at first but then it gradually dawned on him that two little words marked the end of the road. His doubts about the reality of his situation

117

faded and his hands started to shake. In the space of three days he had come full circle and this time they would put him away for life.

"How do you know?"

"Detective Chief Superintendent Viner told me. After you've been formally charged, you will be asked if you want to make a statement."

"And if my memory isn't at fault, I can remain silent. Am I right?"

"Yes. And I think you should."

"So when am I likely to appear in court?" He smiled bitterly. "As you can see, I'm familiar with the procedure."

"In this instance the magistrate will come to the police station."

"What?"

"It's perfectly legal when serious charges are to be preferred. The police will ask for a remand in custody but they'll have to present their case in outline and that will give us some idea of what we're up against."

Listening to Elizabeth Eastgate as she then discussed who they should brief for the defence, it seemed to Mills that her voice was coming from a very long way off.

*　　　*　　　*

Vincent too suddenly found it difficult to hear what Elizabeth Eastgate was saying. In his case, however, this was due to the fact that Harper took it upon himself to turn the volume down to the point where the ability to lip read would have been an asset.

"I think we've left her on stage long enough."

The pronouncement could be taken in any of two ways and Vincent wondered if he was being asked for his opinion or whether it was a sort of apology.

"She's done extraordinarily well; in fact, you could say that she deserves an Oscar for her performance."

So he was wrong on both counts. It had been a cue, a hint that he and Drew should make their entrance and bring down the curtain on the third act, but only after they had prepared the ground for Harper's appearance.

"It's now or never, Harry. Mills is unlikely to be in a more receptive frame of mind than he is at this moment."

"I'll get hold of Drew and the rest of the supporting cast then."

"Do they know their lines?"

"I should hope so; we've had enough rehearsals." Vincent stared at the monitoring screen. "You know something?" he said thoughtfully. "I'm beginning to feel really sorry for the poor bastard. I mean, look at the expression on his face. He genuinely believes this is for real and he can see those prison walls closing in on him."

"You'd better keep your fingers crossed, Harry. If things don't go our way, we could end up in the same boat as Mills."

There was a smile on Harper's face but Vincent was damned if he could see the joke.

*   *   *

Liddell paid off the taxi in the Place du Sourg de Four and then set off to walk the rest of the way to the house owned by Ziegler's lawyer. The cab driver had said that the address he wanted in the old quarter of Geneva was inaccessible by car but there was no such indication on the street map he'd picked up at the airport. Leaving the Square, he took his bearings from St Peter's Cathedral and entering the Rue de l'Hôtel de Ville, turned left after a hundred yards to climb a long flight of steps into the Promenade de la Croix-Rouge. A 'Pedestrians Only' sign at the entrance to the cul-de-sac proved that the cab driver had been right after all.

There was nothing to distinguish Number 17 Promenade de la Croix-Rouge from the houses on either side except a brass plate set into the tall privet hedge which showed that it was the home of Jean-Paul Solange, Attorney at Law. Although they had never met face to face, the CIA possessed an extensive file on the lawyer and Liddell knew his background and life history by heart.

The maid who answered the door had only a smattering of English, which was a little awkward because his French wasn't any too good, but in the end, Liddell managed to make her understand that he was from the United States Embassy in Berne and wished to speak with Monsieur Solange on a matter of some delicacy. To ensure the lawyer received him, he gave his name and an address in the Eaux Vires District. His name wouldn't mean anything to Solange but he thought the address would do the trick since precious few people in Geneva were aware that Ziegler's former house-keeper was living in retirement at Number 24 Rue Agasse.

The message didn't produce the immediate response Liddell had hoped for, but eventually the maid returned and ushered him into a small room off the hall. Solange was forty-eight but looked younger. Small, well-groomed and possessed of a stiff and reserved manner, he seemed the sort of man who might be taken for one of the mythical Gnomes of Zürich the British were always complaining about. His handshake was as cold as his personality.

Liddell said, "It's a pleasure to meet you, sir."

Solange bowed his head. "Perhaps we should dispense with the polite formalities? After all, yours is hardly a social visit, is it, Mr Liddell?" His lips met in a bleak smile. "Correct me if I'm wrong, but I understood there was some delicate matter you wished to discuss with me."

"Yes, it concerns Kiktev."

"Who?"

"Professor Yuri Kiktev of the Leningrad Institute of Technology. He was a close friend of Joachim Ziegler."

"So?"

"Well, I have to tell you that Kiktev died on Sunday the twentieth of June. Of course, there's been no official announcement in the Soviet Press as yet but we have it on good authority that he had a massive brain haemorrhage."

"Naturally I'm sorry to hear it but it's really no concern of mine."

"I think it is," Liddell said quietly.

Solange refused to be drawn; his face was impassive, expressionless as a death mask.

"Ziegler was a good man but we both know that he went into the witness box and committed perjury in order to protect his old friend. The KGB forced him to do it and that's why he almost certainly took out an insurance policy."

"An insurance policy?" Solange repeated mockingly.

"A written statement explaining why he'd acted in the way he had, a statement which was only to be made public should Kiktev die from unnatural causes. I think he gave the KGB a copy back in '64 to let them know what would happen if they decided to execute Kiktev."

"You have a very vivid imagination, Mr Liddell."

"Really? Well, I'm prepared to bet a year's salary that you

know where to find this letter and that it's addressed to the British Ambassador in Berne. Now I don't expect you to show me the contents but I strongly recommend that you take steps to ascertain that Kiktev is dead."

"How?"

Liddell smiled. The champagne question, the one he'd hoped for. "We could always go to the American Consular Office in Geneva."

Solange hesitated for a moment and then nodded his head in agreement.

13

THE FRIENDLY neighbourhood policeman had gone off duty, replaced by a tall, lanky constable with a sallow complexion whose size ten boots creaked with every step. The passageway was still deserted but as they passed the stairwell, Mills heard a telephone ringing above the clatter of a typewriter, which made a change from the stomp of heavy feet and the low murmur of voices. There was no Elizabeth Eastgate waiting for him in the interview room this time, only a fit-looking man of about fifty with brown hair neatly parted on the left side.

"I'm Harper," he said, "Cedric Harper."

Mills shook his hand briefly and then sat down at the table. "I presume you're from SIS?"

"Somebody's been talking out of turn."

"Detective Chief Superintendent Viner – he said the spooks would want to have a chat with me."

"A quaint turn of phrase."

"Oh, he's quite a character," Mills said dryly. "The magistrate was certainly impressed with him, he granted Viner the seven days remand he asked for."

"Does that surprise you? Viner tells me he's got a cast-iron case."

"Have you ever met a policeman who didn't? Viner's got his pinch and that's all that matters to him."

"Whereas you think you were framed." Harper leaned over to one side and opened the Gladstone-style briefcase standing on the floor close by his chair. Sorting through the contents, he produced a thick buff-coloured file and placed it on the table. As he opened it, Mills noticed that his name was on the cover, picked out in Dymo tape. "Isn't that so?"

"I didn't kill them."

"But somebody else did?"

"I would have thought that was bloody obvious," Mills said angrily.

Harper turned over several pages and then looked up with a quizzical smile on his face. "It would seem that you've had a busy time since being released from Leicester. I see that between noon on Thursday and Friday evening, you assaulted a Sergeant Chesterman of Special Branch, a Mr and Mrs Ray Walters and Mr Stanley Walters; all in all, not bad going for a day and a half. Given another month or so, I daresay you could have filled the hospital casualty ward several times over."

"And don't forget, I tried a little extortion on the side."

"That's right, so you did." Harper turned to the previous page. "The sum involved was three hundred and eighty-nine thousand and sixty-one dollars."

"And thirty-six cents."

"No, you told Chesterman you'd forget the odd cents. Of course, this was all part of your campaign to expose this character you call the man in the shadows, wasn't it?"

"I was trying to push him into a corner but he stayed one jump ahead of me all the time."

Harper sensed that the interview had gone off the rails. Mills was no longer angry but listless, as if he'd suddenly lost all interest and didn't care what happened to him. It occurred to him that they might have undermined him to the point where he had lost the will to fight back and survive. Perhaps it was time he fed Mills the idea that Elizabeth Eastgate was not the only one who believed him.

"This man in the shadows?" he said carefully. "Am I right in supposing he used Gilchrist to keep an eye on you?"

"I believe he wanted to know which way I was going to jump when I came out of prison and so Morris was the ideal choice."

"And then when he realised that you were not prepared to let things slide, he decided to kill the Gilchrists and pin the blame on you. After all, there was always the chance that Morris Gilchrist might put two and two together and start asking some awkward questions."

"You make it seem as if the whole business was premeditated, and I don't think it was."

"I'm surprised to hear you say that. I thought it was his intention to destroy you."

"He did his best to keep me inside but when that failed, who knows what he had in mind?" Mills stretched out his legs, crossing them at the ankles and draping one arm over the back of his chair in an attitude of bored indifference. "Look, for what's it's worth, I believe the Gilchrists and Mrs Yelf were killed on the spur of the moment. Poor old Morris was never cut out to be an under-cover man and I had an inkling that something was wrong when he practically twisted my arm to accept the offer of his flat in Moravian Place. The Special Branch men weren't exactly clever either and so I guessed the apartment had to be bugged."

"And naturally you were very angry with Morris."

"To begin with, but then I thought I could turn Morris round and convert him into a sort of double agent; a good enough idea except that it didn't work out in practice. I think he lost his nerve and the man decided he had to go. If it's possible to be objective, it was a brilliant piece of improvisation. I mean he knew that even if I had wiped the flat clean, he could still rely on Special Branch to keep me under surveillance. It was a perfect set-up."

"Providing he had people on tap who were willing to kill for him," Harper said quietly.

"Yes, I admit that takes a bit of swallowing."

"And these same people had to get in and out of the Gilchrists' place without being seen by anyone."

"You mean Special Branch?" Mills shook his head. "I think they were relying on Morris to keep them informed. I doubt if they came close to the house, they were probably watching it from a distance."

Harper fingered his upper lip, a subterfuge to hide a satisfied smile. Mills had come alive again and was slowly warming to him, a development he welcomed because it was a step in the right direction.

"Let's talk about Albany and Durham," he said abruptly.

"That's a sudden switch, isn't it?"

"I like to hop about, Edward." His eyes crinkled in amusement. "My wife says I've got a mind like a grasshopper."

It was the con man's glib disclaimer. He knew that men like Harper didn't flit from one subject to another unless they had a reason.

"You had a rough time in Albany."

"I wasn't exactly popular."

The understatement of the year. Traitors ran child-molesters a close second in the hatred stakes. That he'd been sentenced to seven years for theft was of no consequence; the other prisoners had sat in judgment and pronounced him guilty, and the inevitable scuffles in the exercise yard and the fist fights in the washroom had led to disciplinary action.

"How did you get on with the staff?"

"I thought Patterson had it in for me."

"According to Usher, he was hard but fair."

"You've obviously been doing your homework."

"You're avoiding the issue, Edward." Harper's tone was quiet but insistent.

"I had a chip on my shoulder and Patterson tended to side with the other prisoners. He thought I'd been treated too leniently by the authorities and so he used to turn a blind eye when things got rough."

"And your man in the shadows?"

"He didn't have to lift a finger, I did it all by myself. But Durham was different."

It was different because Albany had taught him a lesson and he'd tried to keep his nose clean. Sharing a cell with Boxall had been a help, at least to begin with, but then something had happened to sour their relationship. It wasn't anything he could put his finger on but over a period of time, Boxall had gradually made it clear that he wanted nothing to do with him.

"Why was it different? You got an extra five years for Grievous Bodily Harm."

"I didn't attack Boxall."

"Two eye witnesses said you did."

"That's right; one happened to be a queer who was easily intimidated while the other was a frightener, a specialist in violence. The queer took to drugs after he was released and died as a result of an overdose. The frightener, who's a handy man with a razor, eventually went to Brazil where he's safe from extradition."

"And Boxall?"

"He was paid to keep his mouth shut." Mills felt a yawn coming on and stifled it behind his hand. "I don't pretend to know how the man arranged it, but he did. They say every prison is a labyrinth, Mr Harper."

125

"So I've heard. I suppose Ollenshaw could have worked it but since he was killed three years ago, he could hardly be pulling the strings today." Harper consulted the file again, turning over several pages to give the impression he was searching for a particular folio to refresh his memory. "Ever run into a man called Ingold?" he asked casually.

"Who?"

"Richard Spencer Ingold; he's on the Directing Staff of the Institute for Political and Strategic Studies."

"No, I can't say I have. Why do you ask?"

"No special reason, except that he and Ollenshaw used to be on very good terms."

One down, two to go. Ingold had been top of the list Liddell had shown him but it was evident that his name hadn't rung a bell with Mills. He toyed with the idea of trying either Quarry or Thurston on him but decided it would be a little premature at this stage of the interrogation. Take your time, he thought, there's no need to rush it, Mills isn't going anywhere.

"They belonged to the same club."

"Yes?"

"The Lansdowne." Slowly and deliberately, Harper began to drum his fingers on the table.

Vincent saw the gesture on the monitoring screen in the control studio and immediately reached for the telephone. Glancing over his shoulder at the policeman with the lank hair and the hollow cheeks, he said, "You're on in two minutes; Harper's just signalled that he wants to take a break."

The constable folded his newspaper away and stood up. "No peace for the wicked," he said laconically. "What about the second Grundig? Shall I switch it on?"

"Yes, you'd better do that small thing; Mills would smell a rat if there were no sound effects in the corridor." Vincent rang through to the interview room, waited for Harper to answer the phone and then said, "One moment, sir, I have an outside call for you."

*   *   *

Liddell wished he hadn't listened to Solange. He'd wanted to take a cab but the lawyer had insisted that it would be an unnecessary extravagance since his office was only a few minutes walk from the American Consulate. In the event, the few minutes had stretched into half an hour while the walk had become a route march clear across town, which was why he now had a painful blister on one heel. Sinking gratefully into a chair, Liddell removed his right shoe and inspected the damage.

"I have a Band-aid somewhere." Solange opened the roll-top desk and sorted through the compartments. "At least I thought I had," he muttered.

"Don't give it another thought, it's only a small blister." Liddell pulled the nylon sock above his ankle and replaced the shoe.

Solange nodded and closed the roll-top desk, locking it with a small key which looked as if it rightly belonged to a child's piggy bank.

"Your Consul is a very charming man, Monsieur Liddell."

"And helpful too." He thought it wouldn't do any harm to remind Solange the Consul had pulled out all the stops to raise the appropriate high level source in Washington who'd confirmed that Kiktev was dead.

"Oh yes, he was very helpful. Unfortunately, my instructions from Joachim Ziegler were very specific."

"What are you trying to say?"

"That I can do nothing until news of Kiktev's death is released by the Tass Agency or his obituary appears in the Soviet Press."

"But that could take weeks."

"It might indeed." Solange clasped his hands together and sat up, prim and erect, his manner suggesting that he was about to deliver a homily on the law and his responsibilities towards the late Joachim Ziegler. "However, I think it's possible to satisfy your curiosity to some extent. I do not know if a letter exists but I was entrusted with a key to a safety deposit box in the vaults of the Zeiss Exchange Bank."

"Forgive me for asking, but where do you keep it?"

"In the safe."

Liddell followed his gaze. The safe was a vintage Chubb model, one which he guessed had been built in the late eighteen sixties. It looked solid and reassuring, undoubtedly tough enough for the Victorian age but scarcely a major obstacle for a determined thief today.

"Of course the bank is closed, but we could go there first thing on Monday morning."

"Monday?" said Liddell. "I can't afford to hang around in Geneva all weekend. Look, Monsieur Solange, you're an influential man – can't you persuade one of the directors to open it up for us?"

"I'm afraid that's out of the question; it would be contrary to normal banking practice."

"But this is an emergency, you must know that. I mean, for Chrissakes, we just can't sit back and twiddle our thumbs all through tomorrow on account of some stupid rule."

From the expression on his face, it appeared that Solange didn't agree with him. He wondered if he should point out that the Zeiss Exchange hadn't got rich by being inflexible but as it happened, he didn't have to say anything. The frosty look gave way to one of resignation, as if the lawyer had accepted that the CIA man was unlikely to budge unless he got some action.

"I'll do my best," Solange said wearily, "but I don't hold out much hope."

"Well, at least you'll have the satisfaction of knowing that you tried."

Liddell opened his street map and finding that the Zeiss Exchange Bank was in the Rue Chaponnière, four blocks down from the Gare de Cornavin, decided they'd take a cab this time, provided Solange had some good news from the oracle.

*   *   *

It transpired that Solange was something of a pessimist and that the bank, far from being inflexible, was quite the reverse. Running one of the directors to ground on a Saturday afternoon involved an expensive number of phone calls but the lawyer's persistence paid off in the end. At ten minutes past five, a despondent-looking under manager had met them at the bank and let them in through a side door, furtively, as if they were being admitted to a blue cinema.

The vaults of the Zeiss Exchange were impressive enough to gladden the heart of even the most hard-bitten of insurance brokers. The walls, ceiling and floor were reinforced concrete, the double gates were pure tungsten carbide and there was a triple photo-electric alarm system. The safety deposit boxes, however, were less resilient, a trifling risk since in Liddell's opinion, the vault was virtually proof against a Sheridan tank armed with a Shillelagh missile.

Solange produced a letter of authorisation from the late Joachim Ziegler to dispel any qualms the under manager might have and then, taking the key out of his pocket, he unlocked the appropriate box with a flourish. Within the space of a few seconds, his face went through most of the colours of the rainbow. Liddell didn't have to be a clairvoyant to guess that the damn thing was empty but the lawyer told him anyway.

"There should have been a large sealed envelope," he said in a voice hoarse with disbelief, "but it's gone. I don't understand. How can it have vanished?"

"Well, that would depend on how long the key has been in your possession."

"I've had it since 1964."

"And when did you last check the box?"

"February, or was it March?" Solange frowned, trying to recall which month it had been. "It must have been shortly after Monsieur Ziegler was admitted to the clinic in Kandersteg."

"And the letter of authorisation?" Liddell asked quietly.

"It was kept in the safe at my office."

Ziegler had died on the ninth of April, more than ten weeks before Kiktev. Ten weeks – plenty of time for the KGB to recruit a locksmith, open the Chubb safe, take a wax impression of the key, check the letter of authorisation to identify the bank and then have a nominee hire a safety deposit box from the Zeiss Exchange Bank in order to gain access to the vaults. Beautiful, simple, foolproof; the whole goddamned security system ripped open like a can of peaches. Liddell began to emulate Solange, turning first pink in the face, then red, then puce.

*　　　*　　　*

The tea was hot, strong and sweet, the sort of brew Harper's batman used to produce for him in a mess tin back in '43 when he was a nineteen-year-old infantry subaltern in Sicily. Listening to the playback of his interview with Mills while he drank from the standard issue cup with the WD hallmark, it occurred to Harper that life had been simpler in those days when the enemy wore a distinctive uniform. It wasn't that you actually saw him very often but at least the battle lines were drawn on a map in chinagraph pencil and you knew roughly where to look for him. Thirty years on, the enemy was a faceless person in a crowd, a chameleon who changed colour to merge with the background. Thirty years on, the enemy was the man or woman next door who traded in classified information, the terrorist who planted a bomb in a crowded restaurant, or the influential civil servant who swayed opinion in high places.

Vincent stopped the tape recorder the instant he heard the drumming noise which marked the end of Harper's conversation with Mills.

"The quality's good," he said thoughtfully, "but it's a pity he didn't mention Ingold by name. Still, I daresay we can solve that problem if we have to."

Harper placed his cup in the saucer. No matter what some people thought, Vincent was not a slouch and it was obvious he'd guessed that he intended to doctor the tapes, cutting words out here and there to fake an entirely different sort of conversation.

"We've got plenty of time, Harry."

"Yes, sir." Vincent tugged at the lobe of his right ear, squeezing it between index finger and thumb. "So what happens now?"

"Oh, I think I'll have one more session with Mills. Try him with number two on Liddell's list – Matthew Quarry. If there's still no reaction, then we'll call it a day."

"And tomorow?"

"Much of the same except that we can afford to stand a few of the actors down." Harper swung round in his chair to face Gattis. "You've done your stuff, Iain," he said, "we shan't be needing you again. As a matter of fact, we can get by with just one CID officer."

From his artless tone of voice, Vincent knew that Harper was leaving the choice open for him to decide. He supposed he and Drew could toss a coin, but that was a pretty evasive solution. Drew wouldn't be keen to stay on; he had a trim little number waiting for him back in London, the honey blonde with the impeccable New England background who'd had to forego the questionable pleasure of his company yesterday evening. What about Jean? Vincent nibbled at his lip; well, Jean had been married to him long enough to accept the irregular hours.

"I'll stay on watch tonight," he said.

"Good," said Harper, "that settles it. Gattis and Drew can push off."

Drew said, "Thanks Harry, I'll make it up to you some day."

Some day? Vincent smiled to himself; that was nice and vague. When was some day? When Drew got tired of screwing around and decided to settle down? Hell, he'd be dead and buried long before then.

"Tomorrow is Sunday." Harper picked up his teaspoon and rapped it against the cup as if sounding a bell. "We'll need to do something about the newspapers."

"Mills has a fairly wide taste – *The Observer, Times, Express* . . . ?"

"You'd better make it the *Sunday Express*, Harry; it's more in keeping with the image of this place. A small insert would help to sustain the illusion."

Without actually saying so, Harper had made it clear that he wanted the forgers to alter the contents. Removing one small paragraph and replacing it with another was no great problem but it would mean working through the night, setting the type up in a hand press to reprint one, possibly two complete pages.

"How much longer do you think we can keep it going?"

"The deception?" Harper frowned. "Mills thinks he's been remanded for seven days."

"Won't he expect to be transferred to Wormwood Scrubs?"

"We can always fake a transfer, Harry."

"Yes?"

"But of course he'll escape from custody on the way."

Allowing Mills to escape was a last resort solution which might have to be put into effect if the CID made life too hot for comfort. It would probably get the Department off the hook but in washing his hands of Mills, he knew he would be walking away from a situation that stank to high heaven. Unless he got a lucky break, defeat was just around the corner. A lucky break? Harper twisted his mouth in a sour grimace; he needed a miracle and miracles were in short supply these days.

Harper didn't know it but a small one was in the making and several people would have a hand in it. The Detective

Chief Superintendent of 'V' Division had an enquiring mind and he was unable to understand why Mills had used a piece of wire to bypass the ignition switch on the Marina after he'd apparently stolen the keys to the car from a handbag belonging to Mrs Gilchrist. It was only a small point but there were others to reinforce a feeling that they could be looking for the wrong man. The pathologist who'd performed the autopsy on Morris Gilchrist had submitted a report which stated unequivocally that the stab wounds had been inflicted by someone who was left handed, an assertion that was born out by the finger prints on the carving knife. The one major piece of evidence, however, which really gave him food for thought was the fact that while CRO had been able to match these prints to Mills, they were adamant that, according to their records, he was right handed.

*　　　*　　　*

The telephone woke Farren instantly and groping in the dark, he found the cord above the bed and gave it a sharp tug. The light from the hundred watt bulb temporarily blinded him and he rolled over on to his left side, shielding his eyes against the glare with one hand while he reached out with the other to lift the extension phone off the hook.

The caller said, "Mr Ormerod?"

The voice was soft, even a little muffled, but quite unmistakable and his pulse began to beat faster than normal.

"Yes." Farren moistened his lips seeking to remove the mucus that had collected in both corners. "Yes, who's that?"

"Cable and Wireless. I have a telegram for you which reads as follows: Consignment has arrived and available for collection at usual address tomorrow provided you call before ten a.m."

"Thank you."

"Should I send you a confirmatory copy in the morning?"

"No," said Farren, "that won't be necessary."

A nagging fear that he and Rooney had been left in limbo had suddenly been removed. Temple was back in touch again and there was a message waiting for him in the dead letter box on Hampstead Heath.

14

THE WASHROOM didn't have that used look about it. The chromium-plated taps gleamed, the basins weren't chipped and the mirrors were exceptionally clean. There were no scuff marks on the plastic-tiled floor and there was nothing wrong with either of the two lavatories, which Mills thought was a little odd because ordinarily he would have expected to find at least one cubicle with the drawbolt missing.

"This place deserves at least two stars." Mills stopped lathering his face and smiled at the reflection of the friendly neighbourhood policeman in the mirror. "For the loos," he added, "not the food."

"The grub isn't that bad, a bit monotonous but definitely edible. You'll fare a lot worse in the Scrubs."

"It figures."

"What does."

"That they'll hold me in Wormwood Scrubs while I'm on remand."

"Now look, that was just a figure of speech."

"If you say so." Mills put the shaving brush on the glass shelf and picked up the safety razor. "Of course, it all depends on this man Harper, doesn't it? I mean, you people would like to get shot of me but you can't make a move until he gives the word?"

"I wouldn't know, I'm just an ordinary copper."

"And a pretty overworked one at that. Don't you ever get a rest day?"

"Yes, every now and then." The constable looked up at the ceiling, his eyes narrowing thoughtfully, as if he was still mulling over the question and wondering how best to answer it. "On average, it's roughly one in eight."

One in eight sounded about right but it had taken him long enough to work it out. Duty rosters were often pretty elastic but Mills couldn't recall having met anyone else who didn't have the days on, days off figures at his fingertips. Perhaps he was reading too much into the man's hesitation but, coupled with the two-star washroom, it rekindled a feeling that the whole set-up was a sham, a ruse to gain time so that SIS could take him apart before putting all the bits and pieces together again.

They used to call it brainwashing in his day but he thought they probably had some fancy new name for it now. Not that it made any difference because the final objective remained the same and at the end of the day you aimed to finish up with a man who was programmed to do exactly what you wanted.

As for Harper, his indoctrination methods were a little off beat. He didn't make things clear, he confused you with names; names like Richard Spencer Ingold of the Institute for Political and Strategic Studies, and Matthew Quarry, next in line to be head of the Civil Service. Mills still couldn't understand why Harper had thought he knew either of them. Quarry had always been an Olympian figure, someone he'd heard of but had never met either before the Kiktev affair or afterwards when the great man had served on the Royal Commission appointed in 1967 to consider the future structure of the SIS in the mid 1970s. What was it Harper had said? The conventional spy is yesterday's man; the most dangerous agent today is the intellectual in the Think Tank who helps to shape foreign policy, the civil servant who has the ear and the mind of his Minister, or the expert adviser on the Eastern Bloc with a subtle line on appeasement? The detailed recommendations of the Royal Commission had never been made public but it was a fair bet that some of their proposals had given the SIS a nasty turn, and if Quarry had been the dominant voice on the committee, that would be enough for Harper to view him in an unfavourable light.

Unfavourable light or not, nobody was standing over Quarry watching his every move. Quarry ate his food with a knife and fork instead of a plastic spoon, kept his pants up with a belt, wore a tie when he felt like it and didn't have to shave with a dull blade while a twelve-stone attendant hovered in the background anxious to relieve him of the razor the moment he'd finished with it, but then Quarry still had his freedom and that was the difference between them. The way the friendly neighbourhood policeman reached past him to pocket the Gillette while he was drying his hands and face on the issue green towel merely underlined this obvious point.

"That's what I call service," Mills said dryly.

"We aim to please." The constable plucked the face towel from his grasp and dropped it into the pedal bin. "In fact, you could say that this is the best and cheapest hotel in town. I mean, where else would you get a first class valet and breakfast in your room for nothing?"

It seemed to Mills that the best and cheapest hotel in town was short of staff. Some ten minutes after locking him in the cell, the erstwhile valet returned in the guise of a waiter bearing a singularly unappetising meal of hard fried eggs and two strips of streaky bacon. The management had also provided him with a newspaper – a copy of the *Sunday Express* that had been folded in half and half again as if to ensure that the small paragraph on the Wimbledon murders would immediately catch his eye. Had they not made it so obvious, he might have swallowed the insert, hook, line and sinker.

*   *   *

Farren stepped into the phone booth and closed the door behind him. Placing a handful of loose change on top of the coin box for the sake of appearances, he felt inside his other trouser pocket and brought out the scrap of lined notepaper which he had found in the dead letter box on Hampstead Heath. Printed in block capitals was a brief message which read: CALL BOX (435-29971X) ENTRANCE TO POST OFFICE IN ROSSLYN HILL, ELEVEN ZERO SIX. He glanced at the number on the dial, saw that it tallied with the one Temple had written in brackets and pulled one of the directories out of the bin, leafing through it at random while he waited for the call to come through. At five minutes past eleven the telephone rang twice, stopped, and then rang again exactly one minute later.

Answering it, he reversed the exchange number and gave his name.

Temple said, "I assume you've been reading the newspapers and watching television?"

"It helps to pass the time."

"It help to pass the time." Temple's voice dripped venom. "In that case, you may have noticed that our mutual friend is receiving very poor coverage."

"He did all right on Friday."

"But we now have a complete blackout. How do you account for that?"

Farren rubbed his nose on a knuckle, trying to still an itch in the right nostril. "I can't," he said finally. "I'm no good at guessing games. Anyway, what are you worried about? They'll find him soon enough."

"What if he's been found already and by the wrong people?"

Temple and his damned euphemisms. Who did he mean by the wrong people – Special Branch or those freaks in the SIS? Farren felt a shiver run down his spine and clenched the phone a little tighter. "I doubt it, he's probably gone to ground."

"It's possible, but I think we ought to make sure."

"How?"

It was a spontaneous reaction, a derisive comment, not a question, but Temple took it as such.

"I have two names – Larissa Fedorovna Pavlichenko and Elizabeth Eastgate. Either of them might know something. You will try the Russian first."

He didn't like it. It was a risk and an unnecessary one at that. But Temple's voice was cold and hard, brooking no argument, and he knew that he didn't have any choice because Temple was holding all the cards. Farren closed his eyes, silently cursing the Chief of Staff in Dublin, the fanatic who was prepared to sacrifice anybody and everybody for the sake of the cause, the man who'd got him into this jam for the sake of two hundred Kalashnikov AK47s and a crateful of Strella missiles, a small arsenal that would continue to sit on the dockside at Stettin until Temple gave the word.

"Where do I find her?"

"Alford Street; she's rented a flat in Curzon House. It's on the second floor, the number's twenty-three."

Farren repeated the address, committing it to memory before moving on to the inevitable question, the one he was reluctant to ask. "And when I get there?"

"Talk to her, see what you can find out and then call me at

five this evening on 444-53132. You'd better make a note of the number."

"I already have and I'm thinking you just made your first big mistake."

"I'm sorry to disappoint you," Temple said smoothly, "but it happens to be the number of a public call box in Highgate Wood."

A sharp click preceded the purring tone. Slamming the phone down, Farren shouldered his way out of the booth and started walking towards the Underground station at Belsize Park, angry that Temple was still able to manipulate him.

*   *   *

There were eight rooms in the basement but, as far as Mills could make out, only the washroom, one cell and the interview room at the far end of the passageway were presently in use. Of the remainder, he knew that there were three other cells in the detention block but there was no telling what lay behind the two doors on the right hand side of the corridor beyond the stairwell. At a rough guess, he thought the building dated back to the turn of the century when the Borough of Wimbledon couldn't have been more than a tiny village and knowing something of their thrifty attitude towards public expenditure, it was inconceivable that the Victorians would have built such a fortress in the depths of the Surrey countryside.

Harper was waiting for him in the end room, the one with the depressing information posters furbished by HM's Stationery Office. Wearing a cheviot suit, he looked type-cast for the part of the affable but vague country gentleman in a Ben Travers farce, an eccentric character which, in real life, Harper in no way resembled. The charismatic charm of the natural born actor was there on the surface, a disarming and beguiling trait that served to conceal a ruthless personality. Although theirs was only a brief acquaintance, Mills was quite sure there were no shades of grey with Harper, only black and white, which made him the sort of man who could be either a staunch friend or an implacable enemy. That much was straightforward; deciding where he stood with him was far more difficult. There were times when he thought

Harper was on his side, others when the reverse seemed to apply.

"You look tired, Edward." Harper waved a hand, indicating the empty chair. "And a little down in the mouth. You're not feeling off colour, are you?"

The solicitous note of concern was false and to Mills it was just another way of saying, "Good morning, and how are you today?" If he had one, Harper would probably have addressed the same question in the same tone of voice to his pet goldfish if one morning it happened to be lying on its side near the surface.

"I didn't get very much sleep last night."

"I'm sorry to hear that. Perhaps your mind was too active thinking about Ingold and Quarry?"

"No." Mills was wary. "As a matter of fact, I was trying to figure out what I stood to gain by helping you."

"The boot's on the other foot," Harper said firmly. "I'm trying to help you."

"You have an odd way of going about it."

"I imagine Sergeant Chesterman isn't exactly enamoured of your methods, come to that." Harper turned to the buff-coloured file at his elbow. It was getting rather tatty now, the cover creased and some of the folios dog-eared. "Let's talk about your account with the Banque de France at Lyon."

"My account?"

"Don't be coy with me, Edward. You were identified by the bank manager and the Notary in Avignon who furnished you with a letter of introduction. The record shows that the account was opened on Friday the twentieth of June 1964, the day before you allegedly woke up to find yourself in a seedy apartment house in Geneva, the one your accomplice rented for you in advance."

"In my name," Mills said acidly. "Now wasn't that clever of him?"

"He intended to double-cross you all along. At least, that's the theory held by the Fraud Squad, and he did end up with the lion's share of the one million dollars. Or did he?"

"You think I'm guilty, don't you?"

"I have an open mind."

An open mind – Harper? No, he was just being ambivalent, blowing hot one moment, cold the next; the oldest trick in the book, one lifted straight from page three of the official pamphlet on 'Methods of Interrogation'.

"The bank account in my name came to light when the title deeds to the villa showed up in July '65."

"So?"

"So then the Fraud Squad held an identification parade and I was picked out from the line-up."

"I'm aware of that."

"Well, suppose you take a good look at my face," Mills said angrily. "It's not exactly unique, is it? Not the sort of face you'd remember a year later. But the bank manager and the Notary did. Oh, they weren't very positive but that didn't bother the Fraud Squad because they had enough documentary evidence to support their case. The ID was just a bonus as far as they were concerned."

"You seem to have thought of everything, Edward."

"Not me – but the man in the shadows did."

"Ah yes; you can't help admiring him, can you? I mean, he's quite brilliant." Harper clucked his tongue. "Almost as brilliant as Giles Thurston."

Another name, another tack, another walk down memory lane. Mills clenched his hands, digging the nails into both palms in an attempt first to stem and then to cool the rising tide of fury. This time they wouldn't go off at a tangent wandering around every bloody mulberry bush that sprang from Harper's fertile mind. This time Harper would have to come clean and tell him where he stood.

"I think it's time we placed our cards on the table," he said in a controlled voice.

Harper stared at him, his eyes narrowing. "Precisely what do you mean by that?"

"I want to know what's in it for me. Can you, for instance, get the police off my back?"

"That depends on you. We've got to help each other."

The perfect equivocal answer, the kind you might expect from a man who was a dissembler. Harper wasn't going to lift a finger to help him, and in that instant he knew that survival was the only thing that mattered to him now. The conspiracy? Best to put it out of his mind and get the hell out of it, make a bid to escape before the walls closed in on him for good.

"Did you ever run across Giles Thurston?"

"No."

"He used to be with the Foreign Office, ran the Economic Intelligence Department before he was co-opted into the Government Advisory Board."

Escape? It would be dangerous but he had nothing to lose. If his hunch was right, SIS had probably circumvented the law and that would mean he was in a position to twist their arm. He could use Elizabeth Eastgate as a go-between, just as Harper had done.

"A trifle conceited but no more than you'd expect from a man who got a double first at Cambridge."

"Who are we talking about?"

"Why, Giles Thurston, of course."

Of course, of course; who else would they talk about but Giles Thurston? Well, let Harper rabbit on if it makes him happy; use the time to plan, use Harper as he is using you.

"In Whitehall he was nicknamed the Hight Priest."

"Why was that?"

"Because I suppose we all thought he was infallible."

Tonight; he would make the break tonight and then, with any luck, he would have this smug little bastard by the short and curlies.

"This High Priest," Mills said softly, "was he a friend of Ollenshaw's too?"

The interest was feigned, a ruse to lull Harper into thinking he was getting somewhere.

*   *   *

Curzon House, where Larissa Pavlichenko was staying, was a product of the nineteen-twenties. Designed by an architect who'd borrowed most of his ideas from New York, it had self-service lifts, wall to wall carpeting and central heating at a time when such innovations were confined to the larger hotels in London. Fifty years later, it seemed positively old-fashioned, an impression that was further enhanced by the hall porter.

The hall porter was sixty, an ex-sergeant-major of the Coldstream Guards, a man steeped in the tradition of service who saw himself more as the guardian and confidant of the residents than as a mere commissionaire. Since most of the thirty-two apartments were leased on a quarterly basis, people were always coming and going, but he made it his business to get to know each new arrival and make them feel at home. He lived on the premises and while Sunday was usually his day off, it so happened that he was passing through the lobby when Farren arrived. A brisk "Good morning" would have sufficed but Farren, over confident, made the mistake of smiling at him.

The hall porter said, "Can I help you, sir?"

Farren froze in mid-stride and then turned to face him. "No, it's all right." He smiled again to hide his annoyance. "Actually, I'm calling on Miss Pavlichenko."

"Oh yes?"

"She's expecting me."

He could see that the explanation, far from satisfying him, had only excited the hall porter's curiosity still further.

"You're from the London Coliseum then, are you, sir?"

Friendly, cheerful but nosey, the sort of man he tried to avoid, the sort of busybody who'd probably read 'Who's Who' from cover to cover.

"No, I'm a police officer." Farren allowed him to catch a brief glimpse of his forged ID card before tucking it back inside his jacket. "The theatre management's got the wind up."

"What about?"

"The cranks have been at it again and they've received a few of the usual threatening letters. It's nothing to get alarmed about but we have to go through the motions. Of course, this is just between you and me." Farren placed a finger against his nose and winked. "Keep it to yourself, okay?"

"Mum's the word."

"That's right, squire, mum's the word." Farren moved past him and took the lift up to the second floor.

The Portuguese maid who answered the door struck him as being none too bright, which was all the more unfortunate since he had some difficulty in making himself heard above the noise of the record player that was booming away in a room off the hall. As patiently as he knew how, Farren tried to explain why he wanted to see Miss Pavlichenko but it wasn't until he resorted to a combination of pidgin English and sign language that she finally got the message.

Larissa Fedorovna Pavlichenko was not at all like the newspaper photographs. Farren had always been under the impression that she was a fairly tall woman, whereas she was a diminutive five foot three. The cameras had also lied about her face. If it was true that the character of a person was reflected in their features, then he thought the gossip columnists were right when they hinted that she was vain, greedy and selfish. The black leotard she was wearing emphasised the tiny breasts and narrow pelvis, making her seem painfully thin except for the calf muscles which were hard and disproportionately large for such slender legs.

"My maid tells me you're a policeman, Mr Ormerod." She switched the record player off and sat down on the settee, curling herself up in one corner like a cat. "Is that not so?"

"Yes, I'm attached to Special Branch."

"Ah, yes, the British Secret Police." Her eyes regarded him with some amusement. "And why should the British Secret Police be interested in me again after all these years?"

"Because we're looking for Mills; Edward James Mills, the SIS man who became a double agent."

"And you think he may try to get in touch with me."

It was an assumption, not a question, and he knew instinctively that it wasn't prompted by womanly intuition either. Somebody had obviously been there before him. But who? Certainly not Special Branch because she would have made some acid comment about the left hand not knowing what the right was doing. CID then? No, they wouldn't have any reason to interview her in connection with a murder case.

"It's possible."

"Yes, that's what Mr Liddell said. He must be a very important man."

"Who? Liddell?"

"No, your Mr Mills. Why are the Americans so interested in him?"

For American read Liddell; for Liddell read CIA; the correct but disturbing solution to a simple equation.

"Well, like us, they reckon he can supply the answers to quite a number of questions." His hands were moist now, the sweat oozing from the palms. "I take it you haven't seen him?" he said.

"No, he hasn't been here."

"Yes – well – I'm sorry to have troubled you."

"You English policemen," she said, "so polite, so considerate."

"You think so?" Farren edged his way towards the hall. "I know some people who wouldn't agree with you." Droll, he thought, oh, very droll.

"What should I do if he does come to see me?"

He wondered if her question was really as innocent as she made it seem. If he was right and the CIA had got to Pavlichenko first, then they would have told her exactly what to do, who to call. Vain, greedy, selfish? Well, he had news for the gossip columnists – they'd left out a couple of adjectives like cunning and devious.

"Didn't Mr Liddell leave you his number?"

"Yes."

"He's a smart man is Mr Liddell. You call him if there's any trouble he'll know how to handle it."

His advice was good, almost prophetic, if he had but known it. Barely five minutes after the Portuguese maid had shown him out of the apartment, Larissa Pavlichenko was on the telephone to the Grosvenor House Hotel asking to speak to Mr Gordon Liddell in Room 408.

15

VINCENT SWITCHED OFF the video tape machine, waited until Mills and the police constable were leaving, framed in the entrance to the interview room, and then cut to camera two. For some reason the picture on the monitor screen started to roll, and leaning forward, he adjusted the horizontal hold and turned up the brightness, bringing the long corridor into sharper definition. Mills had almost reached the detention block when Drew suddenly appeared in camera at the foot of the stairwell, and then the picture went on the blink again and began to break up. Clenching a fist, Vincent gave the box several thumps. He was still swearing under his breath when Harper walked into the studio with Drew close on his heels.

"Say a few for me while you're at it." Harper sank into the swivel armchair and crossed one leg over the other. The old snap and fire was missing and Vincent thought he seemed strangely lethargic. "I don't have the energy."

"I'm sorry."

"What for, Harry? It's not your fault."

Not his fault? Vincent glanced at the monitor screen and was surprised to find that it was behaving itself again.

"I'm the one who can't get through to Mills. There's a wall between us and it's getting thicker all the time."

"I thought he was showing an interest for once."

"In Thurston?" Harper shook his head. "That was just a pose." He stretched both arms above his head and yawned. "I think we'll call it a day."

"Yes, sir."

"Any messages for me before I push off?"

Vincent reached for the clipboard on the table. "Only one," he said, "from the duty officer. A Mr Gordon Liddell wants you to get in touch with him as soon as possible."

"What about?"

"He didn't say, but the duty officer got the impression it was fairly urgent."

"It always is with Liddell."

"Yes – well, you can reach him at the Grosvenor House Hotel, the number's 01-499-6363. Should I get it for you?"

"If you wouldn't mind, Harry."

Vincent dialled the number, asked for Liddell, waited until the hotel switchboard had connected him with Room 408 and then handed the phone over to Harper. The ensuing conversation was brief and rather one-sided, with Harper doing most of the listening. By the time Liddell had finished there was a very thoughtful expression on his face.

"Bad news?" Vincent asked quietly.

Harper stroked his chin. "I'm not sure. Liddell's been to Geneva, chasing after a letter that Ziegler is supposed to have written some twelve years ago, back in '64."

"Oh?"

"Needless to say, it's vanished into thin air."

It didn't make sense. Vincent pursed his lips; surely there had to be more to it than that? There were times when Harper was singularly uncommunicative, when he held the cards so close to his chest that no one in the Department really knew what he had in mind. Vincent noticed that he was busy with the telephone again and wondered who he was calling this time.

"I want you and Drew to hear this."

Harper hooked the telephone into the speech amplifier and leaned back in his chair, looking oddly pleased with himself. There was a faint clatter and then the gruff, unmistakable voice of Chief Superintendent Wray of the Special Branch said, "All right, Cedric, let's hear the worst."

"You know Pavlichenko . . ."

"Who?"

"Larissa Fedorovna Pavlichenko – the ballet dancer."

"What about her?"

"She's had a visit from one of your people, a man called Ormerod."

Wray grunted, making a noise that sounded like a distant rumble of thunder. "He's not one of mine."

"I had a feeling he might be an impostor. Look, I don't

want to tread on your corns, Stanley, but I think somebody ought to have a word with the young lady."

"That's exactly what I was thinking." Wray sounded resentful, aggrieved that Harper had stolen a march on him. "Where do we find her?"

"She has a flat in Curzon House."

"I'll get Chesterman on to it."

"Good. I'll tell Gattis to meet him in the lobby at six thirty."

"That's unfortunate; they'll miss one another. You see, Chesterman will be there within the hour."

"He'll have a long wait then," Harper said cheerfully. "Larissa Pavlichenko's gone to the Zoo to have her picture taken with the animals. I'm told it's some sort of publicity stunt."

"I would have thought a prima ballerina would have been above that sort of thing."

"So would I, Stanley, but you know how it is these days, people will do almost anything if the money's good enough." Harper broke the connection and unhooked the telephone. "Interesting."

"Yes, sir." Noticing the purposeful expression on his face, Vincent thought it was time he put the record straight before he found himself landed with another job. "Drew is here," he said diffidently.

"So I see." Harper's voice was cold and brittle like thin ice.

"Gattis was planning to take his kids for a picnic this afternoon." Drew frowned, trying to recall their conversation of yesterday. "I think he mentioned something about Burnham Beeches."

"Then you'd better get in touch with him before he disappears." Harper slapped his knees and stood up. "I'll be at home if you need me." Half way to the door he suddenly stopped, snapped his fingers and turned about. "One more thing – don't forget to warn Gattis that he'll need his picture box."

"His picture box?" Drew repeated blankly.

"The Identikit," Harper said peevishly. "I want a pen and ink drawing of friend Ormerod."

*   *   *

Farren left the Underground station in Leicester Square and walked round the corner into Newport Court. The antique

146

and secondhand furniture shops were closed but the porn books and girlie magazine forum was open for business behind the plastic strip curtain in the doorway. Farther up the street, two middle-aged men were furtively taking down the telephone numbers of the call girls whose special and personal services were advertised in the display case outside a newsagent's. Turning right into Gerrard Place, he strolled towards the public call boxes outside the open air car park, seemingly in no great hurry until, noticing a Chinese girl leave the nearest booth, he suddenly quickened his stride. Although he still had several minutes in hand, it was better to be safe than sorry. To kill time, he deliberately mis-dialled a number and then leafed through the E to K Telephone Directory for the benefit of any onlooker.

Promptly at five o'clock he lifted the phone off the hook and rang the call box in Highgate Wood. Temple answered it swiftly and reversed the exchange number, observing a security procedure that was becoming more tiresome every day.

Farren said, "Brace yourself for some bad news. We're in trouble."

There was a moment of silence and then he heard a sharp intake of breath, a sort of hissing sound which reminded him of a cat spitting.

"What sort of trouble?"

"The CIA. I think they're using Larissa Pavlichenko."

"In what way?"

The question was automatic, the instinctive reaction of a worried man who needed time to think.

"As an informer. She's been got at by a man called Liddell, if that name means anything to you."

"It does." Temple was breathing heavily now, making a rasping noise like an asthmatic. "He's no fool."

"Neither is Larissa Pavlichenko. I think she may be on to me."

"Assuming you are right, how does this affect your cover?"

He sensed that Temple was calmer now, more in control of himself and seeing things in perspective, analysing the risks before deciding what their next move should be.

"She knows me as Ormerod, but that won't be of much help to the CIA or Special Branch. My landlord knows me by a different name."

"Quite."

There was a longish pause and he knew what Temple was thinking. Larissa Pavlichenko would be able to describe him, perhaps not in any great detail but enough maybe to match some of the physical characteristics with the Identikit likeness that the police in Belfast had on record.

"I can handle Liddell."

"Good."

"But you'd better lie low for a day or two."

"You'll keep in touch?"

"Of course."

The assurance was too glib, too quick for his liking, and Farren had a sinking feeling that he and Rooney were about to be left in limbo again. And this time it might well be for good. With his contacts, Temple would be the first to know whether or not the situation was likely to blow up in their faces and if it did, there was always the chance that he would simply cut and run, leaving them to fend for themselves.

"I think we'd better come to a firm arrangement, Mr Temple."

"What on earth are you talking about?"

"From now on, I want you to call me every night at six thirty on the dot."

"That's quite out of the question, you don't seem to realise . . ."

"No," Farren said firmly, "no, you just listen to me for a change; you've been calling the tune for long enough and now it's my turn. If I don't hear from you within thirty minutes of the appointed time, I'll drop the police an anonymous letter. It's true I don't know an awful lot about you, but I can give them a few pointers."

"You're out of your mind. How do you suppose your people back home will react when I tell them why the deal is off?"

"I could end up either with a bullet in each kneecap or doing thirty years in an English jail, and I know which I prefer."

"Have you gone mad?"

"No, Mr Temple, I'm merely trying to make you understand that we either sink or swim together."

Temple sighed and in that instant, Farren knew that he was going to capitulate.

"All right, if it'll make you happy, I'll telephone at six thirty tomorrow night."

"And leave your number."

"What for?"

"So that I can call you back to check that you're still in this country."

"It's like that, is it?"

"If you mean that I no longer trust you," said Farren, "then yes, that's the way it is."

*   *   *

The wood lay off the A10 roughly two miles beyond the oddly named village of Ponder's Leap in Hertfordshire which, in turn, was only some twenty minutes by car from the suburb of Enfield in North London. Once a local beauty spot, it had gradually become a favourite dumping ground for unwanted rubbish following the eviction of a Romany encampment in 1969. Some of the villagers believed the gypsies had started it off out of spite while others placed the blame squarely on the Urban District Council for having closed the local tip. No matter who was at fault, it still didn't alter the fact that the place was now an eyesore. Abandoned cars, rusty bicycles, refrigerators, washing machines, pots, pans, bedsteads and old mattresses littered the wood from one end to the other. But favourite dumping ground or not, the former beauty spot still attracted its quota of courting couples and young children.

The Ford Zephyr was an old, familiar landmark as far as the two boys were concerned. A Mark II 1970 model, eaten through with rust and minus all four wheels, it had been standing there in the clearing for close on two years, hedged in on three sides by a tangled mass of blackberry bushes and tall clumps of stinging nettles. Just as flies and wasps are drawn to the honey pot, so the car had proved a magnet for the litter bugs and with each passing week, the bits and pieces of junk scattered about in the long grass and cow parsley had grown and multiplied. The latest addition which immediately caught the two boys' attention, was a deep freeze, oblong in shape and with a capacity of twenty-four cubic feet.

Leaving their bicycles propped against the car, they moved

across the clearing to take a closer look at it. It was easy to see why the freezer had been dumped there, for the enamel finish was badly chipped and there were several large dents in the body. Discovering that the lid was either locked or jammed, they searched round for something which they could use to force it open, a quest that seemed pretty hopeless until they found a rusty ball-pane hammer and a tyre lever lying underneath the Zephyr. Armed with these tools, they then attacked the lock, raining blows at it until the housing buckled and the catch was sprung.

The naked man lay on his back, his knees bent upwards in an inverted 'v', his head stuffed inside a plastic bag which had been tied about the throat. Smaller plastic bags which enveloped both hands as far as the wrists had accelerated the process of decomposition so that the body was bloated, turning black in parts and alive with maggots. The boys took one horrified look at the corpse and then dropped the lid. Fear gave impetus to their flight and it took them only eight minutes to ride back to Ponder's Leap on their bicycles.

Half an hour later, having listened to their incoherent account, the village police constable drove out to the wood to verify their story before telephoning the County Police Headquarters in Bishop's Stortford. At twenty minutes past six, two CID officers arrived on the scene where they were joined shortly thereafter by the medical examiner, the official photographer and a team of forensic experts from the Regional Crime Squad.

16

ONE LOOK AT his mutinous expression and Chesterman knew that, like Queen Victoria, Gattis was not amused. Apart from wearing a sour face, Gattis had also advertised his ill humour by using the attaché case as a battering ram to push the swing doors open before stomping into the lobby of Curzon House with all the enthusiasm of a Palestinian refugee compelled to enter a synagogue.

"You look full of the joys of spring."

"It's all right for you, George." Gattis reached past him and pushed the call button for the lift. "You haven't got a wife and kids to contend with."

Chesterman knew that he hadn't put the knife in deliberately but it was the sort of thoughtless remark that hurt. Even though Margaret had been a first-class bitch, he still missed her.

"Been giving you a rough time, have they?"

"What do you think? Look, we were just setting off on a picnic when the bloody telephone rings and I have to go and answer it."

"Tough." Chesterman followed him into the lift and closed the gate. "You shouldn't have joined."

"That's what Mary said."

"And?"

"And so I was tactless enough to point out that the Department was paying me three times as much as I got when I was a Detective Sergeant."

"I bet that went down well."

"Like a lead balloon," Gattis said morosely.

"Cheer up, this won't take long."

"You reckon?"

"Well, you don't think Pavlichenko is going to keep us here all night, do you? She's got better things to do with her time than play footsie with the likes of you and me."

Although he had clocked up sixteen years with Special Branch, Chesterman was still an incurable optimist. Larissa Pavlichenko might have had better things to do with her time but she was one of the most vacillating eye-witnesses either man had come across in a very long while. Any woman had a God-given right to change her mind but Gattis thought she stretched this feminine trait to the point of absurdity and it took them over an hour merely to establish that Ormerod was about five ten, had dark hair and weighed between eleven and twelve stone.

They fared little better with the Identikit, substituting one overlay for another as they endeavoured to match the changing characteristics of nose, eyes, mouth, ears and jaw line. Even the hair caused problems, with the parting first on the left and then to the right and reverting from short back and sides to a more trendy style that covered the tips of both ears. Looking at the finished effort, Gattis was inclined to believe that they had been wasting their time. It was only his opinion however, and knowing that Harper wouldn't be satisfied unless he saw it for himself, he took several shots of the likeness with a Polaroid camera and then made a pen and ink trace so that the lab would be able to photocopy it if necessary.

After that, it was just a question of taking their leave, thanking Larissa Pavlichenko for being so helpful and apologising for any inconvenience they might have caused her. In return, she made the usual, almost obligatory remark that the English police were wonderful and then had the Portuguese maid show them to the door. With his customary patience, Chesterman waited until they were riding the lift down to the lobby before he passed judgment.

"We've got ourselves a lemon," he said philosophically, "the Ad man's creation – a face to fit any face in a crowd."

"We did our best." Gattis eyed the attaché case at his feet and gave it a kick to relieve his feelings. "No one, not even Harper, can deny that."

"There's always the hall porter."

"Oh yes, you can always find another eye witness if you try hard enough. Of course, the chances are that he'll be half blind and have a memory like a sieve."

"Well, what do you say, Iain?"

"I've got to hand it to you," Gattis said wearily, "you're a glutton for punishment, George."

"Come on, it'll only take a minute."

Chesterman was wrong again. It took them a good five minutes to drag the hall porter from his bath and very nearly another five to persuade him to take the door off the chain.

Glancing at Chesterman's ID, he said, "I've known times when you couldn't find a copper anywhere but today it seems you're practically crawling out of the woodwork."

"You saw him then?"

"Who?"

"Ormerod, the man who called on Miss Pavlichenko this morning," said Chesterman.

"Yes, I had a few words with him. He had a funny sort of accent, one that was difficult to place. He sounded as if he came from the Midlands but I think he was faking it."

Gattis took the pen and ink sketch out of his attaché case and held it up. "Would you recognise him from this?"

"No," said the hall porter, "that isn't a bit like him. What's he been up to anyway?"

"We think he could be a tea leaf," Chesterman said glibly. "Do you think you could spare us a few minutes of your time?"

"Yes, of course." The hall porter stepped to one side and beckoned them into the hall. "I'll put the kettle on," he said. "You wouldn't say no to a cup of tea, would you?"

Gattis picked up his attaché case and followed Chesterman into the flat. He had a feeling that the few minutes would stretch into at least another hour.

*　　　*　　　*

Harper dug the fork into the earth and then straightened up, rubbing his aching back. The garden was big, far too big for Muriel and him to cope with and none of his labour-saving ideas seemed to work. The roses had gone, replaced by a shrubbery, but the weeds had remained, finding a new and formidable ally in the dock which had infiltrated the bed. The dock had spread from the railway cutting at the bottom of the garden, advanced through the line of silver birch trees and wormed its way under the strip of lawn to establish itself amongst the rhododendrons. Impervious to every known brand of weed killer, undeterred by his expensive flame gun, it marched on, stretching its tentacles towards the house.

The house in West Byfleet had cost him five and a half thousand when he bought it in '58 but now it was worth between thirty and thirty-five and, with the way inflation was soaring, there was a distinct possibility that it might even fetch fifty thousand when he retired in eight years' time. Of course, the asking price was entirely academic; for all that his wife frequently expressed a desire to live in the country, Harper knew that Muriel would never agree to sell up and leave. Like the dock, her roots were too firmly embedded in West Byfleet and the cottage in Sussex with honeysuckle climbing over the porch was merely a pipe dream, one that was destined never to be fulfilled.

"Cedric." Her voice reached him clearly in the still air and he grabbed the fork hastily. "Cedric, you're wanted on the telephone. It's Matthew Quarry."

Harper averted his face and smiled. After four hours of solid, back-breaking work, this was one occasion when he welcomed an official call from the Permanent Under-Secretary. Leaving the fork where it was, he walked across the lawn with a spritely step, the dull ache suddenly vanishing from his shoulder blades.

"You'd think Matthew would leave you in peace," Muriel said reproachfully, "after all, it is Sunday."

"Yes, it's very tiresome of him." Harper kicked off his shoes and shoved his feet into the pair of carpet slippers that she had thoughtfully placed on the back doorstep. "But you know Matthew – always busy like the proverbial bee."

"You're not thinking of traipsing through the house like that, are you, Cedric?"

"You know me better than that."

Harper stopped, brushed the dirt from his trouser legs, and then went into the study and answered the phone. Moments later there was a loud clatter on the line as Muriel banged the extension down in the kitchen to show her displeasure.

Quarry said, "I suspect I'm not exactly popular with Muriel."

"You are with me," said Harper. "What can I do for you, Matthew?"

"Well, we're hoping that you can tell us what Liddell is doing in London?"

"I'm afraid I forgot to ask."

"You've seen him then?"

From the tone of his voice it was obvious that Quarry didn't expect him to deny it.

"He came to my office on Friday. It was just a social call. Gordon and I are old friends."

"He didn't express an interest in Mills by any chance?"

"Who?"

"Edward James Mills, the former SIS man."

"Oh, that Mills," Harper said airily. "Good heavens, Matthew, why should Gordon be interested in him?"

Quarry hummed and hawed, the wind taken out of his sails. "It would seem that we've been misinformed," he said lamely.

Harper noticed that he was using the royal 'we' again, the second time in as many minutes. It was one of his less endearing mannerisms.

"Yes, I think you have."

"A word of advice might not come amiss, Cedric."

"There's always that possibility," Harper conceded gracefully.

"Don't get involved with Liddell; he could be an embarrassment."

"Oh? In what way?"

"The CIA has been taking a lot of stick in recent weeks. Surely you must have read some of the exposés that have appeared in the newspapers?"

"I seem to recall some journalist naming their top man in Athens."

"Quite – and look what happened to him – he was assassinated. God forbid that that sort of thing should happen in London but one can't be too sure these days."

"No, I suppose one can't."

"What I'm really trying to say is that we don't want the CIA conducting any of their clandestine operations in this country."

"I take your point, Matthew."

"Good. I know I can rely on you to be discreet."

Harper slowly replaced the telephone, unsure whether Quarry's final remark had been an expression of confidence or a veiled warning that he was skating on thin ice. The Home Office would obviously know that Liddell was in town but he wondered why Quarry should connect the purpose of the CIA man's visit with Mills.

*   *   *

Mills raised himself up on one elbow and, craning his neck, gazed at the window. The night sky was now a dark velvet tinged with the ambient light of the stars and a dying moon in the last quarter of life. They had deprived him of his wristwatch, a move that was intended to disorientate his sense of time, but the pangs of hunger were a reliable guide and while the view could still be a fake, he reckoned it was somewhere between ten thirty and midnight. Swinging both feet on to the floor, he sat up and then, cradling his head, groaned loudly and rocked backwards and forwards as if in pain, continuing an act that had started with his refusal of the supper meal.

He wished he'd thought to steal a piece of soap from the washroom; the opportunity to do so had been there but the idea hadn't occurred to him at the time. Swallowing a mouthful of carbolic soap would have been unpleasant but it would have lent substance to the act, raising his temperature until his body was bathed in sweat. Lacking this refinement, Mills relied on sound effects and kept his face hidden from the concealed eye of the TV camera which he believed was mounted in the ceiling behind the heavy glass dome protecting the light bulb.

In the studio farther down the corridor, Drew stubbed out his cigarette and glared at the monitor screen. Mills was bent double now, both arms hugging his chest and stomach as if trying to relieve a pain that was stabbing through his body. The tall, lanky constable with the sallow complexion left his chair in the corner and moved towards Drew, leaning over his shoulder to take a closer look at the picture on the screen.

"I don't like it." His tone was suitably morose, lending weight to a sketchy diagnosis. "He looks pretty bad to me."

"He could be putting it on."

"No, he's got all the symptoms of appendicitis." The constable picked his teeth with a fingernail, trying to remove a sliver of meat that was wedged in a gap between the front incisors. "I should know, my old man died of peritonitis while they were rushing him to hospital."

"I still think he's play acting," Drew said obstinately.

"Well, if you want to stick your neck out, it's no skin off my nose, but Mr Harper will be down on you like a ton of bricks if he snuffs it."

"You've got too vivid an imagination, that's your trouble."

The constable looked at the sliver of meat under the little fingernail and grunted. "Maybe I have, but in your shoes I'd call a doctor. There's one in Goring-on-Thames we've used before who can be trusted to keep his mouth shut."

"There's nothing wrong with Mills."

Feeling in need of another cigarette, Drew was about to reach for the packet of John Player Special when Mills suddenly collapsed and pitched forward, striking his head against the floor before rolling over on to his left side. For some moments he lay there in a semi-foetal position, his back to the camera, and then he pushed himself up and started crawling towards the door on all fours.

"Shit," said the constable, "that does it; I'm calling the quack."

"Like hell you are." Drew grabbed his wrist and pulled it away from the telephone. "We're going to take a look at him first. I want to see if he's sweating because I don't trust that bastard."

"Now who's got a vivid imagination?"

Drew snapped his fingers and opened the palm of his right hand. "Your truncheon," he said, "let's have it."

"What for?"

"Because you're going in first and I don't intend to be caught with my trousers down."

Mills heard their footsteps in the corridor and crouched lower, leaning forward over his supporting fingertips, his legs angled and braced like a sprinter pushing against the starting blocks. A key turned in the lock, the bolt was drawn and then the door started to open, swinging outwards and away from him. There was no finesse, he merely came at them fast, his right shoulder catching the door to smash it into the uniformed policeman who staggered back, the blood spurting from his broken nose.

Unsighted until that moment, Drew lashed out with the truncheon and missed. A split second later, Mills bored into his stomach and his feet left the ground. The impact had knocked the breath from his body, leaving him winded and helpless, and then his back struck the concrete wall with a sickening thud and the night stick slipped from his grasp.

Mills scrambled to his feet and turned to face the other man, jabbing him in the kidneys as he stood there still nursing his shattered nose in both hands. The scream began on a high note but dropped several octaves as the police constable sank down on to his knees and then slowly keeled over on to his left side, the bile dribbling through his open mouth. Jumping over his body, Mills raced down the corridor, heading for the stairwell.

There was only one security guard on duty in a cubby-hole off the hall above, and he was curled up in an armchair, his attention evenly divided between a play on TV and the *News of the World*. The play wasn't very enthralling but he had it on loud enough to wake the dead. By the time it occurred to him to wonder why anybody should be running through the hall like a greyhound after a hare, Mills had already reached the front door and was unbolting it. Alerted by a sharp clunk as the last bolt was drawn back, he leapt out of the chair and ran into the hall. There were standing orders which covered just this sort of emergency and he followed them to the letter. Opening the dummy fuse box on the wall outside the morning room, he pressed the alarm bell inside and then went after Mills.

Avoiding the gravel drive, Mills turned left on leaving the house and raced across the lawn in his stockinged feet. The element of surprise which had worked in his favour was now gone and he knew it was vital to get well clear of the house and grounds before the opposition could box him in. Attracted by an orange glare of light on the horizon, he changed direction and ran towards it, convinced that somewhere beyond the line of trees in the middle distance, he would find himself on the outskirts of a small town.

Moments later, the wrought-iron gates at the end of the drive were thrown into sharp relief by a battery of arc lamps, and then one of the security guards in the Lodge released the dogs. The Alsatians were eighty pounds of bone and muscle and there were three of them. Schooled to work silently and as a team, they left the pen behind the lodge and fanned out across the lawn. Picking up a scent, their leader suddenly wheeled to the right and loped off into the shadows, gathering speed with every stride.

Mills heard him coming and veered away in the opposite direction. Head lolling from side to side, he pushed himself to the limit and beyond, ignoring the stitch that was lancing into his ribs. Half blinded with sweat, he didn't notice the false crest in front of him and losing the rhythm of his stride on the reverse convex slope, he took off in a low forward dive. Landing awkwardly on his right shoulder, he rolled over twice and then staggered to his feet. He was less than twelve feet from the river when the leading Alsatian came at him like a bullet.

The dog went for his right arm and seized it just below the elbow, his jaws tightening like a vice. Reeling back under the impact, Mills sank down on one knee to steady himself and then, wielding his left arm like a flail, he smashed the Alsatian between the eyes with his clenched fist. Fear and desperation gave him added strength and he hit the animal again and again and again.

Even though stunned, the dog was reluctant to let him go and it was some moments before the vice-like grip began to slacken and he was able to prise the jaws apart and free his arm. Trembling like a leaf, Mills stood up and took a pace forward. A deep-throated snarl warned him not to take another and he froze, standing there like a statue with one foot still in the air, the blood coursing down his arm.

The other Alsatians, one on either side of him, lay on the grass with their teeth bared and their haunches coiled ready to spring. The river was tantalisingly close, just eight maybe nine strides away and he wondered if he could make it in one piece. As if able to read his thoughts, the Alsatian on his left suddenly edged a little nearer, squirming forward on its belly. Ten, twenty yards to the rear, one of the handlers called out, "Stay, Thumper, stay."

"Yes, that's right, Thumper," Mills whispered, "you bloody well stay."

Hardly daring to breathe, he walked slowly towards the bank, pushing one tentative foot in front of the other. Three, four, five paces; the security guards were running hard now and closing in on him from the flanks, but the dogs hadn't moved. Seven, eight; he stepped off the bank on to a muddy shelf and the water came up to his knees. He took another pace and went straight under, his feet eventually touching bottom some fourteen feet below the murky surface.

He came up quickly, like a cork popping from a champagne bottle, coughed the water from his lungs and then, still gasping for breath, struck out for the far bank. He swam lazily, doing just enough to make some headway against the current which was carrying him downstream.

Twenty minutes later, Mills hauled himself out of the river and lay face down in the grass, too exhausted to move another step.

17

THE SODDEN CLOTHING chilled his body rapidly and within a few minutes Mills was shaking as if he'd gone down with a bout of recurring malaria. Although the bleeding had stopped, his right arm was throbbing now and, rolling the sleeve up, he saw that it was already badly bruised and swollen. The Alsatian had missed the main artery but his teeth had gone in deep and the wounds looked ugly. They would have to be cleaned, disinfected and dressed, an obvious but impracticable remedy in the circumstances. As of that moment, his first priority was to find a temporary refuge in case the security guards decided to come after him. A treacherous voice urged him to take another five minutes rest; ignoring it, he struggled to his feet, moving stiffly like a tired old man.

The current had carried him well downstream so that the orange glare of light was farther away than before, a somewhat irrelevant fact seeing that he could scarcely walk into town looking the way he did. As well as tending to his arm, he needed a change of clothing, and that meant breaking into an isolated house. He glanced up at the sky and taking his bearings from the Plough, he decided to go north, following a middle course between the river and the town over to the right.

Leaving the meadow, he picked up a meandering path which led him through a sprawling clump of hawthorn bushes before suddenly petering out in front of a strip of rough pasture land. Beyond it, and running in a straight unbroken line from roughly south to north, was a tall hedgerow. As he drew nearer, Mills could see that somebody had spent a lot of time clipping and trimming the privet into shape. Turning south, he moved towards the river, hoping to find a way round the obstruction that wouldn't involve him in another soaking.

The cabin cruiser was moored in a narrow inlet screened from the river by weeping willows. A rich man's plaything, the boat obviously belonged to the owner of the mock-Tudor house that stood in one and a half acres of inflation-proof real estate with a couple of tennis courts and an outdoor swimming pool. There were no lights showing anywhere in the house, which meant that either the occupants had retired for the night or else nobody was at home. Not that it made any difference either way because he didn't intend to go near the place; any residence that could fetch between two and three hundred thousand on the market was bound to be stiff with burglar alarms and infra-red intruder systems. The launch, however, was a different proposition.

The main cabin was locked, but a search of the engine compartment on the well deck yielded a screwdriver which he assumed the owner must have overlooked since it was lying near the sump in a small patch of grease. The blade forced into the door jamb made an effective jemmy and using the screwdriver as a lever to splinter the mahogany overlay, he was able to spring the lock. The atmosphere below deck was stifling, a sign that no one had been near the boat that day.

Once his eyes became accustomed to the gloom, Mills could see that he was standing in a lavishly furnished saloon which extended some ten feet beyond the flying bridge. A small cocktail bar on the starboard side of a dividing bulkhead immediately caught his eye. The owner had taken the precaution of locking the drink away but the cabinet was only made of three-ply. Breaking through the door was child's play; identifying a bottle of brandy in the dark was a little more difficult because it was hard to tell the difference between Benedictine, Vat 69 and Courvoisier by touch alone. Fortunately, he had a nose for it.

The brandy revived him, sending a warm glow through his stomach and, still clutching the bottle in his left hand, he opened the communicating door in the bulkhead and moved forward, looking for the sleeping accommodation. Of the three cabins in the bows, the one adjoining the well-equipped galley was the largest, having a shower en-suite. It also had everything he needed, from iodine, boracic lint and a reel of adhesive plaster in the medicine cabinet above the wash basin to a roll-neck sweater, jeans and a pair of canvas shoes which had been left in the fitted wardrobe.

Stripping off his sodden clothing, Mills bathed his arm under the tap and then dabbed it with iodine before covering the bites with lint which he taped from wrist to elbow. The bandage was crude but effective and finding a pair of nail scissors, he gripped the reel between his teeth and hacked off the spare adhesive plaster. Ten minutes later, wearing a sweater and a pair of jeans that were several sizes too big for him, he returned to the saloon to think out his next move over a large brandy.

The eight-day clock above the cocktail bar was registering ten fifty-two, a fact which surprised him as he'd thought it was much later than that. He had five hours of darkness then, say four and half to be on the safe side, because first light would begin to show around three thirty in the morning at this time of the year. Two hundred and seventy minutes ought to be time enough for him to walk into town, steal a car and make his way to Elizabeth Eastgate's house in Ravenscourt Park before daybreak. His whole future depended on Elizabeth Eastgate and yet he knew next to nothing about her. All right, so he liked, perhaps even loved Elizabeth, but where did that leave him? After what had happened in the last thirty-six hours, he wasn't so sure that she could be trusted, but when it came to the crunch there was no one else he could turn to for help.

Mills eyed the bottle, wondered if he dare have another drink and thought why not? If the police did stop him, getting breathalysed would be the least of his problems.

*　　　*　　　*

The bubbles grew and multiplied to form an unbroken chain and then, quite suddenly, the milk boiled over on to the ring. Taken by surprise, Harper made a frantic grab for the saucepan and poured what was left into the cup; at least, that had been his intention, but since he had crossed hands like a concert pianist while attempting to turn off the stove at the same time, most of the milk ended up in the saucer. Undeterred by this setback, he drained the saucer into the cup and topped it up with hot water from the tap. Some of the drinking chocolate coagulated and floated to the surface to form something akin to an oil slick, which he attacked with a spoon, mashing it into a paste against the rim until

163

it was thin enough to disolve. Harper was not the most domesticated of men but he always insisted on making a hot drink for Muriel last thing at night and he knew she appreciated the thought.

Cup and saucer in hand, he left the kitchen and turned off the fluorescent lighting from the switch in the hall before closing the door behind him. He had one foot on the bottom stair when the telephone rang in the study. It was the green one, not the black, and that meant trouble.

Drew sounded breathless and in pain, as if he'd broken even time for the hundred metres dash and half killed himself in the process.

He said, "I'm afraid we've got a problem. Mills has broken out and fled the coop."

It was the sort of bald statement that raised a whole shopping list of questions but, as of that moment, there was only one that mattered.

"When did this happen?" Harper asked quietly.

"About forty minutes ago. There was some damage – one of the security guards has a busted nose, my back feels as if it's been snapped in two and we've got one very sick Alsatian on our hands."

"And Mills?"

"He made it across the river after the dog took a lump out of him. I suppose I could have sent an unmarked car into Goring-on-Thames on the offchance that we could lift him before he was nicked by the police, but it seemed to me that we were in enough trouble with the law as it was. I've already put the carpenters and decorators to work altering the lay-out of the basement, but you may have other ideas?"

Whatever his faults, Drew was no fool and he'd kept his head where others might have lost their cool and combed the town for Mills, risking a head-on collision with the police. As far as he could see, Drew had things pretty well in hand. By the time the workmen finished, the washroom would be sealed off behind a false wall, while the rest of the basement would be transformed into a record office, each cell in the detention block becoming a strong room for the more confidential documents. The papers were genuine but years out of date, data no longer required by the Central Statistical Office but which the Department had acquired for just such an emergency as this.

"What have you done about the extra clerical staff?"

"Nothing," said Drew. "I thought we could play it by ear depending on how the situation develops. I've been on to the motor pool and a removal van should be here within the hour to switch the furniture over. It'll be a race against time but I reckon we can change all the rooms upstairs into offices by eight thirty tomorrow morning."

"Good."

"What about Miss Eastgate? Does she have the telephone number of this place?"

"She does, but you don't have to worry about her. She's in this right up to her neck, and she won't cause any trouble."

"Thank God for that," said Drew.

"The tapes . . ."

"What about them?"

"I want them on my desk first thing in the morning. We've got to salvage what we can from this operation."

"Right." Drew cleared his throat with a nervous cough. "Nothing like this has ever happened to us before and it's largely my fault. I let Mills take me for a ride."

"He took us all for a ride but this isn't the time to hold a post-mortem."

"No, I guess it isn't."

"I think you've done a good job."

"What?"

"In tidying things up."

Harper replaced the receiver and leaned back in the chair. The ache between his shoulders had returned, but it was purely psychosomatic, unconnected with the hours he'd spent digging over the garden. He had compared Mills to a hand grenade, a lethal but inanimate object, something to be stripped, cleaned and primed for use. Well, they had tried to do just that, only now the pin had been withdrawn inadvertently to release the safety lever, and the fuse was smoking, burning down to the fulminate of mercury detonator, only four seconds away from the inevitable explosion. Of course they had longer than four seconds in which to do something to minimise the damage but he doubted if they could avoid all the fragments.

Mills would probably get in touch with Elizabeth Eastgate, might even use her as a go-between if he decided to bring pressure to bear on the Department. Perhaps in the circumstances, it might be wise to re-establish contact with her. Harper mulled it over for several minutes and then reached for the black telephone. By the time he had finished talking to Elizabeth Eastgate, the drinking chocolate was stone cold.

*   *   *

Mills found himself a car in the small council estate on the outskirts of Goring-on-Thames. A 'C' registration Ford Cortina, it was parked in the road opposite one of the pre-war semi-detacheds that had been built without provision being made for a garage. The nearest lamp standard was a good twenty yards away and since nearly every house in the street was in darkness, he thought it safe to assume that most of the neighbourhood were already in bed.

Satisfied that nobody was watching, Mills jammed the screwdriver into the quarter light and prised it open. Reach-inside, he tripped the lock and withdrawing his arm, opened the door. The bonnet release catch was under the facia to the right of the steering column and he gave it a gentle tug, hoping the cable wouldn't twang. The catch yielded with a dull clunk which, to his sensitive ears, sounded loud enough to wake the whole street. He fully expected to hear the angry owner shouting at him from an upstairs bedroom window at any moment, but nothing happened. Setting the choke, he moved round to the front and raised the bonnet. He had an ample length of wire to bypass the ignition circuit in the plug lead he'd also stolen from the cabin cruiser but there were any number of things that could go wrong at this juncture. The starter motor could jam, the carburettor flood or there could be such a hole in the exhaust silencer that the Cortina would fire into life with a deep-throated snarl like a Formula One Ferrari. Holding his breath, he pressed the starter solenoid.

The engine behaved itself perfectly, catching first time to tick over silently. Anxious to get the hell out of it while his luck still held, Mills closed the bonnet and scrambled into the car. The clutch wasn't all that hot and there was a slight grating noise as he shifted into gear but it wasn't anything to get alarmed about. Resisting the impulse to jam his foot down on the accelerator, Mills pulled away from the kerb and drove off, keeping to the thirty-mile-an-hour speed limit until he was clear of the town.

The M4 was no distance away but, remembering what Boxall had once told him, he avoided it; the motorway was fine for high speed driving but not if you had the police on your tail: it didn't matter a damn if you left them standing because they could radio ahead and have every exit blocked. At least, that was Boxall's opinion and Mills thought he ought to know since he'd been one of the best wheelmen in the business.

Sticking to the minor roads until he was beyond Reading, Mills eventually picked up the A4 Trunk and followed it into London.

*   *   *

Sunday had been a day of rest for most people but not for the forensic experts of the Hertfordshire Regional Crime Squad or the pathologist who'd worked late into the night to complete the PM. That it had been impossible to fix the time of death with any degree of certainty was explained in a preamble to the autopsy report, which stated that the normal process of decomposition had been artificially stimulated. If the time of death was uncertain, the cause wasn't; two small calibre bullets fired into the back of the skull from close range had exited below the right eye within half an inch of each other.

Under the heading of physical characteristics, it was noted that the deceased weighed approximately one hundred and fifty pounds, had brown eyes and light brown hair and was five ten and a half. There were no visible distinguishing marks but an examination of the mouth showed that two molars were missing from the upper jaw and one incisor from the lower. Both hands were badly decomposed but the forensic experts had been able to lift a palm print from the right hand, a job that called for a light touch and a strong stomach. In accordance with normal police procedures, the print had been sent to Scotland Yard in the hope that CRO could establish the identity of the deceased.

18

MILLS LEFT THE A4 at the Brentford Market roundabout and turned into Chiswick High Road, a decision that was largely based on an instinctive feeling that the trunk route would take him too far to the south. For a few uncomfortable minutes it looked as if his bump of direction had let him down but then, in the beam from the headlights, he caught a glimpse of a directional sign which pointed the way to the Underground at Chiswick Park and he knew that he was running parallel with the Piccadilly and District Lines. Half a mile beyond Stamford Bridge Station, he pulled into an open air car park behind the main shopping arcade and deliberately stalled the engine.

The neighbourhood was dead, which was a positive advantage provided he didn't have the bad luck to bump into the fuzz because they were bound to take an interest in anyone out walking the streets at three o'clock in the morning. They would take an even harder line if they found him in possession of a tool that could be used for breaking and entering. Weighing the screwdriver in his hand, Mills debated whether or not to leave it behind; after some hesitation, he decided it wouldn't make any difference, the police would probably take one look at his appearance and stop him for questioning anyway. Abandoning the Cortina in the car park, he walked towards the railway arches at the bottom of Hamlet Gardens.

Practically every B and E man he'd met in prison had maintained that getting caught in the act was simply a matter of bad luck, of being in the wrong place at the wrong time. With their chronic shortage of manpower, the police couldn't be everywhere at once and it was an accepted fact that more often than not, they reacted to rather than prevented a crime. It was a comforting hypothesis and one that was founded on a large grain of truth but it didn't stop Mills from feeling apprehensive.

Turning right at the T junction with Westcroft Road, he began to feel a little easier when he realised that the Royal Masonic Hospital in Ravenscourt Park was just around the corner. The park would have offered a short cut but since the gates were locked, he was forced to go the long way round via an alley below the railway embankment as far as Ravenscourt Road which eventually joined Frogmore Gardens on the far side of the recreation ground.

The MGB was parked outside the house, which was a relief because he hadn't the faintest idea what he would have done if Elizabeth hadn't been at home. Opening the front gate quietly, he walked across the lawn and sticking close to the overgrown privet, edged towards the kitchen. Some instinct made him try the back door before ringing the bell and contrary to expectation, he found she had forgotten to lock it. Or so he thought.

He had almost reached the hall when a flashlight played on his face and his heart skipped a beat.

A very composed Elizabeth Eastgate said, "Hullo, Edward, I've been expecting you."

Mills raised a hand, shielding his eyes from the glare. "You and how many others?" he asked angrily.

"I'm alone."

"I'm glad to hear it. Now suppose you put that damned light out."

"I'm sorry." The beam moved away and picked out the kitchen table. "There's a chair behind you," she said. "Why don't you sit down?"

The note of concern in her voice was indicative of something and he had a feeling that Elizabeth was about to offer him a piece of gratuitous advice.

"You look tired, Edward."

"I feel it."

Pulling a chair out from the table, he sat down and leaned forward resting both arms on his knees. As if satisfied that he was going to be reasonable, she suddenly switched off the torch and settled back in the fireside chair near the solid fuel boiler.

"Harper has been in touch with you, hasn't he?"

"Yes, he wants to help you."

"Save you breath," he said harshly, "I'm not interested in what Harper has to say, he's just out to save his own skin."

"And yours too."

"What are you, his glove puppet?" Mills shook his head. "I've got to hand it to you Elizabeth, that was some performance you gave on Saturday. You really convinced me that I was going to be charged with murder."

"I did what I thought was best for you. I don't like his methods but I'm positive Harper is the only man who can help you."

Elizabeth might be an intelligent young woman but Harper had obviously been plausible enough to pull the wool over her eyes. Although tempted to enlighten her, to make her understand that you couldn't trust men like Harper, he knew that he would only be banging his head against a brick wall. Elizabeth simply had no conception of the sort of people he was up against.

"I can guess what you've been through, Edward."

"I wonder if you can."

"Mr Harper was very frank."

"Then he's a lot more cunning than I thought he was."

"And that's precisely why you need him. Look, why don't you call him later, after you've had a rest? I've got his telephone number."

"No."

"But you've got to trust him, Edward." Her voice was low but insistent. "Can't you see that you've no alternative? I very much doubt if the police will believe one word of your story."

"Have they been here asking for me?"

"No, not yet."

Anticipating how the opposition would react was always something of a hit or miss business. His whole thinking had been based on the erroneous proposition that once CID were satisfied that he wasn't in Glasgow, they would naturally assume that he'd turned to Elizabeth Eastgate for help. With his record, however, it made sense from their point of view to sort through everyone who'd ever done time with him. Only when that line of enquiry had been exhausted would they look to the staff of Wells, Bull and Dixon. Even so, they would be obliged to tread warily until they could prove that Elizabeth had been in contact with him after the Gilchrists had been murdered. The Cortina? His fingerprints were all over it, but the car could lie there in the parking lot for weeks before the police found it. Weighing it up, Mills came to the conclusion that he would be reasonably safe in Frogmore Gardens for a day or two.

"I need time to think," he said. "Can I stay here until I get things sorted out?"

"Of course you may. The bed's still made up in the spare room."

"I don't have any money."

He supposed he must have sounded apologetic because she laughed, apparently seeing the funny side of it.

"That's no problem," she spluttered, "I won't charge you for board and lodging."

"Could you lend me a hundred?"

"A hundred?" Suddenly she was serious again.

"This sweater feels as if it's crawling. I'd like a complete change of clothing from head to foot."

"Yes, I should have thought of that."

It was much lighter now and he could see her clearly, a slim figure sitting upright in the chair, one leg crossed over the other, the housecoat parting at the knee to show a pale blue nightdress. A thumb crept to her mouth and she nibbled at the nail, an unconscious habit that told him she was puzzled.

"I'm stock size so you should be able to get everything off the peg from Marks and Spencers."

"Yes. I'll go to the bank in my lunch hour."

The response was automatic, a smokescreen to hide what she was really thinking. Possibly, it had already occurred to her that a hundred was more than enough for a change of clothes and she was wondering what he intended to do with the rest of the money. If her womanly intuition was really sparking on all six cylinders, she might even guess that he was aiming to buy a one way air ticket to Dublin. Dublin was as good a refuge as any and you didn't need a passport to get there. Not that it made any difference, because the ball was in her court and she could play it any way she liked and there wasn't a damn thing he could do about it.

"What's the matter, Edward?"

"Matter?" he said blankly.

"With your right arm, you're nursing it."

171

"One of the guard dogs sank his teeth into it." Her eyes widened and she stared at him, her lips parted as if she had difficulty in breathing. "Didn't Harper tell you?"

"No, he did not."

"That doesn't surprise me."

There was a moment of total incredulity and then she was at his side, gently rolling the sweater above the elbow. From the stains on the bandage, the arm had evidently been bleeding again.

"Let me take a look at it, Edward."

"It's nothing."

"You're an awful liar," she said. "Let me see it, please; it might be infected. I promise to be careful."

It was obvious that she wouldn't take no for an answer but moments after giving way, Mills knew that he'd made a big mistake. Elizabeth Eastgate was careful, all too careful; instead of ripping the bandage off in one merciful go, she unwound the adhesive plaster a bit at a time, dragging the hairs out. Removing the boracic lint, she took one look at the pus on the dressing and caught her breath.

"I'm going to phone my doctor."

"No."

"Don't be silly, Edward. I know you've got a stiff upper lip, you don't have to prove it to me."

"You're not thinking straight." Mills clutched her wrist. "Call him and we'll be asking for trouble."

She was quick on the uptake and saw at once what he was getting at. "I'll bathe it then."

"Yes, do that."

Her face was only a few inches away and leaning forward, he kissed her gently. One eyebrow rose quizzically as if she was more amused than offended and then, just as he was about to mumble an apology, she closed her mouth on his, her lips parting to return the kiss.

*   *   *

Harper glanced at the tapes which Drew had stacked on his desk and wondered if he was going to run into the same kind of trouble that had finally defeated Nixon and forced him out of office. The storm clouds hadn't gathered yet and there was still time to prevent a minor Watergate, but he was curiously reluctant to have the tapes wiped clean. However illogical it might seem, he couldn't help feeling that their destruction would be tantamount to admitting defeat and he was not the sort of man to throw in the towel when things got a little rough.

Ingold, Quarry or Thurston? It had to be one of those three. And somehow they would have to be pressured until the man he wanted lost his nerve and made a false move. It was a sound idea but one that was difficult to execute because he didn't have a scrap of evidence to put before his Minister. If he could only lay his hands on some damning piece of information from an independent source, it would be a different story. It needn't be precise, any inference that one of these men had consistently acted against the best interests of Her Majesty's Government over the past fifteen years or so would be enough to set the wheels in motion.

Harper glanced at the spools again and frowned. With a little bit of plumbing, Mills could be that independent source. It was an idea he'd floated before and then rejected because it was too risky, but now he'd run out of options and there was no alternative.

"These tapes," he said abruptly, "I want them doctored."

Drew sat up, arms akimbo to support his aching back. "In what way?" he asked.

"I want you to remove our voices; yours, mine, Iain's and Harry Vincent's so that only Mills is left. When they're edited, each tape should then be handed to Miss Nightingale because once we've got a transcript, we can make certain revisions that will enable us to splice the tapes to produce a coherent statement from Mills."

"You hope."

"It's almost a quarter past nine," Harper observed mildly, "so I'll expect the edited tapes and the transcript on my desk in three hours from now."

Harper waited until Drew had left the office and then called the printing section on the intercom. Gift wrapping often helped to sell a product and in this case, half the battle would be won if he could prove that the doctored tapes had reached him through the post. With some justification, he had every confidence that the forgers could produce a crumpled piece of brown paper complete with franked postage stamps which would show that the parcel had been

173

addressed to the Department of Subversive Warfare by Mills.

*   *   *

Gattis compared the Identikit pictures of Ormerod with the likeness in the Northern Ireland Wanted File and decided it might be prudent to get a second opinion before he saw Harper. Lifting the receiver, he rang the switchboard at New Scotland Yard and asked for Extension 331.

Chesterman answered the call and recognising his voice, said, "All right, Iain, what is it this time?"

"Ormerod."

"Whose version? Pavlichenko's or the hall porter's?"

"You can scrub Larissa Fedorovna Pavlichenko."

"I'd be glad to," said Chesterman, "any time she's ready, willing and available."

"Do you want an excuse to see her again?"

"What do you think?"

"I think you should look up my DSW oblique stroke NI oblique stroke seven six of the twenty-third of January."

Chesterman sighed, muttered something about "bloody riddles" and laid down the receiver. A few moments later, Gattis heard him wrestling with a filing cabinet, opening first one sliding drawer and then another in mounting exasperation. A loud, plaintive voice in the background said, "For Christ's sake, George, let's have a little less noise around here, some of us are trying to work." Chesterman told the owner of the voice to get stuffed and picked up the phone again.

"You're a bright specimen," he said testily, "you might have told me it was a covering letter. If you'd been a bit more explicit, I'd have gone straight to the Rogue's Gallery."

"Sorry, George."

"So am I. Anyway, what's so special about the Identikit picture you sent us under your DSW oblique what ever it was?"

"Why don't you compare it with the hall porter's description of Ormerod?"

The seconds ticked away and became a minute. After what seemed an eternity to Gattis, Chesterman finally stopped behaving like a Trappist monk and said, "You know something? I think this guy Ormerod is the dead spitting image of Farren, the IRA gunman."

"And we know Cathal Farren and Terence Rooney are inseparable, right?"

"Yes, but why the hell should the IRA be interested in Mills?"

"Wray and Harper . . ."

"What about them?"

"They're the high-priced help," said Gattis, "suppose we let them figure it out."

19

THE HOME OFFICE was only a brisk five-minute walk down Whitehall from the Department of Subversive Warfare, past the Admiralty, Horse Guards, the Treasury and the Foreign and Commonwealth Office. A mere quarter of a mile from door to door and an all too familiar path for Harper who'd lost count of the number of times he'd called on Matthew Quarry in the last three years to exchange information on the IRA Active Service units operating in England. It was usual for them to meet once a week but there had been several occasions, notably in the aftermath of the Birmingham bombings and the attack on Scott's Restaurant, when Harper had virtually lived in the Home Office for days on end.

One of the irritations of being required to work under the direction of the Home Office in matters affecting internal security was the fact that Quarry invariably treated his Department in a somewhat condescending manner. It was especially annoying because the so-called exchange of information was largely one way with most of the hard intelligence being supplied by his Department's undercover surveillance teams stationed in Belfast and Londonderry. Harper smiled to himself thinking how satisfying it would be if Quarry turned out to be the man they were looking for.

Entering the large cathedral-like hall, Harper showed his ID card to the messenger on duty, signed the visitor's book, and was conducted to Quarry's office on the ground floor.

The office had all the trappings appropriate to a Permanent Under-Secretary; a large Victorian mahogany desk, silver pen and ink tray, two leather armchairs, a bookcase, hat stand, velvet curtains in the windows and a fitted Wilton carpet. It was also more spacious and airy than Harper's rabbit hutch, but then Quarry enjoyed a salary of nineteen seven fifty a year and moved in more salubrious circles. A rather small

176

man with a lean Cassius face, he was wearing striped trousers, white shirt with detachable starched collar and the inevitable club tie. Outwardly courteous, Quarry greeted him with a superficial smile that flashed on and off like an electric light, and invited him to sit down.

"I understand you wish to see me on a matter of some importance, Cedric."

Quarry hadn't used the royal 'we' but his manner was no less regal for all that. Repressing a faint smile, Harper opened his Gladstone-style briefcase and extracted a large buff-coloured envelope which he placed on the desk.

"I thought you might be interested to see the enclosed transparencies."

Quarry reached for his paperknife, a Queen Anne piece of silver that was more decorative than functional, and then found that the flap had not been sealed down.

"Cathal Farren and Terence Rooney." He looked up with an irritated frown. "Aren't these the very same Identikit pictures you forwarded to Special Branch some four months ago?"

"Not quite; the one of Farren is more up to date. It was completed with the help of a witness who reported seeing him in London."

"When was this?" Quarry asked sharply.

"Yesterday."

"It was probably a false sighting. In May, he was rumoured to be in Amsterdam buying arms for the IRA."

"My information comes from an unimpeachable source," Harper said calmly. "Larissa Fedorovna Pavlichenko."

"I would hesitate to describe her as an unimpeachable source."

"Farren is posing as a police officer under the name of Ormerod. He told Pavlichenko that he was with the CID of 'V' Division and was anxious to trace Edward Mills."

Watching the expression of incredulity on his face, Harper knew that his distorted and embroidered version had shaken Quarry to the core. It would be a different story, however, once Quarry recovered his poise and he thought it best to pre-empt some of the more awkward questions with a glib explanation, one that did not involve the CIA.

"It's just as well we did look her up when she arrived in London last Thursday." Harper smiled. "I mean, if Gattis hadn't left his telephone number with Pavlichenko, this information might never have come into our hands. It really was a stroke of pure luck."

"You're being unduly modest, Cedric."

"Well, it makes a change, doesn't it?" Harper said affably.

Quarry picked up one of the transparencies and held it at arm's length as if long-sighted. "I take it you've been in touch with Special Branch?"

"I've spoken to Chief Superintendent Wray."

"And what does he think?"

"He's just as puzzled as I am. Neither of us can understand why Farren should be interested in Mills." He lied effortlessly and without any qualms. Experience had taught Harper that the best way to handle Quarry was to plant the germ of an idea in his head and then leave him to develop it.

"Farren is alleged to have said that he was from 'V' Division?"

"That's correct."

Quarry placed the Identikit picture on one side and clasped his hands together, the index fingers forming a church steeple. "It is possible that there might be a connection."

"A connection?" Harper contrived to appear bewildered.

"With the Wimbledon murders."

"Ah yes, Wray was thinking on much the same lines. As a matter of fact, he implied that he might take a run out to Kingston on Thames."

Wray hadn't inferred anything of the kind and it had taken all of Harper's considerable powers of persuasion to convince him that he should have a word with 'V' Division. At this moment, all being well, he ought to be closeted with the Detective Chief Superintendent trying to make the hard sell.

"What about Rooney?"

"We don't have a line on him but it's pretty safe to assume that he's still working with Farren."

"Yes, they've been together for a long time."

"Quite." Harper avoided looking at Quarry and gazed at the heavy velvet drapes in the window instead. "We were wondering . . ." he said hesitantly.

"What?"

"Well, I know it's rather unorthodox, but both Wray and I feel that we should consider releasing their Identikit pictures

178

to the Press. We believe they might well panic and come out of hiding if they were splashed in the newspapers."

"I'm not sure the Director of Public Prosecutions would approve." Quarry rubbed his hands together as if washing them under a tap. "Still, I suppose I could consult our legal department."

"That might be an idea," Harper said quietly.

"Of course, one would also have to seek the advice of 'V' Division."

"And if the police have no objections?"

"Then we'll take the Press into our confidence."

Harper nodded and rose to his feet. "Thank you, Matthew," he said deferentially, "I'm sorry to have taken up so much of your time."

"Not at all, Cedric; it's always a pleasure to see you." Quarry's handshake was firm and the electric smile came on again. "Do remember us both to Muriel; it's ages since we saw her."

"You must come and have dinner with us sometime; I'll get Muriel to drop Pauline a line."

"Patricia," Quarry said firmly.

"Patricia, yes, of course." Harper snapped his fingers. "How stupid of me, I'll be forgetting my own name soon."

"You haven't asked me when their pictures will appear in the newspapers either."

"Oh no, so I haven't, but it's not a decision I can take, is it?"

The fencing match had entered a new phase and Harper had an uncomfortable feeling that he had lost the initiative and that Quarry was pressing him, trying to find a way to slip the foil past his guard.

"No, the ball is with CID."

Quarry placed a hand on his shoulder and he felt himself being gently steered towards the door.

"However, you can rest assured that they will make the front page tomorrow."

The hand squeezed his shoulder in a gesture that was not exactly friendly.

"Now you can do me a favour, Cedric. When you see Liddell again, tell him to keep his nose clean while he's over here."

"I'll be only too happy to oblige," Harper said casually,

"provided you can tell me where to find him, Matthew."

The riposte wasn't up to his usual standard but for once, Quarry's parting shot had caught him flat-footed.

*   *   *

The sun was always there shining in through the curtains no matter which way he turned in bed; unable to ignore it any longer, Mills gave up the unequal struggle and reluctantly opened his eyes. The note had been propped against the alarm clock on the bedside table where it was only a few inches from his nose but, even so, it was some moments before he noticed it. Written in a bold hand with plenty of flourishes and exclamation marks, it read 'Back at six! Eggs and bacon in fridge! Use non stick pan on top of the gas stove and you should be all right! Love E.' Rolling out of bed, he pulled on the pair of blue jeans that he'd left draped over the chair and then opened the curtains.

The car caught his eye immediately. A blue 1960 Vauxhall Victor on its last legs, it had obviously been dumped some time during the night in the alleyway beyond the fence at the bottom of the garden. No doubt the previous owner had figured it would remain there for several weeks before anybody thought to contact the local council, but if so, he hadn't reckoned with the woman in the flowered apron. Looking at her more closely, Mills could understand why the Town Hall had responded with such alacrity; if appearances were anything to go by, she was the sort of belligerent woman who could nag the hind leg off a donkey and still have breath to spare. He pitied the council workman who had his head inside the engine compartment looking for a serial number, because you didn't have to be a lip reader to guess that she was giving him a piece of her mind.

A council workman in dark blue trousers and a light blue shirt? Mills backed away from the window a split second before the disgruntled police constable surfaced from beneath the bonnet. Grabbing the roll neck sweater from the chair, he retreated into the bathroom. What was it Boxall had said? You can plan as much as you like but in the end it all depends on the element of chance; if the fuzz happens to be in the wrong place at the wrong time, you've got yourself a spell of free board and lodging. Well, he could think of one policeman who'd come close to being in the wrong place at the wrong time and all because some damned woman was determined that nobody was going to leave a heap of junk at the bottom of her garden and get away with it.

Mills picked up the tiny battery-operated lady's razor that was lying on the glass shelf and tried it out on his face. A Vauxhall Victor, dark blue like the one in the alley; he stared at his reflection in the mirror, recollecting the early summer of '62 when he was home on leave from Bonn. Janet Rayner had borrowed the Victor from a girlfriend and they had driven up to Cambridge on the Saturday to attend some college ball, spending the night at the Blue Boar before returning to London on the Sunday via Saffron Walden. They had stopped for lunch at a pub and had then turned off the main road to follow a meandering route through Rodwinter and Great Samford and were just about a mile from Fitchingfield when it had dawned on him that the offside rear tyre was flat. He'd just got the car jacked up when the rain storm had hit them and they had sat there in the Vauxhall waiting for the downpour to stop. Suddenly Janet had pointed to a thatched cottage across the fields on their left and had said something to the effect that they could always ask 'the high priest' to put them up for the night. When he had asked who that might be, she had seemed surprised that he didn't know it was a nickname for Giles Thurston around the Foreign Office.

He switched off the razor, filled the basin with water and then washed, using his hands in lieu of a face flannel. Giles Thurston, a name that Harper had dropped into their conversation, a name that had failed to strike a chord until now. Mills thought it was curious how the mind suddenly recalled some long-forgotten and quite inconsequential incident. Drying his hands and face on the towel, he slipped the sweater on over his head and went downstairs.

The Daily Telegraph was lying on the kitchen table and it was obvious that Elizabeth had read it over breakfast because the paper was inside out and back to front. He noticed without surprise that the Wimbledon murders appeared to have dropped out of the news for the time being but there was a small paragraph at the foot of page one which dealt with another case in Hertfordshire where the body of an unidentified man had been found in a deep freeze.

*　　　*　　　*

181

Compared with the Victorian edifice of Cannon Street Police Station which Wray had known as a young police constable on the beat, 'V' Division at Kingston on Thames was as different as chalk from cheese. Housed in a modern concrete and glass structure that reminded him of an office block, it was boxed in by one-way streets as if, having sited the building near the centre of town, some practical joker had then decided to make it almost inaccessible by car. The reception area downstairs looked as if it had been designed not only to impress the public but also to put them at their ease. Anyone seeing the black, vinyl-upholstered bench seats and low occasional tables along both walls inside the main entrance might well think they'd entered one of the more swish job employment centres by mistake.

Upstairs, however, the accommodation was a good deal more cramped, especially the office of the Detective Chief Superintendent which was little more than a box room with a walk-in cupboard. Considering the telephone hadn't stopped ringing in the past hour and that half the detective force had been in and out of the shoe box on one pretext or another, Wray wondered how he managed to put up with it, let alone keep on top of the job.

"You've caught us at a busy time."

Wray struck a match and re-lit his pipe. "Would you like me to come back when things are less hectic?" he said amicably.

"It's never quiet around here; crime's one of the few growth industries we've got in this country. Still, it's being busy that keeps you going, or so they tell me." The burly Chief Superintendent glanced at the pictures on his desk and grimaced. "You've come up with a bright pair of specimens in these two. Rooney looks young enough to be a choirboy and Farren has the sort of face you'd find reassuring in a secondhand car salesman."

"They're a couple of bastards in anybody's language," Wray said harshly. "They've killed fourteen people between them, seventeen if they did the Gilchrists and Mrs Yelf."

"Where do I find this Russian ballerina that Farren is supposed to have called on?"

"Pavlichenko is staying at the Curzon House in Alford Street off Park Lane. If you're thinking of interviewing her, you'd better see the hall porter too. He bumped into Farren in the lobby and had a few words with him."

"Curzon House, Alford Street." The silver propelling pencil was barely visible in the outsized fist. "I hope you're not giving me a load of bull." He looked up from the scratch pad and smiled at Wray. "Like your Sergeant Johnson did."

Wray shifted on his chair. He might have known he'd not be forgiven easily for the cover-up after Johnson's surveillance job on the Gilchrist house.

"You can always check with the Home Office; they know why I'm here."

"I don't think that's necessary."

It was a nice diplomatic touch and one that didn't mean anything. Minutes after leaving 'V' Division, Wray was prepared to bet that he would be on the phone to the Yard asking his superior to check the story with the Home Office.

"You know something, Stanley? This case is about as straight as a corkscrew. Everything points to Mills – we've got his prints on a bottle of whisky, a glass, the carving knife and the Marina he stole. We know that he threatened Gilchrist because we have his voice on tape, but the pathologist says that Gilchrist was killed by someone who was left handed, and Mills isn't. And now you tell me that Farren is looking for him."

"Well, I'm sorry if I've upset the apple cart."

No apology was called for but Wray contrived to appear suitably contrite.

"You should worry, we'd already lost a wheel off the cart before you showed up. There are too many blanks on Gilchrist's tape for my liking, and that isn't the only thing that bothers me. You see, we know Gilchrist cancelled his wife's appointment at the hairdressers a good twenty minutes before Mills arrived at the house. The girl he spoke to said he sounded very strange, as if he were tensed up and on edge."

The PM report had undoubtedly caused him to have second thoughts, but Wray could name several equally experienced police officers who might have discounted the pathologist's opinion and built their case on the mass of forensic evidence that pointed to Mills. The Chief Superintendent was obviously a shrewd, inquisitive man and a modest one too; tracing Gilchrist's last telephone call had been a fine piece of detective work but he'd refrained from blowing his own trumpet.

"So what are you going to do about Farren and Rooney?"

"After we've talked to Pavlichenko, we'll make house to house enquiries in Wimbledon; you never know, one of the neighbours might have seen them."

"There is one way you could save yourself a lot of trouble," Wray said tentatively.

"By giving their pictures to the newspapers?"

"Well, it's a thought, isn't it?"

"You're a cunning old devil, Stanley, you want us to do your dirty work." His eyes narrowed thoughtfully. "Of course, your people will have to keep an eye on the air and sea ports. I mean, I'd hate these two to slip through our fingers."

"They won't. I'll stake my pension on it."

There was a very long pause before the Chief Superintendent said, "All right, Stanley, we'll play it your way. If nothing else, it might have Farren and Rooney running to the bog."

20

Harper glanced at the cassette which Drew placed on his desk and pursed his lips.

"This is the final version, is it?" he asked.

"I certainly hope so," Drew said with feeling.

"So do I." Harper placed the cassette inside the Philips tape recorder and pushed the control tab forward.

Mills said: 'I'll call him the man in the shadows because it's too early to put a name to him yet, and after all, this is a mystery story. The record shows that I was sentenced to seven years' imprisonment for theft, but that wasn't good enough for him, he wanted to keep me inside until the system had turned me into a harmless vegetable. He didn't have to lift a finger while I was in Albany; I did it all by myself. I went in there with a chip on my shoulder and I wasn't exactly popular with the staff or the other prisoners. But Durham was different, different because I'd learned to keep my nose clean and I had a friend in Sidney Boxall. Does that surprise you, Mr Harper? It should; I got an extra five years for Grievous Bodily Harm but I want you to know that I didn't attack Boxall. Oh, there were a couple of witnesses all right but one happened to be a queer who was easily intimidated while the other was a frightener, a specialist in violence. The queer took to drugs after he was released and died as a result of an overdose. The frightener, who's a handy man with a razor, eventually went to Brazil where he's safe from extradition. And Boxall? Well, he was paid to keep his mouth shut. I don't pretend to know how the man arranged it, but he did. They say every prison is a labyrinth, Mr Harper.'

There was a slight pause and then Mills continued in much the same vein except that his voice was a lot harsher.

'He couldn't touch me while I was in Leicester because I spent most of my time there in hospital with TB so you can bet he wanted to know which way I was going to jump when I came out of prison. If it's possible to be objective, he was brilliant, quite brilliant. He obviously knew that I'd kept in touch with Gilchrist so he decided to turn Morris round and convert him into a sort of double agent, using him to ensure that I accepted the offer of a flat in Moravian Place, a flat that had been bugged by Special Branch. It was a perfect set up; I mean, he knew that even if I wiped the apartment clean, he could still rely on them to keep me under surveillance. Now who do you suppose was in a position to pull all those strings? Somebody like Matthew Quarry, the man who did all the donkey work for the Royal Commission on the future of the SIS? How does that grab you, Mr Harper?'

The final question was delivered in a provocative tone and its impact was such that it was some moments before Harper realised that there was nothing more to come.

"What do you think?" asked Drew.

"It's good," said Harper, "very good. You've repeated some of his sentences word for word while others have been cut up or quoted out of context."

"Yes. I only wish we could lay our hands on some of the bugged material that Special Branch must have in their possession. If we had their tapes, we might be able to put a little more flesh on the bones."

"No, I think it holds up very well as it is, well enough to give it a trial run."

"Oh?" Drew raised an inquisitive eyebrow. "Who are you going to use as a guinea pig then?"

"Ingold. He was with the Government Code and Cipher School at Bletchley Park during the war; one could say that he's forgotten more about the Intelligence game than you and I will ever learn." Harper slipped both arms into the grey single-breasted jacket which he'd left draped over the back of his chair. If anyone wants me in the next hour or so, I'll be at the Institute for Political and Strategic Studies."

*　　　　*　　　　*

Harper thought it wholly appropriate that the Institute for Political and Strategic Studies should be situated in the heart of Bloomsbury, an area well known for its weird bunch of intellectuals. Modest to the point of being coy, the Directing

Staff had settled for a Georgian town house in Gaten Place behind the British Museum, where they were so well off the beaten track that very few taxi drivers were even aware of their existence.

Ingold's office was on the top floor of the building. A chubby, fresh-faced man with an untidy thatch of light brown hair, it was hard to believe that he was only a year away from drawing the old-age pension. A brilliant mathematician, he had been persuaded to leave Cambridge and join the Government Code and Cipher School by Admiral Sir Hugh Sinclair, who immediately despatched him to Bletchley to work on the Heydrich-Enigma coding machine which Alastair Denniston had collected from the Polish Secret Service in Warsaw on the twenty-second of August 1939. Although he'd returned to Cambrige after the war, Ingold had found it impossible to settle down in a humdrum routine again and in the spring of '46, he'd asked Admiral Sinclair to get him a job with the Allied Joint Intelligence Bureau in Occupied Germany. Tracking down Nazi war criminals was a far cry from what he'd been doing at Bletchley but he'd taken to it like a duck to water.

Declared redundant when the Bureau folded up nine years later, he'd retreated to Dorset and renting a cottage on the outskirts of Charmouth, had turned his hand to writing, publishing three books in quick succession based on his experiences in post-war Germany. None of them made the best-seller list but he drew favourable reviews from the critics and building on this, he'd branched out into other literary fields, eventually becoming a regular contributor to *Current Affairs Today*. This, in turn, had led to several appearances on television where he was given the opportunity to air his views on global strategy. Once the politicians recognised that he was an original thinker with a first-class intellect, it was almost inevitable that Ingold would be invited to join the Institute for Political and Strategic Studies.

When Harper walked into his office, Ingold was poring over a huge map of South Africa spread out on a work bench that took up the whole of one wall. Casual to the point of being slovenly, he was wearing a pair of corduroys and a sleeveless sweater over a checked shirt. Although the atmosphere was muggy, the heat didn't seem to bother him. Always charming, he greeted Harper with a warm, friendly smile.

"Hullo, Cedric," he said cheerfully, "how's life been treating you?"

"Very well. And you, Richard?"

"The arthritis in my shoulder has been acting up lately, but one mustn't complain."

Harper leaned against the bench and peered at the map. "What are you working on?"

"A projection for the Government Think Tank." Ingold picked up a ruler and pointed to the northern frontiers. "Angola, Namibia, Botswana and Mozambique," he said crisply, "how long do you think Vorster can hold out against that lot?"

"You tell me."

"Within the next decade there will be majority rule in South Africa and it's in our interest to ensure there's an orderly transition."

"Towards what, Richard? One man one vote?"

"Yes."

"Even if it transpires that it's one man one vote once only?"

Ingold creased his eyes, mildly amused. "I know you're trying to needle me, Cedric, but in my view, once only is preferable to no vote ever."

"I'm afraid there's no answer to that," Harper said amiably. "I'm not a political philosopher, only a plumber who's called in to repair the lavatory cistern when it springs a leak."

"Some of us have to do the thinking, Cedric."

"Well, I'm happy to leave that to you and Giles Thurston. I imagine he asked you to make this projection?"

"Yes, as a matter of fact, he did. Can you imagine what would happen to the world's monetary system if all that gold in South Africa ended up in the wrong hands?'

"I'm not an economist either, but offhand, I'd say we'd all be in the shit." Harper drummed his fingers on the bench. "Of course, Giles Thurston may have other ideas. You were at Cambridge together, weren't you?"

"For a few months, but I didn't know him then. Giles was one of the post-war mature students – an ex-RAF bomber pilot. Spent the last year of the war in a prison camp after he was shot down over Munich." Ingold smiled again. "Still, you haven't come here just for a gossip, have you, Cedric?"

"No. I wanted you to listen to this and then give me your

opinion." Harper reached into his pocket and brought out the cassette. "It's a statement by Edward Mills, the former SIS man who was released from prison last Thursday. He sent it to me through the post and I think it's pretty explosive. Do you have a tape recorder handy?"

"No, but I can get one from the typing pool. Anyway, what's he got to say that hasn't already been said?"

"It's mainly about a man called Boxall."

"Not Sidney Boxall?"

Harper raised his eyebrows in astonishment. "Yes – do you know him then?"

"Only from what I've read in the newspaper." Ingold walked over to his desk to fetch his copy of the *Evening News* that was lying in the pending tray. "There are a few lines in the Stop Press at the bottom of page one. Apparently, his body was found yesterday in a deep freeze by two small boys who were playing in a wood near Ponder's Leap in Hertford-shire. It seems the CRO had his fingerprints on record."

Harper stared at the newspaper, scarcely able to believe his eyes at first, but then it began to dawn on him that the four terse sentences in the Stop Press marked a decisive turning point. Armed with the newspaper and the tape, he could go to the Minister and repeat the allegations that Mills had made. Ask for and get the assistance he wanted from Special Branch.

"I won't be a minute," said Ingold.

"Oh, I don't think we'll need the tape recorder now." Harper scratched his forehead. "I needn't have bothered you, Richard, it's all here in the *Evening News.*"

Quarry, Ingold, Thurston. The Minister wouldn't like it but in the end, he would accept that they'd really no alternative but to put all three under surveillance. Arranging a wire tap behind Quarry's back wouldn't be easy but he would find a way round that problem.

"Well, if there's nothing more I can do for you, Cedric . . ." Ingold said doubtfully.

"As a matter of fact, there is something you can do for me."

"Yes?"

"I'd like to use your telephone – do you mind?"

It was a bit like rubbing salt into an open wound but Harper was quite unrepentant.

*　　　*　　　*

Watching her as she walked through the park towards the house, Mills could see that Elizabeth was tired and listless from the heat. Her shoulders were slumped as if the shopping bags in either hand weighed a ton and she could hardly find the strength to push one foot in front of the other. Overtaken by at least half a dozen other people, a middle-aged man finally took pity on her and, despite smiles of protestation, insisted on carrying the larger of the two bags for the rest of the way. For a moment or so, it seemed he was going to follow Elizabeth up the front path but after opening the front gate for her, he returned the shopping, tipped his hat, and walked off in the opposite direction. Leaving the sitting room, Mills went out into the hall to greet her.

Elizabeth was still fumbling with her key, trying to insert it into the Yale lock, when he opened the door. Caught off balance, she stumbled forward into his arms, the bags slipping from her grasp to land in an untidy heap on the floor. The patterned silk dress clung to her like a sheath and he could feel the softness of her body beneath the thin material. Drawing her closer, he kissed her on the mouth. One high-heeled foot came off the ground and pushed the door shut, cutting them off from the street and the noise of the children playing in the park. Presently, a slim hand pushed against his shoulder and he broke away.

"Hey," she whispered, "I need some air."

"You look as if you could use a cool drink too." He backed off a pace and crouched to retrieve the packages. Silk rustled on bare legs and then she was stooping too, her nose just a few inches from his.

"Sidney Boxall is dead, Edward," she said in a low voice.

"Dead?"

"Murdered." She reached inside the smaller of the two shopping bags and fished out a crumpled newspaper. "There's a small piece here in the *Evening Standard.*" She stood up and moved past him towards the kitchen. "Read it for yourself if you don't believe me. His body was found in a wood near Ponder's Leap."

"Ponder's Leap? He thought the name sounded familiar. Ponder's Leap . . . Ponder's Leap . . . Pond Jump. Yes, that was it – Pond Jump – the absurd codeword Ollenshaw had used for Geneva. He could see the small office now, the cigarette smoke eddying below the ceiling like vapour trails, and the incongruous Pirelli calendar on the wall behind Ollenshaw's desk, the one which showed a well-endowed blonde in tennis gear who looked as if she was about to burst out of the tight shorts and the shirt that was unbuttoned to the waist. Wednesday the fourth of June; the date ringed and his initials enclosed in the circle as if Ollenshaw needed to be reminded about the briefing. And the telephone had interrupted them and Ollenshaw had answered it reluctantly. For how long? Two, maybe three minutes, and then he'd replaced the phone and muttered something about Giles Thurston and the Economic Intelligence Department being in a bit of a tizzy because they'd heard that a new assistant had been assigned to Kiktev.

"You've no reason to run away now, have you?" Her voice reached him faintly from the kitchen.

"No," he said, "no, I'm through with running."

"I'm glad to hear it." She turned to face him as he walked into the room, a box of Bryant and May in one hand, a spent match in the other. The gas was flaring under the kettle and needed adjusting but it was evident she had something far more important on her mind. "Why don't you telephone Mr Harper? I've got his office number."

"I might just do that later."

"Why not now?"

"Because Harper will have to wait his turn."

Mills placed both hands on her shoulders and kissed her again and then her arms hugged him close and her body nuzzled into his. The gas continued to flare, the flames licking up the kettle to blacken the sides.

*   *   *

Farren read the newspaper paragraph again and felt his stomach sink. Moments later his hands began to shake and suddenly losing his temper, he wadded the *Evening Standard* into a tight ball and stuffed it into the kitchen wastebin, trampling it underfoot until the newspaper was buried under the rest of the litter. Surveying the mess, he wished he had put Boxall under six foot of earth instead of leaving him in a deep freeze, because now that the police had put a name to the body, there was no getting round the fact that he and Rooney were at risk. They had come close to the brink when they'd sprung their last ambush in Belfast from the

Divis Flats, but this was worse, much worse. At risk? Farren smiled sardonically; Christ, that was the understatement of the year; they were clinging to a precipice, holding on by their fingertips in the hope that Temple would throw them a lifeline. Feeling in need of a drink, Farren went into the living room and dug out the bottle of Irish whiskey from the sideboard.

The Divis Flats had been a perfect set-up while it lasted. Sandwiched between the Lower Falls and the city centre, it was the biggest low-cost development in Belfast, a huge towering complex that dominated the skyline and housed a population of seven thousand, of whom the vast majority were hard-core Republicans. There was no shortage of volunteers in that place and you could always find somebody who was willing to mind your Armalite after you'd sprung the ambush and needed to leave the area in a hurry. As far as security was concerned, the Divis Flats had been on par with the Bogside in Londonderry, which was why it had been their favourite hunting ground until the September of 1975.

Even now with the benefit of hindsight, Farren still could not understand why that last ambush should have provoked such a very different reaction from all the others. They had killed two members of a foot patrol and wounded a third to surpass their previous best score in a single action, and that was something to be proud of, or so he'd thought at the time. It had never occurred to him that anyone who lived in the Divis Flats would regard that simple act of war as an atrocity, but apparently somebody had. Despite the fact that the operation had been extremely successful and that they'd slipped through the cordon with ease, their pictures had subsequently been plastered all over the city.

In '75 there had been a safe haven waiting for them over the border and any number of sympathisers who were prepared to hide them until it was safe to slip across. Things were different this time however, different because they were on the wrong side of the Irish Sea and Special Branch had an efficient network of spies and informers. Farren swallowed the rest of the whiskey and was about to pour himself another when the telephone rang. Leaving the glass on the sideboard, he walked out into the hall and lifted the receiver off the hook.

Temple said, "I'm on 435-99206; call straight back as soon as I ring off."

Farren replaced the phone slowly. Temple had sounded calm enough but he was using a private number, not a public call box, and that was a bad sign. If security had gone by the board, then the situation was a good deal worse than he'd imagined. Lifting the phone again, he rang the number that Temple had given him. It rang just once and then Temple was on the line.

"It's me," Farren said lamely.

"What kept you?"

"I needed time to think. I mean, things don't look too good at the moment, do they?"

"It's just the tip of the iceberg."

The tip of the iceberg? Farren stared at the wallpaper in front of him. "Do you know something that I don't?"

"I've heard a whisper about a publicity stunt, one that could put you both in the limelight tomorrow."

"Maybe it's time my friend and I took a holiday," Farren said huskily. "They tell me it's easy to get a seat on an Aer Lingus flight these days."

"I think you've been misinformed. According to my travel agent, they're fully booked."

Beads of perspiration gathered on his forehead. Fully booked was Temple's way of saying that Special Branch had already been alerted to cover all the exits.

"However, I can put you in touch with a small air charter firm. Belleview haven't been in business all that long but they're very reliable."

"Where do I find them?" Farren was unable to raise his voice above a whisper.

"About a mile beyond Fitchingfield. I suggest you branch off the A11 before you get to Bishop's Stortford and take the road out to Great Dunmow where you'll find a signpost pointing to the village."

"Belleview near Fitchingfield?"

"That's it," Temple said casually. "Try the back door if you find their office is closed for the lunch hour."

"Thanks for the tip."

"You're welcome."

"Will I be hearing from you again?"

"I doubt it, but we may well find ourselves on the same flight." Temple managed a faint chuckle before he broke the connection but there was no mirth in it.

For the first time in weeks, Farren suddenly felt the need to sleep with a revolver under his pillow. Retrieving the oilskin pouch from the lavatory cistern in the bathroom, he carefully unwrapped it to reveal a .38 Police Positive. Carrying the weapon into the kitchen, he then opened the cupboard under the draining board and took out a packet of Omo. Hidden in the washing powder was a small box containing twenty-four rounds of .38 calibre ammunition.

Some twenty minutes later, and in a much calmer frame of mind, Farren got in touch with Rooney to arrange a suitable RV for the following morning.

21

F ARREN STROLLED INTO the Underground station, collected a ticket from the vending machine in the entrance hall and passing through the barrier, rode the escalator down to the Central Line. He calculated that it would take Rooney roughly five minutes to reach Notting Hill Gate from Gloucester Road on the Inner Circle and, provided he'd left his flat on time, Farren thought he ought to be waiting for him now under the train indicator. Weaving his way down the crowded patform, he spotted Rooney standing near an Indian woman in an orange-coloured sari with a white bodice, and stopping just short of the subway leading to the District Line, he edged into the queue. Glancing to his right, he saw that the distant signal was set at green; moments later, a train rattled out of the tunnel and gradually squealed to a halt.

The compartment was packed, the passengers jammed together like sardines in a tin, and he had to elbow a path through the crush near the automatic doors to find a space in the aisle where he could strap-hang. Conscious of the .38 Police Positive in the hip holster, Farren shielded it with his left arm in case anybody accidentally bumped into him. A stout middle-aged woman who'd been standing behind him on the platform just made it before the doors closed and then the train jerked forward and pulled out of the station.

Gazing about him, Farren could see that Temple hadn't been whistling in the dark. Wherever he looked their Identikit likenesses screamed at him from the front page of *The Sun, The Mirror, The Express, The Mail* and *The Daily Telegraph; The Guardian* and *The Times* weren't quite as vulgar about it but he assumed they would be carrying their pictures too on the inner pages. A total nationwide circulation of what? Twelve to fifteen million copies? Whatever the true figure it was more than enough to cover the entire population of London, more than enough to alert eleven million pairs of eyes. Alert them to what? A couple of dead-pan pictures that bore very little resemblance? They'd got his eyes set too far apart, the nose was wrong and so was the hairstyle. And Rooney's too; they had made his face round as a pudding, just as it had appeared in the original likeness that had been plastered all over Belfast to little or no effect.

Eleven million pairs of eyes on the look out? Not if this compartment was anything to go by. They were just so many doughy faces, so many robots of assorted shapes and sizes; clerks, typists, secretaries, cashiers, book-keepers and shop assistants by the dozen on their way to work and loathing every moment of the journey. Wrapped in their own thoughts, they were either too hot, too down in the mouth, too bored or too insular to pay any attention to those around them. It was a comforting thought to hang on to.

He wondered how Rooney was bearing up in the adjoining coach. Not that there was really any need to worry about him; Rooney was ice cold, devoid of normal emotion and seemingly cut off from all human contact, like an autistic child. He hadn't always been that way. Farren could remember when he'd been so nervous that he couldn't stop shaking, couldn't hold the gun steady in his hand, but that had been a long time ago, before he'd developed a taste for killing. Rooney had reached the point now where it was simply a way of life for him and he no longer needed a motive. Farren doubted if seven years ago he would have killed Boxall without compunction; seven years ago, Rooney would have asked him why it was necessary.

What harm had Boxall ever done them? He'd been a nobody, a wheel man with a long record of previous convictions, but Temple had said that he was the one weak link in the chain and therefore he had to be removed. Easy to say and easy to execute, because right up to the very last moment, the poor slob had been convinced that they were Special Branch officers anxious to protect him from Mills. One telephone call to Ealing Police Station and they had known where to find him. One face to face meeting in a café round the corner from Swiftsure Radio Cabs in the High Street where Boxall was working and the ground had been prepared, the victim primed what to say to his landlady and employer so that no one would think it odd when he finally disappeared.

But there was one man who had thought it odd, and Farren still believed that they should have gone for Mills at the same time and arranged for him to meet with a fatal accident. Temple, however, had ruled it out because he'd been convinced that this was the one course of action that could rebound on him, the one false move that could lead certain people to suspect that there might have been something in what Mills had been saying after all. You didn't cure a malignant tumour by leaving it alone, but Temple had refused to budge and since he was calling the tune, they'd had to go along with him.

A general exodus from the train jerked Farren back to reality. Peering through the window, he read the sign on the platform and was shocked to find that they were at Holborn and not Lancaster Gate as he'd thought. At a time when he needed to have all his wits about him, he had been lost in a dream world and the train had stopped at five intermediate stations without him being aware of it. He glanced at the route map sandwiched between adverts for Bravington rings and Kleenex tissues in the roof panel above the window and tried to work out when they were likely to arrive at Epping on the outskirts of London. Fifteen stops down the line was roughly the equivalent of fifty minutes travelling time, a valid enough calculation in its way except that he knew it didn't solve any of the problems that would be waiting for them at the end of the line. Stealing a car was child's play for Rooney but he had a curious premonition that this was going to be the one occasion when everything went sour on them.

*　　　*　　　*

Using a red chinagraph pencil, Miss Nightingale described a neat circle on the talc overlay and then stepped to one side so that Harper could see that she had ringed the Institute for Political and Strategic Studies to bring the map up to date with the Occurrence Log. In her view, both the large-scale street map of Central London and the 1/500,000 Ordnance Survey of the British Isles were unnecessary embellishments, but Harper liked visual aids and she had been with him long enough to know when it was unwise to voice her opinion.

"I should be grateful to the RAF." Harper flashed her a

warm smile. "They trained you very well. I must say you haven't lost the knack after all these years."

It wasn't the most tactful remark. No woman liked to be reminded of her age, particularly if she was approaching forty, and it was evident from her frosty expression that he had offended her. Jean Nightingale had joined the WAAF straight from school at the age of eighteen shortly before the Suez crisis and had just completed her training as a plotter when Duncan Sandys wielded an axe on Fighter Command. Posted to a Meteor night fighter wing at West Malling, she'd served on until the station was disbanded in '58 and had then taken her discharge.

"I was thirty-eight on my last birthday."

"What?"

"You were counting on your fingers, Mr Harper. I thought I'd save you the trouble of working it out."

The cold front was still there despite the faint smile and he realised that he would have to make it up to her. Lunch at his club in the mixed dining room might do the trick, but this wasn't the time to invite her; he would have to wait for a more propitious moment when the atmosphere was less frigid, otherwise it would seem too obvious.

"Well, I think that covers about everything, doesn't it?" Even to his ears, Harper thought he was overdoing the heartiness.

"Except for Edward Mills."

"What about him?"

"I thought I told you that he telephoned yesterday evening while you were seeing the Minister?"

"Really? I don't remember you mentioning it. Did he leave a message?"

"No, but he said you would know where to reach him."

Her manner suggested she knew he remembered very well and would like to know just why he had done nothing about it. Explanations weren't easy. Possibly he was being unduly suspicious but he wasn't sure he could trust Mills after what had happened at Goring-on-Thames. There were two ways of looking at the phone call; either Mills wanted to know whether the Boxall affair had changed anything or else he'd decided the time was ripe for him to apply a little pressure. Whatever the motive, Harper was damned if he was going to contact Mills just yet.

"I'm sorry. You must think I'm an idiot." Harper shook his head as if vexed with himself. "I really am becoming absent-minded in my old age."

"No, Mr Harper, it's partly my fault. I should have left a memo on your desk."

Harper thought it was typical of Miss Nightingale that she should meet him more than half way. There were any number of efficient secretaries in Whitehall but few possessed her tact and charm and he was the first to admit that he'd be exceptionally lucky to find anyone else who was so long-suffering.

"I'll telephone him later this morning."

"Yes, of course."

Her tone was matter of fact, an acceptance that there were other more urgent problems on his mind than Mills, and that her presence was no longer required. The door closed softly behind her and Harper rested both elbows on the desk, hunching his shoulders as he leaned forward to stare at the chinagraph symbols on the map.

Quarry, Thurston or Ingold? He had hoped in vain for some kind of panic reaction from one of them but they were behaving as if nothing had happened. It was difficult to know what to make of it but either the man in the shadows was playing a game of bluff or else he had an ace up his sleeve in Farren and Rooney. Everything hinged now on Farren's visit to Larissa Fedorovna Pavlichenko. If he had a nose for danger, it could be that both IRA gunmen had already slipped out of the country, in which case they could call off their watchdogs and Special Branch might just as well pack up and go home for all the good they were doing at Heathrow and elsewhere.

Harper pushed the thought out of his mind. Negative thinking only made things worse. The man he wanted had all the characteristics of a mole, an appropriate simile if only because he would remain below ground until the ferrets flushed him out of the burrow. Waiting for him to surface would be a supreme test of patience, but that was what the game was all about. Nobody could hide for ever and when he did come out into the open, he'd find that every bolthole was blocked. Every bolthole? Certainly Special Branch were covering the main air terminals and the sea ports but what about the private flying clubs? Thurston, for instance, was a qualified pilot, and the map showed that there was a small landing ground near his weekend cottage at Fitchingfield. Wray was no fool but there was no harm in marking sure he hadn't overlooked anything.

The telephone rang as he stretched his hand towards it and answering the call, Harper found that he had a very irate American on the line.

Liddell said, "I thought we had a deal?"

"A deal?"

"Don't give me that crap, you know what I'm talking about. Last Friday I walked into your office and gave you three names for openers."

"I haven't forgotten, Gordon."

"No? Well, it seems to me that our agreement is pretty one-sided. I practically serve you Farren on a plate and what do I get in return? Nothing. A great big fat zero. You know something, Cedric, for my money you're the biggest asshole in the business."

"Have you quite finished," Harper said mildly, "or is there more to come?"

"The bell's just gone for the end of round one."

"You need a second, Gordon, someone to fan you with a towel. How would you like to have Edward Mills in your corner?"

The sharp intake of breath and the long silence which followed was predictable, so predictable that Harper could envisage and secretly enjoy the puzzled expression he knew would be on Liddell's face. Although Liddell might suspect that there was an ulterior motive behind the offer, curiosity would finally get the upper hand.

"You must think I was born yesterday."

The obligatory riposte and one that was delivered without conviction.

"I'd rather you didn't prevaricate," Harper said crisply. "Things are hotting up and I want to keep this line open."

Another pause; and Harper counted off the seconds to himself. One, two, three, four five – a long drawn-out sigh that told him that Liddell was ready to throw in the sponge – six, seven, eight, nine . . .

"All right," Liddell said wearily, "how do I find him?"

"He's staying with a Miss Elizabeth Eastgate at 21 Frogmore Gardens."

"Where's that?"

"It's over in Ravenscourt Park. I suggest you buy yourself a copy of *Nicholson's Street Finder.*"

"Thanks for the advice."

"I'll give you one more tip. Be careful how you approach Mills – he could turn nasty."

Harper broke the connection before Liddell had a chance to come back at him. He thought he had good reason to be pleased with himself. At one stroke he'd got Liddell out of his hair and provided Mills with a baby-sitter who'd keep him quiet for the next few hours. Lifting the phone again, he called Wray, anxious to check that Special Branch were keeping an eye on the private flying clubs.

* * *

There were only five people left in Farren's compartment when the train pulled out from Theydon Bois. Glancing to his left as they swayed round a curve, he saw Rooney leave his seat in the adjoining coach and move down the centre aisle. Although Epping Station was still some two minutes off, Farren felt compelled to follow his example and lurching to his feet, he made his way towards the nearest exit. None of the other passengers took the slightest notice of him but then, as far as he was aware, nobody had spared him a second glance right from the moment he'd boarded the train at Notting Hill Gate. Eleven million pairs of eyes? Well, he had news for Special Branch; the Great British Public were all suffering from an advanced case of glaucoma.

The wheel bogies began to lose their fast, rhythmic clatter and a signal gantry passed by the window in slow motion. A harsh grinding noise set his teeth on edge as the vacuum brakes came on, and then moments later the train shuddered to a halt alongside the platform, and the doors opened.

Farren stepped out of the coach, turned to the right and sauntered down the platform at a leisurely pace to ensure that he and Rooney would be at the tail end of the exodus. Surrendering his ticket at the barrier to a disinterested collector, he entered the booking hall where he hovered by the phone booths in the entrance until the last of the passengers had left the station. Ignoring him, Rooney walked into the yard and turned towards the car park.

Stealing a car was not exactly a new experience for them

and over the years, Rooney had acquired a master set of keys which covered the whole range produced by the Ford Motor Company. Usually he stuck to Escorts because they were less conspicuous and had a good turn of speed, but it had not been unknown for him to lift a Granada Ghia Coupé if the colour scheme took his fancy. Farren just hoped that Rooney would steer clear of the de luxe models on this occasion. Counting off the seconds, he waited a full two minutes before walking out into the yard.

The long approach road was deserted and glancing in the opposite direction, he got a thumbs-up sign from Rooney who was standing beside a grey-coloured, two-door Cortina. His lips breaking into a slow smile, Farren went towards him. He was less than fifteen yards from the car when the police constable appeared from behind a Bedford Dormobile. One look at the suspicious expression on his face was enough to tell Farren that they were in trouble. Catching his warning nod, Rooney slowly turned about.

The police constable eyed them warily and instinctively patted the right side of his chest as if seeking reassurance from the Pye radio set clipped to the lapel of his tunic.

"Is that your car?" Although his voice sounded aggressive, it was apparent that he was nervous.

"Yes, it is." Farren grinned at him. "Don't tell me we've forgotten to get a ticket from the machine."

"Do you see one?"

"What?"

"A vending machine."

Farren looked round the car park. "No," he said, "but then we only arrived a few minutes ago."

"Do you mind showing me your driving licence?"

"Shit," said Rooney, "I've had enough of this. Why don't you let him see your warrant card?"

"You're both police officers?"

It was a mistake, and a bad one at that. The station sergeant would have briefed him that one of the two wanted men was posing as a CID officer and a slight narrowing of the eyes suggested that he knew their identity.

Reaching inside his jacket, Farren produced his forged ID card. "We're attached to Special Branch," he said in a flat voice.

"That's right," said Rooney, "and I happen to be carrying a side-arm."

It happened fast, so fast that Farren was unable to do anything about it. Snatching the tiny 7.65 mm Beretta pistol from the hip holster, Rooney shot the police constable from point-blank range, hitting him in the chest. As the officer pitched forward, he fired again, blowing a neat hole above the right eye. There had been no deafening reports, no back echoes, merely two sharp cracks as if somebody had snapped a dry twig in half and half again, but to Farren's sensitive ears the Beretta had sounded like a canon.

Rooney said, "For Christ's sake, don't just stand there, help me get the bastard into the car."

For some moments Farren stood there, his mouth hanging open like a stranded fish. Then the adrenalin started to flow and he grabbed hold of the legs and helped Rooney bundle the corpse inside.

Driving out of the car park, they picked up the A11 and headed north towards Bishop's Stortford. Five miles beyond Epping the Pye radio set crackled and a plaintive voice asked Golf Foxtrot Two for his location. To Farren it seemed like an epitaph.

*   *   *

Ingold had first noticed the unmarked van when he arrived at the office. Parked in full view of the Institute for Political and Strategic Studies at the junction of Gaten Place and Bloomsbury Way where there happened to be a double yellow line, the driver had also compounded the original offence by leaving the apparently unattended vehicle within ten feet of a fire hydrant. It was the sort of traffic violation that invited positive action by the police or the traffic wardens but for some curious reason, the Ford Transit seemed above the law. After watching it on and off for almost two hours from his office window with the aid of a pair of binoculars, Ingold decided it was time he did something about it.

As a result of a 999 call, four officers from the Metropolitan bomb squad arrived on the scene at twelve minutes past eleven. Observing them huddled together on the pavement seemingly reluctant to approach the vehicle, Ingold wondered if they were merely waiting for reinforcements or whether they suspected that the call might have been a hoax. Any lingering doubt that they were not taking the warning seriously was removed some ten minutes later when the police turned up in strength to divert traffic away from the immediate area. Thereafter, the carefully staged farce moved towards an inevitable climax which was heralded by the appearance of a Bedford drop-side truck and a Coles crane. Chesterman and Hales, who had been keeping the Institute under surveillance, suddenly found themselves in mid air as the crane lifted the Ford Transit from the kerbside.

There were some people at Scotland Yard who professed to see the funny side of it but Wray was not amongst them, because he reckoned Harper would go through the roof when he heard the news. In view of the recent IRA bombing campaign, it was perhaps only natural that Ingold should have been suspicious when he saw a van standing in a No Parking area, but all the same, Wray had a nasty feeling that he had used this as a pretext to flush them out.

22

MILLS WATCHED THE stranger press the bell for the fourth time and hastily stepped back into the living room, sensing that the man might turn round at any moment and catch a glimpse of him through the net curtains in the window. Despite the conservative style of dress, his posture, the gold-framed glasses and the dark, short, almost crew-cut hair stamped him as an American.

The stranger removed his thumb from the bell button and rattled the letter box. Crouching in front of it, he then pushed it open and said something which sounded like, "Come out, come out, wherever you are." His manner was not unlike a parliamentary candidate trying to persuade a reluctant house-holder to turn out on a wet and windy night and cast his vote before the polling stations closed. The letter box rattled again, louder and more insistent than ever, and as he went out into the hall, he heard him say, "You can't hide from me, Mr Mills, I know you're in there."

"I should think the whole bloody street knows that by now." Mills opened the door and glared at the stranger. "I'm surprised you didn't bring a loud-hailer with you."

"Edward Mills?"

"Yes."

"I'm Gordon Liddell."

A large hand grabbed his and pumped it enthusiastically to set his bruised right arm throbbing again.

"I've been wanting to meet you."

"I'm not interested."

"Come again?"

"In whatever it is you're trying to sell."

Liddell smiled ruefully. "Harper warned me you'd be a difficult character to handle."

Harper? Well, that just about explained everything.

"All right, so now you know he wasn't exaggerating." Mills started to close the door, saw that Liddell had a foot in the way, and said, "You'd better remove it before I tread on your toes."

"You're not going to invite me inside then?"

"Damn right I'm not."

"You should. You see, I think you owe me a few minutes of your time." Liddell leaned against the door and gave it a gentle shove with his shoulder. "I'm the CIA man who persuaded Harper to take another look at the Geneva affair. But for me, your people would have buried you long ago."

It was evident that Liddell didn't believe in selling himself short. A touch of poetic licence was all very well but Mills wondered what really lay behind the smooth line of patter.

"Perhaps you'd better come in after all. The living room's on your right."

He opened the door wider to allow Liddell into the hall and then poked his head outside. The street was empty except for a small group of very young children clustered around a Mr Whippy ice cream van that was parked down at the bottom end near Ravenscourt Road. There were a couple of students in the park across the way but they were lying on the grass with their arms around each other and were too busy necking to notice anybody else. Retreating into the hall, Mills closed the door and went into the living room.

Liddell had made himself comfortable in an armchair and was browsing through a small black pocket book. There was a faint smile on his lips as if he was secretly pleased with himself.

"Can I get you a drink?"

"No thanks; it's a little early in the day for me." Liddell looked up from the pocket book. "How does it feel to be another Dreyfus?"

"Lonely; especially when you're up against people like Harper."

"You don't want to underestimate him."

"I don't."

"Sometimes I think he's Machiavelli re-incarnated." Liddell rubbed his jaw. "Not that he's got anything to learn from that old Italian."

"Do you know what he's up to?"

"You could say he's thrown us together in the hope that we'd stay out of his hair."

"And you'd like to pull the rug out from under his feet?"

Liddell thought that Mills and Harper had one thing in common; they both possessed a highly developed sense of intuition.

"It would give me a lot of satisfaction if I could."

"Why?"

The one-word questions were usually the most difficult to answer. Liddell supposed he could say that he'd always maintained the British had nailed the wrong man and that the SIS investigation back in '64 had smelt of a cover-up, but there was more to it than that. Laos, Cambodia, Vietnam and Angola; enterprises that had been started with the full backing of the State Department but had never come to fruition because of a gradual volte-face. It all added up to twelve years of failure, perhaps even longer than that if you included Dien Bien Phu. He'd been working in Hanoi then, collecting Intelligence data which the CIA had shown to the Pentagon; hot information which had almost persuaded Admiral Radford and the Joint Chiefs of Staff that there was a case for intervening in French Indo China. Almost was the operative word because State wouldn't buy it and in Britain, Eden's star had been in the ascendancy and they'd ended up with the Geneva Agreements of '54, which settled nothing except that he believed it had paved the way for the war in Vietnam.

"There are some blind men walking around Washington," Liddell said tersely, "and I want to restore their sight."

It sounded a whole lot better than saying he was tired of being labelled a failure and was determined to prove a point, one that would convince people like Harper that he'd been right all along.

"How? By nailing Quarry, Thurston or Ingold to the cross?"

"Maybe. What do their names mean to you?"

"Nothing."

"Well, I can fill you in on those characters. It's all down here in my little black book."

"No." Mills shook his head. "No, you can't tell me a damn thing that Harper hasn't already raked up, and they are still strangers as far as I am concerned."

"Like Ollenshaw?"

"Don't be ridiculous, he was my boss."

"Which doesn't mean to say you really knew him," Liddell said coolly. "For instance, would it surprise you to learn that he was a fag?"

"You've got it wrong; everyone knew he was a stoat."

"Because he put it about. Oh, he used to leer at the secretaries, pat their rumps once in a while, but it was all a front. Like the stories you heard about his wife, the frigid lady who wouldn't let the old goat come near her. Hell, if she was a sour, dried up old trout, it was because Ollenshaw refused to sleep with her. Listen, in 1939 he was asked to leave Sherwood College where he was an Assistant Housemaster when it became patently obvious that extra tuition in French wasn't the only reason why some of the fourteen-year-old boys were being invited into his study. I figure the war was a blessing in disguise for Ollenshaw; with his language qualifications he was a natural for the SOE. Sure, he was one of the best agents they had in the field and anyone who collects a DSO, an MC and the Croix de Guerre has got to be a very brave man, but do you know how the Gestapo finally caught up with him in Paris early in '44? They found him in bed with a male prostitute he'd picked up at the Bal Montaigne-Sainte Genevieve."

"You know what your trouble is?" Mills said contemptuously "You've been poking about in the gutters for far too long."

"My source is unimpeachable, a former member of the French National Liberation Committee whom I met while attached to our Embassy in Paris back in '67. I'm not saying that Ollenshaw was definitely a traitor, but he sure was open to pressure."

"From whom?"

"Well somebody like Giles Thurston. By a strange coincidence, Thurston was educated at Sherwood College; in fact, he left a year after Ollenshaw got his marching orders. I'm surprised Harper didn't tell you."

Ollenshaw a fairy? It wouldn't be the first time a dead man had been pilloried by malicious, unfounded gossip. Liddell was wrong. Or was he? Mills frowned, suddenly remembering how Ollenshaw had been in the habit of clapping an arm around his shoulders and giving him a hug like some fatherly, elder brother. He had always looked upon Ollenshaw as one of those hearty extroverts who couldn't resist slapping people on the back, but now he couldn't help thinking he must have been more than a little naive in those days.

"When Ollenshaw briefed me before I went to see Ziegler, he led me to believe that I'd been chosen because I was supernumerary to establishment at Bonn. But what if . . . ?" Mills broke off and massaged his aching arm. "No, that's ridiculous."

"What is?" Liddell asked sharply.

"Well, whoever leaked the news that Kiktev was going to defect obviously decided that he would have to protect himself, and I was just wondering if this man in the shadows persuaded Ollenshaw to send me to Geneva. You see, when I left Bonn on the thirtieth of May, it didn't occur to me that I would never return."

"You've lost me."

"I left all my personal things behind including the Olympia portable that was used to type the various letters of instruction to the Notary in Avignon. The SIS collected my gear on the twenty-fourth of June, so the man had almost a month in which to set me up."

"Yeah; the KGB could pre-date the letters and forge your signature for him, but he would have to know an awful lot about your private life."

"You mean Janet Rayner?"

"Yes."

"She was acquainted with Thurston, well enough to know he had a weekend retreat at Fitchingfield." Acquainted could be an understatement for all he knew. Looking back, it seemed to Mills that Janet Rayner must have been on everybody's party list. But that was understandable; Janet had been very attractive and voluptuous too, like the girl on the Pirelli calendar, the one Ollenshaw had ringed. "I'm not sure whether it's significant but I remember Thurston called Ollenshaw while he was briefing me on the fourth of June."

"Does Harper know this?"

"No."

"Then I think I'd better tell him." Liddell got up and

209

walked towards the door; half way there, he turned about. "Do you think Miss Eastgate would mind if I used her phone?"

"I'm quite sure she wouldn't," Mills said quietly.

If she had been in his shoes, Mills knew that Elizabeth would have been elated but instead, he merely felt tired. It was difficult to grasp that it was almost over, that it could end like this with one stranger talking to another when there were so many questions still unanswered. How could a man like Thurston fix Boxall up with a job without drawing attention himself? And why would two Irish gunmen kill for him unless he had some sort of deal going with the IRA? But what sort of deal? Arms and ammunition? Yes, that could be it, especially if Thurston was in a position to control the date of delivery.

A faint ping out in the hall told him that Liddell had finished talking to Harper and he waited expectantly. The door opened slowly and then Liddell walked into the living room with a puzzled expression on his face.

"It would appear we've fingered the wrong man," he said thoughtfully.

"Oh?"

"Ingold has just been apprehended at London Airport. It seems he intended to board an Aer Lingus flight to Dublin."

"Two minds with but a single thought." Mills smiled wryly. "I almost did the same thing."

"Yes? Well, Harper's on his way to Heathrow, so I guess that's it."

He had a mental picture of Janet Rayner staring moodily at the misted windscreen, her lips compressed in a thin line as she watched the rain belting down from a leaden sky, and then she had craned her head to one side, frowning as if puzzled by something and then he too had heard the drone of a low-flying aircraft. The Tiger Moth had descended below the cloud base, banked over the road and skimming above the thatched cottage, had disappeared from sight behind a copse.

"There's a flying club near Fitchingfield."

"So what?"

"If I were Thurston and Ingold was a friend of mine, I think I'd use him to create a diversion."

"Do you have a car?"

210

"There's an MGB outside. I'm sure Elizabeth won't mind us borrowing it."

*   *   *

Leaving Drew to park the car behind the Heathrow taxi rank, Harper walked into the Terminal Building and headed for the Aer Lingus desk where Wray had said that Sergeant Johnson would be waiting to meet him. The Dublin flight had already departed and there were only two people at the counter, a dark-haired attractive-looking young woman and a broad-shouldered, lean-waisted man in a brown suit who was busy chatting her up. Suddenly aware of footsteps behind him, the man turned slowly about and appraised him thoughtfully.

"Mr Harper, sir?"

"Sergeant Johnson?"

"Yes, sir." His face creased in a ready smile. "If you'd like to follow me, I'll take you to Mr Ingold. We're holding him in the Customs and Immigration interview room."

"Good." Harper fell in step beside him. "How's he taking it?"

"Philosophically." Johnson flexed his shoulders. "In fact, he seems to think it's all a huge joke."

"He would," Harper said grimly.

Ingold looked fairly presentable for once. The sports jacket had leather patches on both elbows and the cavalry twill trousers could have done with a pressing, but Harper thought they were a considerable improvement on the corduroys, checked shirt and sleeveless sweater he'd been wearing yesterday. Seated on a tubular steel chair, his arms folded and resting on the small table in front of him, Ingold seemed quite unperturbed, despite the presence of a plainclothes man who was keeping an eye on him.

Looking up, he grinned at Harper and said, "Hullo, Cedric, I had a feeling you would show up sooner or later." He ran a hand over the thatch of light brown hair in a vain attempt to make it a little tidier. "Now that you are here, perhaps you'd be good enough to tell me what's going on?"

Harper glanced at Johnson, waited until both Special Branch officers had withdrawn, and then sat down facing Ingold across the table. "I was hoping you could enlighten me, Richard."

211

"Well, until I was forcibly detained by that rather objectionable Sergeant Johnson, I was planning to go to Dublin."

"On business or pleasure?"

"Oh, business unfortunately. Mind you, I'm very fond of Dublin."

"I presume this trip of yours must have been a fairly sudden decision," Harper said mildly.

"As a matter of fact, it was. You see, I only heard this morning that Doctor Kevin Cohalen had been recalled to Dublin for urgent consultations."

"Cohalen?"

"My dear Cedric, he's their resident Minister to the United Nations and an expert on African affairs. He was Dag Hammarskjöld's trouble-shooter in the Congo. Giles Thurston suggested I should go to Dublin on the off-chance that I could wangle a short talk with Cohalen before he returns to New York later this afternoon. Giles thought it would be a good idea to pick his brains in connection with the study I'm working on."

"Thurston spoke to you this morning?"

"Yes, he called shortly after I had telephoned the police. You can always check with him if you don't believe me."

Ingold was very self-assured but then he had every reason to be confident. Harper thought that, in all probability, there had been a telephone call but unless Thurston's PA was in the habit of eavesdropping, their conversation would remain private. The wire tap only covered their home numbers; extending it to blanket the official telephones would have involved far too many people. It had been a difficult decision but on balance, he still believed the Minister had been right to limit the electronic surveillance.

"Did I do wrong?"

"What?"

"To alert the police about the van?"

"Certainly not. Why do you ask?"

"Because I can't think why else I have been detained, unless you are thinking my call was a deliberate hoax?"

"I'm beginning to think it was a smoke screen."

"I don't like your tone," Ingold said coldly, "and you've no right to detain me. It's not in my nature to threaten anyone, Cedric, but unless you put a stop to all this nonsense, I intend to phone my solicitors and Matthew Quarry."

"Why Quarry?"

"Because he happens to be the Permanent Under Secretary to the Home Office and I would like him to explain why he decided to have me watched by Special Branch."

It was hard to know whether Ingold was bluffing or not. He was an old hand, a man who'd spent most of his life dabbling in the twilight world of the Security Services and there wasn't much he didn't know about the game. Breaking his story would take days, possibly weeks, and even then it was highly likely that they would have to let him go for lack of evidence. Still, it was worth a try and there was no harm in making him sweat.

Harper pushed his chair back and stood up. "By all means call your solicitor and Quarry too if you feel like it, Richard. Tell them that you're being held for questioning."

"By whom? You, the police or Special Branch?"

"SIS," Harper said, "they'll be here to collect you shortly. In the meantime, I'll leave you in the tender care of Sergeant Johnson."

Ingold pulled a face. "Couldn't you find someone less uncouth?" he asked in a plaintive voice.

*   *   *

Drew hung up and was about to get out of the car when he spotted Harper amongst a group of people leaving the Terminal Building. Glancing at the radio telephone beside him, he wondered if he should get the Department back on the line but on reflection, decided it would be better to wait. Of the various messages which had been relayed to him, the one from Chief Superintendent Wray was somewhat involved and he thought Harper would need time to think about the implications. Leaning across the passenger's seat, Drew opened the nearside door for him.

"You look as if you're busting to tell me something." Harper closed the door, tugged the inertia-reel seat belt across his chest and pushed it home into the socket between the seats. "I hope your news is favourable because I don't think we'll get anywhere with Ingold."

"That's unfortunate. Special Branch aren't too sure whether they are getting anywhere either. Apparently, Thurston, has hired a Piper Cherokee from the Venture Flying Club at Fitchingfield but it appears he made the booking early yesterday morning. He also submitted a flight plan at the same time with an ETA at Linton-on-Ouse set for eighteen hundred hours tonight."

"That's an RAF airfield, isn't it?"

"Yes; he's attending some sort of reunion. Chief Superintendent Wray said that the Station Commander gave him the impression Thurston had virtually asked the RAF to arrange a special dinner night for him in the Mess."

Thurston had been stationed at Linton-on-Ouse during the war, had flown his last mission from there, the one which had led to his Lancaster being shot down over Munich in March '44. Harper supposed it was just conceivable that Thurston intended to make some sort of nostalgic trip back into the past but if so, it was out of character. He had been labelled arrogant, conceited, gifted and insufferable but no one had ever accused him of being sentimental. On the other hand, Thurston was intelligent enought to anticipate their every move and the flight plan could be a clever ruse designed to satisfy their curiosity.

"A Piper Cherokee?" Harper said.

"Yes. It's a small, single-engine, four-seater job with a maximum range of eight hundred and forty-five miles and a cruising speed in excess of a hundred and forty miles an hour."

Harper wasn't too sure of his geography but he had an uncomfortable feeling that Thurston could easily make it to East Germany in one hop. He would have to leave his wife behind but theirs had always been a marriage of convenience; Cynthia had supplied the money and Giles the social position, and there were no children to complicate the issue.

Guessing the ulterior motive behind the flight plan was one thing, preventing Thurston from carrying it out was quite another matter. Thurston hadn't put a foot wrong so far and unless he could tie him in with Farren and Rooney, there wasn't much he could do except sit back and wait for something to happen. He could ask the Ministry of Defence to alert the RAF, arrange for the Piper Cherokee to be kept under radar surveillance, but once Thurston decided to drop below the screen, they would lose track of the aircraft and that would be it. Another defector, another howl of outrage from the Press and one more Ministerial Inquiry that would get them nowhere.

"Were there any other messages?"

"Mr Liddell phoned from Frogmore Gardens at twelve forty-five and asked if you'd ring him back on 98264. Ten minutes later, he was back on the line again telling Miss Nightingale to forget it because he was going to take a look at the Real Estate around Fitchingfield."

Fitchingfield? Harper frowned. It was too much of a coincidence and he wondered what Liddell was up to.

"And Epping Police Station appears to have mislaid one of their officers. He hasn't been seen since nine thirty this morning, but they found his Panda car parked near the railway station."

"I think we'd better get back to the office."

"Right."

"And then I think you and the Armourer should take a good hard look at that Piper Cherokee."

"You want us to examine it?"

"In a manner of speaking," Harper said casually.

Drew nodded, understanding exactly what Harper had in mind. Firing the engine into life, he pulled out from the taxi rank.

*   *   *

Farren heard a faint but deep-throated snarl and reached for the pair of binoculars which he'd left on the windowsill. From the vantage point of the bedroom, he had a reasonable view of the surrounding countryside and focussing the glasses on the narrow road in the middle distance, he spotted the car as it appeared round a sharp bend some four hundred yards away. As it grew in size, he saw that it was a green-coloured MGB with a black hardtop and mentally crossing his fingers, he waited to see if the driver would turn into the lane leading to Belleview Cottage. Temple – his lips moved, silently mouthing the name over and over again – Temple – it had to be Temple.

The car went on past the turning, skidded to a halt and then backed up. For a moment, Farren almost allowed himself to be persuaded that Temple had simply overshot the lane until he realised this was just wishful thinking. Temple would know the route like the back of his hand and would, therefore, ease his foot on the accelerator when he came into the bend. A nagging worry that something was wrong became all too apparent when the MGB turned into the gravel drive and he saw that there were two men in the car. Leaving the binoculars on the window ledge, Farren raced downstairs to warn Rooney.

*   *   *

The sun was in his eyes and squinting through the windscreen it looked to Mills as if the drive came to a dead end just beyond the thatched-roof cottage. Common sense told him that it did no such thing and he automatically shifted from third into second. Even so, the nearly right-angled bend almost caught him on the hop and he had to put the wheel hard over to the left, the offside mudwing just clipping the gatepost as he swept into the yard.

Liddell whistled softly. "You cut that pretty fine."

"Too fine," said Mills, "I've dented the bloody wing."

"Tough."

"That's an understatement. I know someone who's going to raise Cain."

Liddell laughed. "Not to worry, when the times comes, I'll be there to lend you moral support. Right now we've got things to do."

"Like what?"

"Like finding out if there's anybody at home." Liddell pushed open the door and scrambled out.

Mills thought the cottage would have looked well on the lid of a chocolate box. The white distempered face was almost entirely hidden by a mass of deep red and blush pink roses that had climbed the trellis frames on either side of the oak door and then spread outwards to form a tapestry below the upstairs windows. In front of this colourful backdrop were dwarf and standard fuschias planted in four tubs that had been spaced equidistant and dressed off from the right like Guardsmen on parade. From the gravel drive, a well-kept lawn stretched as far as the line of blackberry bushes interlaced with honeysuckle that marked the boundary. Just inside the gates and to the right, was a ramshackle outhouse covered in ivy which obviously served as a garage.

Liddell said, "I'm not getting any answer. I guess Thurston isn't here."

"Somebody is." Mills pointed to the outhouse. "Otherwise, what's that Cortina doing here?"

216

"Suppose you take a look at it." Liddell raised the heavy door knocker again and slammed it against the boss, beating out a tattoo loud enough to wake the dead.

The police constable was lying on the floor curled up in a tight ball between the seats, his knees drawn up in a pyramid, his head over to one side and resting against the nearside door. There were black powder burns around the neat hole above his right eye and the blood had caked on his cheek.

"There's a body in here." Mills raised his voice. "There's a dead man in the car."

"And there'll be two more any minute."

Mills turned about. The man facing him some twenty yards away with a small pistol in his left hand looked incredibly young. There was a curious lopsided smile on his face and although he bore only a passing resemblance to the Identikit picture he'd seen in the newspapers, he knew it was Rooney. And the other framed in the cottage doorway as he covered Liddell with a snub-nosed revolver, had to be Farren. He supposed they must have been watching them from inside the cottage, waiting for an opportunity to jump him and Liddell, and seeing it, Rooney had left by the side entrance to take them in the flank. A simple and obvious deduction, but one that was quite irrelevant now because Rooney was raising his left arm, extending it like an accusing finger, the right hand grasping the left wrist to steady it while he took aim.

Farren saw his finger curl around the trigger to take up the first pressure and knew that Rooney would pump one round after another into Mills unless he put a stop to the whole bloody business.

"Hold it." His voice was cold, incisive. "Drop the gun, Terry, we need him."

"You're wrong, Cathal, we don't need him at all, we should have killed Mills a long time ago."

"As a hostage."

"A hostage?"

"That's what I said."

The gun was wavering now and the lopsided smile had given way to a puzzled expression. Out of the corner of his eye, Mills saw Liddell edge a pace nearer to Farren and held his breath, hoping and praying the American would forget the heroics and play it cool. Another step, and he knew it was fatuous to go on praying. As Liddell launched himself at Farren, Mills sprinted for the MGB, jinking and swerving so as to present Rooney with a difficult target. The Beretta cracked twice in rapid succession, the bullets ricocheting off the gravel drive to buzz over his head like angry bees. Diving forward, Mills hit the ground and rolled behind the car.

There was an age gap of at least fifteen years between them and Liddell knew that all the long hours spent on the squash courts and all the sweat-inducing work-outs in the gym at Langley could never bridge the difference. The fight, once started, would have to be finished quickly if he was to come out of it in one piece. Flailing his right arm in a scything motion, he chopped down on Farren's wrist to send the Police Positive spinning from his numbed fingers. Moving in close, Liddell tried to gouge his eyes but Farren brought a knee up into his groin and he went down, pitching forward on to his face.

The .38 landed within ten feet of Mills and he went after it, scrabbling on hands and knees to grab the revolver as Farren came charging towards him. There was no time to take deliberate aim and still on both knees, he simply pointed and fired. The bullet smashed into Farren's mouth and continuing upwards on an inclined plane, exited through the crown of his head.

Moving sideways down the near side of the car, Mills looked under the body and spotting Rooney's feet on the far side of the MGB, came up fast, the gun kicking in his hand as he emptied the remaining five chambers. Hit in the abdomen, stomach, chest and forehead, the combined impact lifted Rooney off his feet, and falling backwards, he rolled over on to his left side and lay still.

"Jesus." Liddell climbed painfully to his feet and shook his head. "Jesus, for a moment there I thought we'd had it."

"So did I." Mills dropped the revolver and leaned over the bonnet. "I haven't smoked a cigarette in years," he said in a flat voice, "but I could use one now."

"Be my guest."

The packet of Lucky Strike landed at his feet.

"Do you want a light?"

"There's a cigar lighter in the dashboard."

Liddell nodded as if Mills had uttered some profound truth. "I'll phone Harper then, tell him what's happened here."

"Yes, you do that."

Mills bent down and picked up the packet of cigarettes. Mechanically he ripped off the cellophane wrapper, took out a cigarette and reaching inside the car, pushed the cigar lighter home. Gripped by a paroxysm of coughing the moment he lit up, Mills hastily dropped the cigarette on to the gravel and trod on it.

"Harper said to wait here."

"What?"

"Thurston has broken cover and he's running." Liddell was jubilant almost to the point of being incoherent. "I've just spoken to Harper, got Miss Nightingale to patch me through to him on the radio telephone."

"Yes?"

"You don't seem to understand. This is really it; we've got the bastard by the short hairs."

"Great," said Mills. "Should I give three cheers now or wait till later?"

So the long years in the wilderness were definitely over. He supposed he ought to be on top of the world, but there was only a feeling of emptiness. All his energy had been directed towards one objective and now that it had been attained, there was nothing left to strive for. Nothing left? Mills frowned. There was Elizabeth Eastgate and she was worth striving for every inch of the way.

*   *   *

Thurston glanced into the rear-view mirror, saw that the road behind him was clear, and smiled. Ingold had served him well, providing the smoke screen he'd needed to throw Harper off the scent. Harper would turn Richard over to the SIS but they would never break him no matter how hard they tried.

It was a pity everything had to end while he still had so much to contribute but he had been living on a knife-edge ever since the Kiktev affair. Of course, things might have been different if it had been possible to detain Mills in prison or if Farren and Rooney hadn't bungled it. Farren and Rooney – two of the best gunmen in the Provisionals? His lip curled in disgust. If they were the best, then the IRA would be well advised to call a truce while they got themselves reorganised.

Thurston caught a brief glimpse of the milestone on the grass verge and eased his foot off the accelerator. With the road and track junction outside Fitchingfield less than a mile ahead, the time had come to make a decision. The choice was simple enough; either he went straight on through the village or else he took the short cut out to the airfield and bypassed the cottage. A simple decision too when he came to think about it, because Farren and Rooney had outlived their usefulness.

The road and track junction was in sight now and dropping into third, Thurston flicked the indicator to show that he was turning right.

*　　*　　*

Liddell stepped away from the window and said, "All right, let's get on with it – Thurston's coming."

Mills opened one eye as he heard the crunch of tyres on the gravel. "I wouldn't bet my shirt on it."

"It's got to be him," Liddell said fiercely. "You saw the note he'd left for Farren and Rooney. He said he'd pick them up at sixteen thirty. Right?"

"Yes."

"Well, as of now, it's twenty-five minutes past four. I'd call that pretty good timing, wouldn't you?"

Liddell broke off and turned to face the window once more as the car pulled up outside the cottage. Two doors opened and closed in quick succession and then Liddell, swearing under his breath, stormed out of the sitting room.

When Mills joined him on the porch, he was talking animatedly with Harper and Detective Sergeant Garrett, except that Garrett had apparently changed his name to Gattis. After all that had happened, Mills wondered why he should find the switch so surprising.

Harper said, "What have you done with Farren and Rooney, Gordon?"

"We figured Thurston would get here first so we hid them in the outhouse."

"That was very sensible of you, Gordon, but you needn't have bothered. You see, Thurston has gone straight to the airfield, which is much more convenient for us."

"Convenient?"

"We're hoping he will defect."

Liddell stared at Harper in total disbelief. "You've got to be out of your head. For Christ's sake, Thurston has been hoodwinking your politicians for years, selling them a load of crap, and you – "

"Selling them, Gordon?" Harper shook his head. "This isn't America, you know. For more than half the time, Giles was telling them exactly what they wanted to hear, wanted to believe. Making a case against him would mean turning over far too many awkward stones. That's why it's wise to let him go."

"You think it's that simple? Thurston can still hurt us with the knowledge he's got locked away in his mind."

"Well, it's true Whitehall will have to do some re-thinking but I don't suppose it will do them any harm."

"I guess that about wraps it up then?" Liddell said bitterly.

"Not quite. It would be churlish of me to let you go without expressing my appreciation for all your invaluable help, Gordon."

"Forget it." Liddell swung round to face Mills. "I want to get the hell out of here before I throw up." His eyes glittered angrily. "Will you give me a lift back to town?"

Mills nodded. To all intents and purposes he was in the clear. Yet from what Harper had said, it was quite evident that the whole business was going to be swept under the carpet. In the circumstances, he thought it might be a good idea if Elizabeth Eastgate obtained a written statement from Liddell before the American had time to cool off. When you were dealing with people like Harper, it was advisable to have an insurance policy.

"I take it I'm free to go?"

"Of course you are, Edward." Harper smiled amiably. "Gattis and I will stay on to clear up the mess."

There were no handshakes, no apologies, no pats on the back, just a vague smile that could mean anything or nothing. Backing the MGB out of the space behind the outhouse, Mills waited until Liddell had adjusted the seat belt and then drove off without so much as a backward glance.

*   *   *

Gattis said, "Shall I telephone the police at Bishop's Stortford about Farren and Rooney, or will you?"

"There's no hurry."

Harper cocked his head in an attitude not unlike that of a well-trained gun dog. To Gattis it seemed he was lost in thought but then, presently, he too heard the faint roar of an engine in the distance. Moments later, a bright red Piper Cherokee appeared in view above the horizon and climbed towards the sun. It had reached an altitude of approximately one hundred and fifty feet when the engine suddenly cut out and rolling over on to its back, the Piper went into a spiral. One wing came off while the aircraft was still some fifty feet from the ground, and then it went in nose first, disappearing from view below the skyline. A dull crump preceded the column of black smoke which rose lazily in the still air.

"My God." Gattis sucked in a deep breath. "Oh, my God, did you see that?"

The question was stupid but Harper supposed it deserved some sort of answer. "Yes," he said, "I saw it. Poor old Giles."

Gattis hunched his shoulders. "Well, at least there are no loose ends."

Loose ends? Harper frowned. What was it Cyril Connolly had written back in '51? 'After the third man, the fourth man, after the fourth man the fifth man, who is the fifth man, always beside you?' Burgess, Maclean, Philby, and now Thurston. Who was the fifth man then? Richard Ingold or Matthew Quarry? Or was there a sixth? Ingold could be quietly retired, put out to grass, because he would be sixty-five in a few months' time, but Quarry was a different problem altogether. Quarry was suspect because he was the one man who'd been in a position to arrange for Mills to be placed under surveillance; he had the ear of the Home Secretary and there were any number of ways he could have hood-winked Special Branch. Thinking it over, Harper came to the conclusion he would have to do something about Quarry.

"What happens to Mills now?"

"Oh, I expect he'll get a free pardon in due course."

"In due course?" repeated Gattis. "What does that mean?"

"I'm surprised you should ask. Mills was convicted for theft and that's one issue we still haven't resolved satisfactorily." Harper dug a heel into the turf and loosened a sod. "We'll have to do a lot of digging before I'm satisfied."

"Digging?"

"Mills inherited a little over eight and a half thousand from his mother; the money came from the sale of her house in Tonbridge."

The sudden switch in conversation left Gattis floundering. Harper sometimes gave the impression that he had a grasshopper mind but from past experience, he knew there was always some definite purpose behind the apparent rambling.

"You can get the name of the present owner from Wells, Bull and Dixon because they handled the contract. And then I want you to have a few words with your contacts in the Fraud Squad and persuade them that it's worth their while to have the garden dug over again. Of course, they'll have to apply for a search warrant."

"What are they supposed to be looking for?"

"Eight hundred and fifty thousand dollars' worth of Bearer Bonds." Harper smiled fleetingly. "I don't believe Mills did steal them, but I would like to make absolutely sure they aren't buried in Tonbridge."